P9-BTM-092

LOST
BOOKS
AND
OLD
BONES

LOST BOOKS
AND
OLD BONES

Paige Shelton

MINOTAUR BOOKS
New York

This is a work of fiction. All of the characters,
organizations, and events portrayed in this novel
are either products of the author's imagination or are
used fictitiously.

www.minotaurbooks.com

Library of Congress Cataloging-in-Publication Data

Names: Shelton, Paige, author.
Title: Lost books and old bones / Paige Shelton.
Description: First edition. | New York: Minotaur Books,
   2018. | Series: A Scottish Bookshop mystery; 3
Identifiers: LCCN 2017050904 | ISBN 9781250127792
   (hardcover) | ISBN 9781250127808 (ebook)
Subjects: LCSH: Booksellers and bookselling—Fiction. |
   Murder—Investigation—Fiction. | Edinburgh
   (Scotland)—Fiction. | Women booksellers—Fiction. |
   Women detectives—Fiction. | Bookstores—Fiction. |
   GSAFD: Mystery fiction.
Classification: LCC PS3619.H45345 L67 2018 | DDC
   813/.6—dc23
LC record available at https://lccn.loc.gov/2017050904

Our books may be purchased in bulk for promotional,
educational, or business use. Please contact your local
bookseller or the Macmillan Corporate and Premium
Sales Department at 1-800-221-7945, extension 5442, or
by email at MacmillanSpecialMarkets@macmillan.com.

First Edition: April 2018

10 9 8 7 6 5 4 3 2 1

For that kid in my college writing class
who told me he loved my writing, even
if he didn't always understand it.

ACKNOWLEDGMENTS

Thank you to my agent, Jessica Faust, and my editor, Hannah Braaten, for everything. You are simply the best.

Thanks to everyone at Minotaur who works so hard to make these pages into real books. A special shout-out on this one to Alan Bradshaw, Amelie Littell, and Tom Cherwin. Your ways with words, grammar, and research are much appreciated.

My guys, Charlie and Tyler, are the best. I'm crazy lucky to have them both. As always, thanks for your support, fellas.

At around the sixth century BC in Scotland, numerous wells with miraculous powers of healing were associated with the names of various saints. Of these, one of the most famous was the Well of St. Triduana, at Restalrig, near Edinburgh. St. Triduana was a recluse of the primitive church, whose tomb after her death became a shrine for pilgrims afflicted with eye diseases. In early life, her beauty had attracted a Pictish chief from whom she fled, and, being pursued by his emissaries, she plucked out her eyes and sent them to him impaled upon a thorn, as they had been the cause of his unwelcome attentions. For many centuries, the Well at Restalrig, afterwards called St. Margaret's Well, was the resort of those [who came to drink the water with the hopes they could mend their eyes].

—From *History of Scottish Medicine to 1860*
by JOHN D. COMRIE

And that was only the beginning.

LOST
BOOKS

AND

OLD
BONES

ONE

The cold liquid splashed the back of my neck before it rolled down and underneath my shirt. I gasped and reflexively turned to see who had sloshed their drink in my direction.

"Delaney! I'm so sorry. Oh dear. Here let's go tae the toilet. I'll get you cleaned up and you can have my shirt," Sophie said loudly with a drunken slur as she grabbed my arm and started to pull me through the crowd.

"But then what will you wear?" I asked, trying to raise my voice.

She didn't hear me above the crowd and band noise. I barely heard myself.

Though loud, the performers weren't, in fact, a band; they were a duo. Mad Ferret was made up of one Irish and one Scottish gentleman. Together they performed upbeat folk songs that brought out the jig in pretty much everybody.

I'd first seen them with Tom, my boyfriend, after the two Mad Ferret members had stopped by his pub one evening and invited him to a show. Tom had taken me to see them in a very dark pub that hadn't seemed quite big enough for the jubilant crowd inside. The setting was much the same tonight, though Tom wasn't with me and my new friends, Sophie and Rena, and my newest friend Mallory, whom I'd just met this evening. All the women were medical students at the University of Edinburgh.

A few crowd dodges later, Sophie and I made our way toward the small back ladies' room, a place where everyone wrote their name on the walls and the liquid soap smelled like the lavender hips scent my mom used in her kitchen back home in Kansas.

The three green-doored stalls inside were empty and the music fell into a muffled tinny bass beat when the bathroom door closed behind us.

"Your shirt is soaked through. I'm so, so sorry. I was careless. I'll have it cleaned," Sophie said as she turned me around so she could inspect my back. Then she turned me again to face her. "Here, take mine."

I stopped her just as she made it to the second button of her blouse.

"It's not a problem. I've been spilled on before," I said. "Don't worry about it."

She blinked her heavily mascaraed brown eyes my direction. Until tonight I'd only seen her and her roommate Rena with light to no makeup and hastily brushed or pulled back hair. They were usually dressed in scrubs or jeans. Their skirts and makeup as well as their post-test Friday desire to blow off some steam had surprised me tonight, though I remembered that feeling from when I was back at the University of Kansas.

I'd lost track of how many gin and tonics they'd downed, though it seemed that Sophie was moving double-time compared with the rest of us. Now, some of her latest drink was beginning to make my back sticky. I was going to smell like a pine tree, but I didn't really mind.

Reluctantly she said, "All right. At least let me buy you a drink tae make up for it."

I laughed. "I'm good, but I'm glad you're having fun."

"I'm going to have a wicked hangover tomorrow, but it's worth it. It's good tae let loose a little."

I smiled and redid the one button on her shirt. She didn't seem to notice as she leaned against the sink.

"It's a lucky twist of fate that we met you," she said.

"I feel the same about you guys. Come on, let's head back out and listen to some more music," I said, sensing an alcohol-induced love fest coming on if I didn't distract her.

A couple of months earlier, Sophie and Rena had come into The Cracked Spine, the rare book and manuscript shop that I'd traveled halfway around the world to work at. They'd brought in some old medical books that had been in Rena's family for decades. Rena's father had given her the books with the hope she could sell them and use the money to help with her own medical school tuition.

An Atlas of Illustrations of Clinical Medicine, Surgery and Pathology was made of up twenty-five books, all of them filled with colorful, gruesome pictures that depicted the many things that could go wrong on and in the human body. The books had been printed in the early 1900s by the New Sydal Society, with hand-drawn illustrations. My boss Edwin's eyes had filled with tears when he'd seen them; he'd swooned.

"Lass," he'd said. "These were from the time of the Industrial Revolution, when we didn't even know how much we were learning until later when we could look back and be utterly amazed at ourselves. These are the most beautiful things I've seen in a long, long while."

He'd pored over the books for days, dreamily. I'd thought that perhaps he'd had more than a few moments over the years when he wished he'd turned his biology degree into something medical, instead of founding and cultivating the most amazing rare and used book and manuscript shop in Scotland.

Edwin had given Rena slightly more than the books were worth. He couldn't decide what to do with them. He wouldn't resell them, but would either keep them for himself or donate them to a library, or perhaps to the University of Edinburgh Medical School. Edwin liked those sorts of happy endings. Someday, Rena might walk past a display case and look upon the books that had helped her and so many others before her learn the most respected of professions.

I found the medical books interesting, particularly when I could manage to look past the stomach-curdling images and let myself be amazed by the knowledge, work, and sheer will of patience that had gone into creating them. I knew that some of Edwin's most beloved treasures weren't the most expensive ones. I suspected he'd keep the books for himself.

Sophie bounced herself away from the sink but then leaned, in a weird slow-motion movement, back into it again.

"I need tae tell you something," she said as she grabbed my arm.

"Okay."

She glanced toward the door and then at the empty stalls. "You can't tell Rena."

"Um, okay," I said.

"I think I'm in trouble. I'm not having a good semester. And that test today; I'm sure I failed," she said.

"Oh, Sophie, I'm sure you're going to be fine. You've been brilliant so far. You're just . . . Well, you'll feel better tomorrow. Maybe not in the morning, but by the afternoon." I gave her a smile, but I didn't think she saw it.

She and Rena *had* been brilliant, attaining notoriety at the University of Edinburgh Medical School as two of its top students. They'd both come from Glasgow, started college twice, once when they were both eighteen and then again at twenty-five. Their first time, they'd flunked out. After a successful second run at undergrad, they'd begun medical school when they were thirty. Friends since they were younger, Sophie and Rena had made a pact to go through life together. They were an unbeatable team.

"No, no." She waved off my words. "Medical school is really, really hard, Delaney."

"I know, but I'm sure . . . Hey, let's not worry about that tonight. When will you know the grade on this test you took today?"

"Should be posted by Sunday."

"All right. I'll come over and we'll look at it together if that would help. Or you can come over to my house. Whatever is easier. I'm sure it will be fine, Sophie. You've had a fair amount to drink, and maybe that's causing some undue emotions."

She looked at me with glassy eyes, blinking heavily again. "I hope you're right."

"I know I am. Come on."

But before I could get her away from the sink again, the bathroom door opened, bringing Rena and Mallory into the already cramped space.

"There you are!" Rena said as she glanced back and forth between Sophie and me. "Everything okay?"

"Yep. We were just heading back out," I said.

Inside the small room, Sophie and Rena's similarities seemed even more obvious. Both were tall and thin with brown eyes and long brown hair. Sophie's hair had a wave to it while Rena's was stick-straight. When you looked closely, you could spot other differences too: Sophie's face was pleasantly round, Rena's was made with slightly sharper angles and she had a stronger chin. They didn't look like sisters, but could pass for cousins. In contrast, Mallory was shorter, curvier, and platinum blond. Her dark roots currently showed and she'd mentioned to everyone earlier that she needed to do something about them, but that there would be no time until the short summer break that began in a couple of months.

"Oh. Let's wait a bit," Rena said.

"Why?" I asked.

Rena and Mallory looked at each other.

"Dr. Eban is out there," Mallory said.

Sophie put her hand to her mouth. "He's here?"

"Aye," Rena said. "And he's taking note of the students he sees, I'm certain. He's rather evil that way."

"He's probably come tae ruin everyone's night," Sophie said. "Fail us all for having a wee bit of fun when we should all be home, crying about the grades he'll be doling out on the exam."

Rena's eyebrows came together as she looked at Sophie and then at me. "None of us want tae make an ill impression."

"He's a tough one," Mallory said to me with a small smile. "He's also a wee bit odd."

"Odd how?" I asked, noting that Mallory seemed more amused than horrified, as Sophie seemed to be. I chalked up the different reactions to the probable levels of alcohol each had consumed.

As I asked the question, a thought took shape in the back of my mind. None of these women, though Mallory was only twenty-seven to Sophie and Rena's thirty-two, was young or foolish. They were grown, long of legal drinking age. It didn't seem to me that they should feel the need to hide their behavior from anyone, including a professor.

Mallory seemed to consider the best way to further explain Dr. Eban, but Rena jumped in. "He begins every semester with a story about William Burke and William Hare. Those names familiar?"

"Of course," I said. "The men who killed for corpses." I cleared my throat. "That's a bit to the point, but . . ."

"Right," Rena said. "Back in the early 1800s they killed and sold the corpses of their victims tae Dr. Robert Knox, who used them for dissection in his anatomy classes at the University of Edinburgh. Anyway, Dr. Eban tells the story, and his rendition is filled with enough drama for a vampire story. He finishes off the lecture by saying that Burke and Hare probably saved more people than they murdered, considering what their contributions did tae assist medical students. He has a point, but it was still murder, and the way he tells the story . . . he's plain creepy. It's a tone he sets for himself early, and it's something he sticks with. That, along with his always-tough attitude, makes him the most talked about, and probably most feared, professor at the medical school."

Mallory added, "Either it's just the way he is, or the impression he wants tae give. And he conducts his classes in a theater that's set up the exact same way Dr. Knox's was, on purpose.

There's a plaque about Dr. Knox on the wall outside the door and everything."

"In his office, he's a totally different man, when no one else is looking," Sophie said.

We looked at her as she leaned against the sink. I thought she might say more, but it seemed like she lost her train of thought.

"I could use a cup of coffee," she said a moment later.

"I think that's the best idea of the night," Rena said. "Come on, I saw a table in the back. It's small, but we'll see if we can grab it."

"I'll go order the coffee," Mallory said.

The musicians told the crowd they were taking a break just as we exited the restroom. I followed behind the other three and kept on the lookout for someone creepy as we weaved our way thought the mostly student crowd in the small pub.

I'd met a few students over the past couple of months. Rena and Sophie shared a flat close to the university. Most of the building's residents were medical school students, but not all. It was immediately obvious who the undergrads were. Other than the fact that they looked the youngest, they also usually seemed to be having the most fun.

As we made our way through the crowd I spotted a familiar woman leaning against the bar next to another woman I didn't recognize. The one I recognized lived on the bottom floor of Sophie and Rena's building, and had opened the building's front door for me a few times. She could spot visitors approaching though her window and seemed to feel compelled to let people in.

Though I'd never met Mallory before tonight, she lived in Rena and Sophie's building too, in a flat all her own. She'd already mentioned that she spent most of her time holed up there, studying, and studying some more. In the brief time I'd known her I'd already noticed that she had a quiet calm about her that Sophie and Rena didn't possess. Maybe Mallory just worked harder to hide her stress.

I waved at the woman from the first floor, someone I'd pegged as an undgrad. I thought she was looking my direction, but she didn't wave back. I followed her line of vision and spotted who she must have been watching instead. A handsome man, probably about sixty, stood not far from the edge of the small dance floor. He wore dark pants and a dark peacoat over his tall, thin frame. His short dark hair was slicked back from his high forehead, and though I thought his nose should be hooked to match the rest of him, it wasn't. It was straight and almost regal. He was lazily holding a tumbler half full of liquid.

He didn't see me looking, and neither he nor the young woman noticed that I saw what happened next. Both the man by the dance floor and the woman sent a quick, furtive glance toward a third person, a man who seemed to be in a hurried exit out of the pub. The only features I caught of the third person were a head full of bushy gray hair and the back of a tall body that moved in defiance of the gray hair; strong and sure.

It could have been my imagination or the happenstance of my timing regarding their expressions, but in those brief beats of time, I thought both the man by the dance floor and the woman were concerned about the leaving man, or at least concerned about something. But the moment was over quickly, and I immediately doubted what I thought I'd seen.

As we approached the table Rena had spied, three men were also about to sit there. They sent us smiles of surrender and let us have the chairs.

After we sat, Mallory approached with a tray of four cups of coffee. "Freshly brewed," she said as she placed the cups in front of us one at a time and then leaned the tray against the wall. She angled herself into the tight space that held the last of the four chairs.

"Did you see him?" Sophie asked Rena.

"Yeah, just standing there being creepy," Rena said.

"The tall man in the dark clothes next to the dance floor?" I asked.

"That's him. That's Dr. Eban," Rena said.

"Did you guys see the gray-haired man leaving?" I said.

They all looked toward the door and said they hadn't.

"He must have left," I said, not sure why those brief seconds had made such an impression on me.

Mallory twisted around in her chair so she could see the man by the stage. "That's Dr. Eban, though. He'll probably just stand there all night and ooze horror, just tae set us all off balance. Take away our fun." Her words were ominous, but her tone was somewhat playful.

I looked at Rena.

She shrugged and said, "Believe it or not, that's probably exactly what he's doing. It's a power thing, I think. He likes bothering us."

"He teaches anatomy, huh?" I said.

"Aye," three voices said together.

"Here's the other part," Sophie said. "He's also one of the best teachers on campus. Really good. He's just . . . difficult."

"Unrealistic expectations," I said before I sipped the coffee.

It wasn't a question, but the three women looked at each other as if searching for the right answer.

"Yes," Sophie said.

"Sort of," Mallory said.

"I'm not sure they're unrealistic, but they are high. We should have high expectations, though. We're going tae be doctors," Rena said.

I watched for Sophie's reaction to Rena's words, but didn't see disagreement.

My back was to the wall. Since I was sitting in the corner seat, I had the best view of the rest of the pub, and I saw Dr. Eban moving in our direction. His eyes caught mine for an instant, and I knew our table was his destination.

"It looks as if he's headed our direction," I said without moving my lips or remaking eye contact with him.

Despite the instantaneous terror that blanched my table-mates' faces, there was no escape now.

TWO

"Ladies," Dr. Eban said as he stepped just a bit too close to the table, causing Mallory and Rena to have to lean sideways. "How are we this evening?"

"Hey, Dr. Eban," Mallory said. "Fancy meeting you here."

"I'm a big fan of the lads' music," Dr. Eban said easily.

"They're very good," Sophie said, working too hard to keep her words from slurring.

"Aye," Rena said.

For a moment I was perplexed by the dynamics. No one was doing anything wrong. But I had no way of knowing what their outside-school lives meant to their in-school lives. I was about to jump in and introduce myself to get us all past the awkward silence that seemed to fall over the table, but Dr. Eban jumped in.

"Will you all be attending the service this Tuesday?" he asked.

Briefly, they seemed as perplexed by the question as I was, but Mallory caught on first.

"Oh! For the corpses?" she asked.

"Aye," Dr. Eban said.

"Definitely," Rena said. "I think it's important."

"Services for the corpses?" I asked.

"Aye," Rena said. "Every year there's a service for the corpses that we are privileged tae . . . work with. We're required tae attend during our first year, but most of us attend after that anyway. These are people who donated their bodies tae the medical school, and we honor them every year with a church service. Sometimes their families show up and we get tae thank them in person. Many medical schools have such an event."

"That's really lovely," I said.

"Aye," Mallory said. "The public is invited if you're interested. It's Tuesday at Greyfriars Kirk."

"I think I would enjoy that," I said. I was curiously intrigued. The church was an architectural masterpiece, and I'd visited the neighboring graveyard a few times.

"Please join us," Rena said. It seemed she was about to introduce me to Dr. Eban, but he interjected another question before she could.

"Are you all pleased with your exam?" he asked, a happy uptick to his tone. Pointedly, he looked at Mallory first.

"I hope so," Mallory said with a smile.

"We'll see," Rena said. "But I feel good about everything."

Then everyone's attention turned to Sophie. Prompted by Rena's firm gaze in her direction, Sophie kept her back too straight as she said, "I hope so." But then, as if someone had unplugged her, she slumped. "But I don't hold out a lot of hope."

Rena closed her eyes and shook her head ever so slightly.

"Aye?" Dr. Eban said.

Without asking anyone, he reached around to an empty

chair at an otherwise populated table and moved it into the small space between Rena and Mallory, causing all spaces to close up even more. We scooted and gave him room, but all of our knees were touching by the time he sat and leaned forward on his elbows, his concentration hard on Sophie.

I wanted so much for this moment not to happen. If Dr. Eban hadn't yet picked up on Sophie's state, I hoped he wouldn't hold anything she said against her.

"What has you concerned?" Dr. Eban asked.

"Everything," Sophie said with an all-encompassing hand gesture. "Every-damn-thing. I wasn't prepared for the test, Dr. Eban. Your exams are—"

"Dr. Eban," Rena interjected. "We're just blowing off a wee bit of steam tonight. Forgive us if we're emotional. You know how it is?"

"I do," Dr. Eban said. He turned back to Sophie. "You're a good student, lass. I'm sure you did fine."

I put my hand on Sophie's knee and squeezed. We weren't good enough friends for me to intervene in such a way, but I liked her enough as a person to jump in and at least try to keep her from continuing. Besides, her knee was practically fused to my own.

She looked at me, sending me another heavy blink. But then she returned my knowing smile.

"Thank you, Dr. Eban," she said as she looked at him again. "I'm sure I'll feel better about things tomorrow."

"Aye! Now, I know all the students at the medical school, and I'm sure you aren't one," Dr. Eban said to me. He extended a hand over the table. "Bryon Eban."

"Delaney Nichols," I said. "No, I'm not a student."

"An American? Visiting Scotland?"

"Yes. I'm living here and working at a bookshop in Grass-market. I've been here almost a full year now."

"Delightful! Which bookshop?"

"The Cracked Spine."

"Aye?" Dr. Eban sat back, and his eyes got big.

Everything he did and said seemed oversized, but not in an off-putting way. Was this why he was considered odd?

"You've been there?" I said. I spent most of my time work-ing in the warehouse but I racked my brain wondering if I'd seen him before. He wasn't one to blend into the background, but I was sure he wasn't familiar.

"A few times." He looked around the pub. The musicians ap-peared to be readying their instruments for another set. Dr. Eban leaned farther over the table. "Tell me about Edwin MacAlister."

I smiled. I'd had this question a time or two. "He's a great boss and an interesting man."

Dr. Eban nodded. "Right. Tell me about his secret room, the place where he keeps all his treasures."

"That's just a myth," I lied easily. I'd had that question be-fore too.

Dr. Eban inspected me. In fact, everyone did. Even Sophie's wobbly attention was fixed on me.

"Come on, lass, you can tell us," Dr. Eban said. "You know, I've heard he has a scalpel from Dr. Robert Knox. He was the doctor who paid Williams Burke and Hare for the bodies they acquired by murder."

"I did know about Burke, Hare, and Knox, but no, there's no secret room. No old scalpels," I said, though I wondered if there were. Were there old scalpels in the warehouse, a place that most definitely did exist? I hadn't seen any. Yet.

"Really?" Dr. Eban said.

"Really," I said.

He watched me a long moment, but I kept my expression firmly neutral, as I'd done with many people over the last year. The secret of the secret room hadn't become a burden; it had become part of my own secrets, and it was one that I protected fiercely.

"Interesting. I'd love tae meet Mr. MacAlister. Any chance you'd introduce us?"

"It would be a pleasure," I said. "Give me a call at the shop, and we'll coordinate a time. I'm sure he'd love to meet you too."

"Aye?" Dr. Eban said.

"I'm sure."

Mad Ferret strummed a few chords and then began their set with a tune lively enough that I began to tap my toes even as they were crowded together.

"That would be wonderful. Ta," Dr. Eban said over the music and crowd noise.

I hadn't heard much of an accent in his voice, but his informal Scottish "Thank you" suddenly, and admittedly strangely, made me like him. I smiled.

"You're welcome. I look forward to your visit," I said.

Dr. Eban scooted the chair back from the table, releasing all the knees underneath.

"I'll ring you next week. A good evening, ladies. And, Sophie: I'm sure your exam will be fine."

I looked at Sophie, thinking she would just smile and maybe say thank you, but I was surprised to see something else entirely.

The smile, though still somewhat booze-infused, was not just a friendly smile. I swung my attention back to Dr. Eban. He had the same sort of look on his face, something that rang of that sort of affection that's supposed to be a secret but isn't.

I zipped my eyes to Rena, who, with big eyes and a frown in my direction, seemed to confirm what I thought I'd seen.

It appeared that maybe Sophie and Dr. Eban were much more than student and teacher.

That couldn't be good.

THREE

"I don't know what went on between them, if anything really. She shares everything with me, except this," Rena said as she and I stood outside the pub, the cold and humid March night air nipping at the tip of my nose.

I hadn't asked, but she must have read my expression. We'd put Sophie into Mallory's car and sent them on their way. Rena had stayed behind with me.

"None of my business," I said. "They're grown-ups and can make those sorts of decisions themselves. I'm sorry if I looked surprised; I was . . . well, I guess I was just surprised." I smiled weakly. The few streetlights around us were dim and cast a yellow glow, creating shiny spots in the small puddles left by an earlier rain.

"Aye, they're grown-ups, but Sophie has gotten in over her head in some way. I'm helping her through it, at least as much as I can without knowing all the details. He's an odd man, tae be sure."

There it was again. Odd. However, what I thought was also odd was Rena's tone. She was holding back something, or forcing something, I wasn't sure which. But I was certain she wasn't giving me a complete story.

"Is he married?" I asked.

"Aye."

"That's not good."

"No, and his wife is . . . fierce."

"How?"

"Wicked smart. Beautiful. She's a professor at the medical school too."

"So, fierce in a good way? Is she easier on the students?"

Rena laughed, the sound seeming too loud in the humid night air. She cleared her throat and said, "A wee bit easier on the students, but not so easy on her husband."

I blinked. "Has she done something, said something to him publicly that would embarrass him?"

Rena bit at her thumbnail and looked down the road Mallory's car had taken. She finally said, "She mocks him with her eyes. It's difficult tae explain."

"I think I get it," I said, but there was still more; I could see her stress. "Are you nervous or scared for Sophie?"

She looked at me and smiled, but didn't answer.

I was caught in that spot between none-of-my-business and the expected intrusion that comes with friendship. I cared for my new friends, but we didn't have that bond that forms after many shared experiences and the passing of time. We'd known each other for three months and had met because of some books they had brought into the bookshop. We'd enjoyed a few coffees out, some lunches, and, before tonight, a smattering of sober evening get-togethers. They'd come into The Cracked Spine a couple of times as a break from their studies and perused the books on the shelves, but their lives were all about medical school. I had enjoyed getting to know them a little here and there, but we didn't know each other well at all. I hoped we might remain friends for a long time, although we were still at the beginning of whatever our relationships would become. Rena didn't owe me the whole truth just as much as I felt I didn't owe them the whole truth about Edwin and his warehouse.

I finally said, "Let me know if I can do anything to help. I'm sorry Sophie is in over her head, but I do think she'll be fine."

"Because she's not a child, or at least she's old enough tae know better?"

"Something like that, but I don't want to be too harsh. It sounds like neither of us really knows the circumstances, but when two adults get involved with each other there are at least two stories there . . . Well, you know." I tried to smile again, but a distinct sense of unease made me swallow hard. A married professor and his student having a sexual relationship was such a cliché, and never a good thing as far as I was concerned.

Rena's eyebrows came together as she looked toward the pub. Her profile moved into some of the yellow light, and it deepened the lines of concern around her eyes.

"What?" I asked. "There's more?"

"This is going tae sound even more dramatic, and maybe ridiculous, but I do have a favor tae ask of you."

"Anything."

"If something should happen tae me, will you watch over Sophie? We've been comrades for sae long that she'd be lost without me, at least for a short while."

Any harsh judgment I had disappeared; any sense of treading lightly because we didn't know each other well yet was gone. Real fear lined her words, and, catching me off guard, her Scottish accent seemed to become thicker. I hadn't really paid attention to the crowd noise still bass-beating from inside the pub, but a knot of concern now thumped with the beat in my stomach.

"What's wrong, Rena? Really, what's going on?"

"Nothing that I'm certain of," she said with a forced smile. "See, I went and made it way too dramatic. I'm sorry. I'm just worried about Sophie, I think."

I nodded. "Hey, let's grab a cab and you come back to my place with me. You can get some rest."

"No, that's okay. I need tae get home, so I'm there when Sophie wakes up. She'll need some support in the morning." The accent went back to light again. "You need tae get home too. I'm sorry, Delaney. I'm . . . It's late, it's been a tough week."

I didn't want to let her out of my sight, but we were going in opposite directions, and I sensed she didn't want me to go with her. "All right, let's get you a cab."

We flagged down two cabs, and I directed her into the first one. She opened the back door, but then turned to face me.

"You'll do it, though?" she asked.

"Take care of Sophie?"

"Just watch over her for a wee bit if . . ."

"Of course," I said. Then I added, "You need to tell me if something else is going on, Rena. I can help. If I can't, I know people who can."

"Nothing's going on. I just want tae make sure." She bit her lip again. "We're all each other truly has. Neither of us have a family who cares. It's just us, and between you and me, I'm the stronger one." She smiled sadly.

"I'm there for anything either of you might need, Rena. Anything," I said.

"Thank you." She got in the cab.

I watched it for so long that my cabdriver honked at me.

My cab smelled of men's aftershave and peppermint. I was sure it was my addition of the smell of gin that made the cabbie roll down his window a small crack. If it wasn't so late I would have called my landlord, Elias, so he could pick me up in his cab, but even though he'd happily have made the trip, he and his wife, Aggie, were early-to-bed and early-to-rise.

"Where tae, lass?" the cabbie said in the mirror.

Besides, I wasn't quite ready to go home. I gave him The Cracked Spine's address.

———

I'd spent a few late hours at The Cracked Spine. Sometimes I worked without any attention to the time; sometimes I went back into the warehouse when I woke up in the middle of the night and felt the need to get back to a project I was working on. I liked the quiet.

Tonight, however, I had a different idea. I'd been spooked by Rena's unsettling request, and I didn't relish the idea of being in the old bookshop building in the middle of the night myself, but I knew someone who could join me.

Tom, my boyfriend, though it had become a habit to call him "my pub owner," was available. He was the proprietor of Delaney's Wee Pub, a place not far from the bookshop that hadn't been named after me, but the moniker given to the business founded long ago felt like a perfect coincidence nonetheless. His employee Rodger was able to close up the pub on his own, so Tom met me outside the bookshop and gallantly paid the cabbie as I got out.

We'd come to that spot in a relationship where we shared these sorts of things all the time. I didn't usually think much about it, but I did notice it that night, and for a moment I marveled at the longevity—almost ten months—of my relationship with this man who allegedly didn't like long-term relationships.

"You're wearing a kilt!" I said as the cab pulled away.

"Aye. I'd say it was just for you, but we had a wedding party in the pub tonight. Rodger and I spiffied ourselves up a bit."

"I like you in a kilt."

"I might have heard that a time or two."

I couldn't see the cobalt of his eyes, but they glimmered off the light from an old-fashioned streetlight on the corner.

I cleared my throat. "Let's go in."

"What are we going to do?" Tom asked as I unlocked the front door.

"Look for some scalpels."

"Aye? Sounds like an interesting adventure."

I gave him a quick rundown of my night with Rena, Sophie, Mallory, and Dr. Eban as we walked through the darkened retail portion of the shop, the side I'd deemed "the light side." I never tired of the book smells, and the constant sense of "messy" all around. Almost a year ago I thought I wanted to straighten everything up, no messes anywhere. Now I knew that the bookshop was just the way it was supposed to be. However, I'd organized most of the mess into a system that not only could I understand, but that my coworkers—Hamlet and Rosie—and even Edwin could as well. My other coworker, Hector the small terrier, even appreciated my efforts with extra smiles and attention when he sensed I was tired from the labors of moving books from one shelf to another, all the while keeping the shop true to its original incarnation.

Tom and I climbed up the stairs, crossed over to the other side—the one I'd deemed "the dark side"—and I flipped the switch that lit a naked overhead bulb. Despite its dust and grime, the dark side was my favorite, because it was where the warehouse, my work space, was located.

We climbed down another flight of stairs, these steps more rutted with wear than the others, and took the short hall back to the oversized and ornate red door. On the way we passed a small kitchenette and the toilet before we came upon this door that hid the secrets.

It hadn't been long into my relationship with Tom that Edwin gave me permission to tell him about the warehouse. My landlords, Elias and Aggie, had also been invited in. For something that was such a big secret, a legend even, Edwin hadn't hesitated to trust my judgment regarding who could be included in our small inner circle.

And even with the warnings about Tom and his love-'em-and-leave-'em ways, and my only knowing Elias and Aggie a short time, I hadn't hesitated to trust them. So far my trust hadn't been misplaced. I'd tried to quit worrying it might happen with Tom, that he'd "leave-'em" me, but every once in a while I'd look at my pub owner, become flummoxed by his cobalt eyes and the way he smiled at me, and think that somehow the universe wouldn't want me to have him all to myself. It was best not to dwell on those worries.

I put the oversized blue skeleton key into the lock and turned three times to the left, unlatching the dead bolts inside.

Because it was the rule, once we were inside and after I flipped on the overhead lights, I relocked the door.

"Cold," I said. "Sorry."

"A wee bit like a dungeon, but in the best way possible."

"Yep." I smiled. I loved my dungeon.

Shelves lined the walls and, as on the light side, things were messy. However, I had a good grip on what was on most of the shelves. I'd inventoried, catalogued, preserved, and filed more over the last year than I had in all the years I'd worked at the museum in Wichita. The warehouse would always be Edwin's, but it was mine too now.

"Over there," I nodded as I checked my desk for messages and found one from Rosie, "are three shelves I haven't done a thing with yet because I've been saving the hard parts for last and these seemed the most packed. If there are scalpels in here, they must be on one of those shelves. Be careful, though, there are some sharp points and edges, and if there really are scalpels, they might still be sharp enough to do damage."

I looked closely at the message. It was from earlier today after I'd left the shop, and said: *Birk needs you, Delaney. He says it's life and death, but you know Birk.*

I could imagine Rosie's eye-roll. The "Birk" she was referring to was a friend of Edwin's. I'd done some research for him, and though Edwin thought Birk took advantage of my skills too often, I'd come to enjoy his flamboyance and general outlook on life. He liked to have, to be, and to throw himself right into the middle of "fun." I'd call him first thing in the morning.

Tom approached a shelf and moved a few large items, uncovering a small wooden chest on the end of one of the shelves.

"Seen this before?" he asked.

"I haven't looked inside it yet," I said.

I didn't remember even noticing the small chest, but there'd been so much to explore that I might have just forgotten about it.

"Gold and doubloons inside this one, you think?" he asked as he carried it to my worktable. I also had an old desk that, true to the ad that I'd answered for the job, had seen the likes of Scottish kings and queens. I hadn't become cavalier about working atop something with such history, but I wasn't scared of it any-more. I'd acquired a roll of white newsprint and, as one would with a doctor's exam table, I changed the paper frequently.

However, Tom was still wary of the desk, so much so that he'd cut a slightly larger path than normal around it. I watched him with the box and smiled at the fact that he'd never even con-sider setting it on the desk.

"Gold and doubloons are distinct possibilities," I said.

I was curious enough to join him at the worktable.

There were sliding latches on three sides of the box. Two moved easily, but we had to use a small screwdriver to budge the last one. With one raised eyebrow and a conspiratorial smile that almost did me in, Tom raised the lid.

"How disappointing," he said as we looked at the empty space inside.

"A nontreasure treasure chest," I said.

"It's a lovely wee box, though."

"It is."

I was glad there were no gold pieces inside the chest. Because of the combined natures of my boss and the warehouse itself, chances weren't nil that there might be gold pieces nearby, par-ticularly hidden in a small treasure chest.

Edwin had tried to allay my concerns about the value of his collections, but there was no escaping my upbringing. He'd al-ways had money. I'd never been poor, but Kansas farm girls were taught more about sticking to a budget and using all parts of everything than Edwin ever had been. There was always some-thing intimidating, magical but definitely intimidating, about the bigger discoveries.

We closed and relocked the box and then Tom put it back on the shelf before we resumed searching for scalpels. We continued to find interesting items, like a boot fastener, a plug-in egg scrambler, and, most surprising to me, a map of Arizona that, according to its accompanying text, might actually lead one to the real Lost Dutchman's Gold Mine.

I tried to call on my bookish voices, that trick of my intuition that recycled lines from books I'd read and spoke to me sometimes when I was at a loss or needed to pay attention to something my conscious self wasn't aware of. Books usually had to be in the general vicinity for the bookish voices to pipe up, and there were plenty of books close by. However, my bookish voices had been communicating with me less and less at the bookshop. I'd worked so hard to keep them under control that they'd come close to muting themselves, become more like silent coworkers that just kept their heads down and their focus on their own jobs.

About half an hour later, just as a wave of tired came over me, Tom moved an old kerosene lamp and said, "Dr. Robert Knox was the doctor, right?" He held up a small chrome container in one hand and the brown leather case it had come out of in his other hand. "This was actually under the treasure chest, but I just got to it. There were other things in the way."

"Yes, Dr. Knox," I said as I followed him back to the worktable.

Gently, Tom set the two things on the table.

"I'm not qualified to touch those," he said. "Have at it."

The chrome container was small, only about three inches wide by four inches high. Its hinged lid made me think of Zippo lighters, and a memory of sitting on my long-gone grandfather's lap flashed in my mind. He'd light a cigarette with a Zippo, click it shut, and put it in the pocket on his shirt. I could still remember the leftover tangy smell.

At first, the engraved stamp on the container was the most interesting part of it. Written in an old cursive font, it said: Dr. Robert Knox, Edinburgh Medical School.

"It doesn't look big enough tae hold scalpels inside it," Tom said.

"They were different back then," I said. "More like a barber's straight-edge razor."

"They folded over, hinged?"

"Yes."

"Then that . . . Delaney, just sitting on a shelf in Edwin's warehouse?" Tom said.

"I know, Tom, it's crazy the stuff that's in here. But, at the moment it seems more than possible."

"Are we going tae have a look?" Tom asked.

I nodded and grabbed a pair of latex gloves from a box under the worktable. After I slipped them on I pulled back on the chrome hinged lid. Packed inside like sardines were what I thought were ivory handles.

I slipped out one of them and then unfolded it.

"A scalpel, or maybe it was called a lancet," I said as I placed it back on the table.

"That belonged tae the man who bought corpses of people who were murdered?" Tom said as he shook his head.

"It appears that way. I'll have to do some research to confirm."

"That's unbelievable," Tom said.

"I know. I've felt that way a few times since I've been here," I said.

"You have an interesting job, love," Tom said.

I smiled at the comment and the term of endearment. I was so taken with the guy in the kilt that I almost thought his words were more interesting than the historically significant scalpels. That was not a reasonable opinion for someone in my position, or something a girl-power girl was all about, but there it was.

"I need to get these in a protective bag before we go," I said. "It won't take long."

Tom watched as I put the leather case into one bag made for preservation and safekeeping, and the chrome case, filled with more scalpels, into another. Then I put the scalpel that I'd pulled out for inspection into its own bag.

"Grab that chest again. We'll put all of the separate bags in it and then the whole thing into a drawer on my desk," I said.

I wouldn't take them with me, because the chances of something going wrong increased the farther they were from the place in which they'd been hiding for who knew how many years. I debated staying in the warehouse overnight—I knew Tom would stay with me. But I also knew that Edwin would think our staying was unnecessary.

I wasn't the only one to double-check the lock on the warehouse door, however. Tom watched as I turned the skeleton key to the right three times, and then he tested the knob after I did. We both triple-checked the lock on the shop's front door.

"Should we call Edwin?" Tom asked as we stood outside in the cold.

"No, he said that only life and death was urgent enough for middle-of-the-night wake-up calls." We'd had a few of those, but I still wondered, were scalpels presumably used by Dr. Robert Knox close enough to life and death? I decided they weren't.

"Your place or mine?" Tom asked as we started the walk up the short hill to his car.

I was stunned and happy about the discovery we'd made. I

was also distracted, wondering if I really had done the right thing by leaving the scalpels behind, but the outside air and the proposition cleared my mind. I made a big deal of eyeing the kilt. "Yours is closer."

Tom laughed, though I could still hear some of his own concern. "Aye, it is. Let's go then."

FOUR

"Extra strong," Tom said as he handed me a cup of coffee. "Just the way I think we both need it today."

"Thank you," I said.

I sent him a tired smile as I took the mug. He looked tired too, but his hair was perfectly messy. I resumed my explorations out the front window of his small blue house by the sea as he turned to go back into the kitchen. His breakfast specialty was omelets, and he'd already cracked the eggs.

I sat in my favorite—in the entire universe, probably—chair and let the sea's waves and foam, both on the mellow side this morning, hypnotize me. I'd already left a message for Edwin, and I had a busy day ahead at the bookshop, so a few moments of contemplation in Tom's chair before breakfast was the start I needed.

I'd thought about texting or calling Rena just to see if she and Sophie were doing all right, but I hadn't done either yet. I'd wait until later in the morning. Though I'd gotten some sleep, the previous evening's events had been playing over and over in my mind all night long. A lot had happened—at the pub and at the bookshop. I had a busy day of follow-up ahead.

It suddenly looked like that busy day was going to begin earlier than I thought. Before I could take a second sip of the coffee, my cell phone rang and buzzed from the bag I'd hung over a hook by the front door.

Tom grabbed the bag and handed it to me just as I managed my way out of the chair.

"Hello," I answered the bookshop's number. It was usually Rosie calling, but not this time.

"It's me," Hamlet said, his voice too high and rushed.

"What's wrong?"

"There's a problem at the bookshop, but Rosie, Edwin, and I are fine," Hamlet said.

"Hector, Regg?" The dog went home with Rosie every night but belonged to all of us, and Regg was Rosie's boyfriend.

"Regg is on holiday in Australia, remember? Hector's fine too. I . . . I think it's just best if you come in. This isn't easy over the phone."

"I'll be right there." I disconnected the call.

Tom was already gathering my things and his car keys.

———

"This is not good," I said as Tom turned onto Grassmarket Square.

Four police cars, their lights blazing, and an ambulance were crammed together in front of the bookshop.

"Hamlet said everyone at the shop was fine," Tom said.

"Something's certainly not right."

Tom parked as close as he could without getting in the way

of the emergency vehicles' expected routes, and we hurried toward the shop.

A police officer, dressed in white crime scene coveralls and with a sour expression on his face, stood outside the door and stopped us.

"Sorry, not open today," he said.

"I work here," I said.

"Are ye Delaney?" the officer said.

"Yes."

The officer sent Tom a look, but then let us both inside.

There were no police officers or EMTs in the shop. Edwin, Rosie, Hamlet, and Hector were all there, but they seemed unharmed as they stood together by the back corner table. Obviously upset in varying degrees, but not visibly hurt.

"Oh, Delaney, it's sae awful," Rosie said when she saw us hurrying to them. "Sae, sae awful." She'd been crying. She held Hector, who leaned into her and looked at me with hopeful eyes. He wanted someone to fix whatever was so wrong.

Edwin stood behind Rosie and put his hand on her shoulder as he grimly nodded for me and Tom to take a seat. Hamlet, who was already sitting, looked at me with wide, scared eyes. When I sat too, Hector squirmed himself away from Rosie and into my lap. Tom sat next to me, closer than normal.

"Delaney," Edwin began. "Hamlet and Rosie came in early this morning. They arrived at the same time and became alarmed when the front door was ajar."

Tom and I shared a look, but we didn't interrupt Edwin's story.

Edwin continued. "They called the police, but then they both came inside." He paused. "The shop was fine, over here, but then they moved over tae the other side and found that things weren't so fine over there."

Hector whined as he must have noticed me become tenser. Absently, I patted his head.

"Over there," Edwin nodded, "they found the window in the kitchen had been broken."

"Was the grate still over it?" I interjected with the first thought that came to my mind.

"Aye, but that led them to wonder further what had happened to the window, so they went back out to explore the close."

"The alley," Hamlet interpreted.

Hamlet had been my interpreter since the first day I'd come to the bookshop. When something distinctly Scottish came up or someone, mostly Rosie and my landlord Elias, used a Scots word, Hamlet would jump in and clarify. I knew what a close was, though. In fact, as Hamlet had offered his help this time, my mind had gone back to that first day, when he'd been the one to greet me in the shop. We'd gathered coffee and tea in the kitchen and he'd first told me about closes, their names, and the stories and histories that went with them.

I nodded and sent him a quick smile, but it was clear that he was just as rattled as Rosie. Rosie sniffed and grabbed a tissue from the box on the table as the tears began to flow down her cheeks again.

"What did they, you, find?" I asked.

"Tragically, they came upon a dead body," Edwin said.

Some words changed everything forever.

"Oh no," I said. Hector snuggled closer. I swallowed hard. "Who?"

"At first we thought it was a stranger, but the police retrieved some identification and it looks tae be someone you might possibly know. You've become friends with some students at the medical school. We all met the women who brought in the books, but only briefly," Edwin said.

I could barely breathe. "Sophie or Rena?"

"No, it's a lass whose identification said her name was Mallory Clacher. Did you know her?"

"I met a woman named Mallory last night, but I didn't catch her last name." I swallowed hard. "Bleached blond hair?"

"Aye," Rosie said as Hamlet nodded.

I nodded and swallowed again as my hands got ice-cold and I began to shake. "I was with her last night, or at least I'm guessing that was her. I'd have to see her to confirm, but I think so."

"Lass, I'm so sorry," Edwin said.

I looked at Tom and then back at Edwin. "Where are the other officers? I, we, need to tell them about last night. Or should we tell the one at the door?"

Tom nodded and took the hand that wasn't on Hector.

Tom said, "We were here last night too, Edwin."

Edwin opened his mouth to speak again, but I jumped in. "We came to search for something. We found things that we put in the desk drawer. I'll give you and the police all the details. But I'm sure we both double-checked all the locks."

"The front door was just open?" Tom asked Rosie.

"Aye," Rosie said.

"Any sign of a break-in?" Tom asked.

"No," Rosie said. "That's why Hamlet and I thought it okay tae come inside. I was the last one oot yesterday and I thought meebe I'd left it open, or meebe Delaney or Edwin was inside already."

"We checked the locks," I said as I looked at Tom. "We checked them all more than once."

Tom nodded. "We did."

"I have no doubt," Edwin said.

But how could he not doubt what Tom and I were saying? I was as sure as I could be that we'd confirmed that the shop and the contents inside it were secure, and I still doubted.

"Delaney, Tom, the door was open but there was no sign that anything had been taken from inside. No damage to anything," Edwin continued. "Other than the window, and that looked to be broken in from outside."

"It looked like no one had come into the shop? Did . . . did the police check everywhere?" They all knew what I meant.

"Aye. I checked the warehouse first," Edwin said. "Nothing seemed out of place, but I wouldn't have thought tae look in the desk for anything. When he got here, the officer in charge walked through everywhere with me, including a brief look inside the locked warehouse. He said they'd probably only need to cordon off the kitchen for now to gather possible evidence. He'd tell me if he needed to look further, but they suspect the bulk of any evidence will be found in the close. I've given them full access to everywhere. I didn't hesitate," Edwin said.

I nodded. "Do you think she was trying to get inside through the window?"

"That's our best guess, but no one would have been able to make it in through the security grate over the window," Hamlet said. "You just met her last night?"

"Yes, I was at a pub with Rena, Sophie, and Mallory. The bookshop did come up in conversation, when one of their professors, a Dr. Eban, joined us at the table. He asked if the warehouse really existed, asked about some scalpels . . ."

"She was curious tae see, maybe," Edwin said.

"Possibly, but she was killed, murdered? Or did she hurt herself out there?" A note of hope lifted my voice. Accidental death was so much better than murder.

"I dinnae think so," Rosie said. "There was . . . She looked . . . Hamlet, please explain."

Hamlet nodded and blinked as he called up some stronger resolve.

"We walked back there and when we spotted her, we hurried, thinking maybe someone needed help. I turned her over and it was clear she was dead. Her . . . her neck was bruised—I'll never forget that." He paused. "There was something else, too. A skull. A human skull had been placed next to the body. As if it had been staged." He shook his head.

It took me a moment to understand why the skull seemed to unsettle him further, but I figured it out. I reached over the table and put my hand on his. "You thought it might be a message to you?"

"I just wasn't sure. It was so eerie and wrong—and the skull. Shakespeare and Hamlet and skulls . . ."

"No, Hamlet, it had nothing to do with you. I met her last night, and it's a good bet that our conversation somehow brought her here and her killer here. Nothing to do with you. The skull . . . well, who knows, but I have no doubt that it has nothing to do with you."

Hamlet nodded.

"It's all right, lad. It's all right." Edwin moved to Hamlet and patted his shoulder.

"Did anyone call Inspector Winters?" I asked. Inspector Winters had become a friend to all of us, though an ever-suspicious friend to Edwin.

No one had.

"Should we call him? Are the other police out in the close? I need to talk to an officer," I said.

"We'll not call Winters yet," Edwin said. "And, I'm afraid I'm going tae have tae intervene and ask you not tae talk tae anyone until you and Tom have an attorney."

"I can just give a statement," I said.

"No, lass. We need to do this the right way," Edwin said. "We can tell them that you want tae talk tae them, but we'll be meeting with them later. Same goes for you, Tom."

"Aye. I have a friend," Tom said. He looked at me. "He'd be happy tae represent us both. He'll tell us if there's some conflict. Let me ring him."

"All right," Edwin said. "If we need more than one, I have a few we could contact."

"Thank you," I said.

"Excuse me. I'll ring him right now and let him know." Tom stood, but then didn't seem to know which direction to go.

"Go on tae the pub, Tom. We'll let the police know you aren't a flight risk," Edwin said. "You should call from somewhere private, and I can't rest assured there's any place around here that is at the moment."

Instead of leaving immediately, Tom crouched next to me. "You okay?"

I nodded. "I don't think we did anything to make this happen."

"Of course not."

"Call me when you've talked to him."

"I will." He kissed my forehead, shared a look with Edwin, and then hurried out of the bookshop.

I looked at Hamlet. "How do you think she broke the window?

"It was just a rock. Nothing unusual, except that it might be unusual tae find one its size around here." He made a five inch or so diameter circle with his hands. "She, or the killer, might have brought it from elsewhere. I don't know. I didn't put all that together in my mind."

"Can I tell you all about last night first? The details, now, before I talk to the police? The things Tom and I found? Maybe you will catch something I'm missing," I said. I had never wanted my bookish voices to speak to me more. Had I missed something that might tell me who had killed Mallory? The voices were silent, telling me my subconscious hadn't picked up on anything either, or maybe it just needed to process some more. I hoped it would process quickly.

"You might want tae wait," Edwin said.

"I don't want to wait." I shook my head.

Rosie said, "Let her tell us, Edwin. We'd all lie for her anyway."

The tiny pull of a smile showed briefly at Hamlet's lips, but he sobered again quickly. Edwin frowned.

"Whatever you're comfortable with, lass," Edwin said.

"I'll let ye know if someone comes back 'round inside," Rosie said as she scooted her chair to a position where she could better see the door.

I told them about the pub. I even told them what Rena had *almost* confirmed about Sophie and Dr. Eban. I mentioned her strange, last-minute concern for Sophie if something happened to her. But mostly, I tried to relay Dr. Eban's curiosity about the warehouse, while mentioning that I hadn't noticed if Mallory had seemed as curious. Had she? Had someone last night done something in the pub, directed toward Mallory, that should have made me worried for her safety, or suspicious? Replaying the events didn't shed any new light.

I tried to recall if anyone had been watching us with evil intentions in their eyes, but nothing came to me. Even the as-described "odd" Dr. Eban hadn't seemed evil, and the sighting of the gray-haired man seemed insignificant—so much so that I was sure my mind had turned the moment into something it really hadn't been.

I remembered finding Dr. Eban endearing at one point. In my mind, the evening still ended with me getting into my own cab after I'd watched Rena get into hers, my concern for her much greater than for anyone else. We'd both seen Mallory drive off with Sophie in tow, but I had no way of knowing if any of them had made it home or if, like me, hadn't wanted to go directly home.

I didn't think Sophie had it in her to kill anyone, but figured maybe the police should look at her and the cabdriver. My concern for Rena was renewed, and I had an urge to call both of the women to ask if they were okay, but Edwin told me to wait.

I hadn't seen anyone else when Tom and I came into the bookshop, but perhaps one of them could have been lurking in the dark close, and unless we'd heard something we would never have considered looking there. I didn't turn the light on in the kitchen and didn't glance even briefly at the window as we passed by it on our way to and from the warehouse. We didn't hear a window break.

"Mallory didnae seem at all interested when Dr. Eban brought up the warehouse?" Rosie asked.

"No, but I was so focused on Dr. Eban at that moment that I wasn't paying attention to the others. I was also worried Sophie might do or say something she would later regret, so I had some attention on her, but I didn't pay much attention to Mallory."

"You're certain you'd only met her last night?" Edwin said.

"One hundred percent sure," I said.

"You don't remember seeing her in the bookshop?" Edwin asked.

"Never," I said. "The three of them seemed to be pretty good friends, but Rena and Sophie didn't mention her to me before. There's no reason to think they would; our friendship is still new. There was a sense of camaraderie between them all. She was a welcome member of the group last night, but so was I. There was no sense that anyone was unwelcome, except for the doctor, and the women weren't rude to him." I took a deep breath. The reality of the murder just kept getting bigger.

"Ye couldnae've seen this coming, Delaney," Rosie said.

"Do you suppose I was followed back to the shop? Tom and I came to look for the scalpels, but we locked the doors. When we left we were both nervous about what we'd found. Tom wanted to call you, Edwin."

"You think the scalpels are genuine?" Hamlet asked.

"Unless they're some sort of novelty items—and we've seen that sort of thing before. They were in a small hinged case with Dr. Knox's name engraved on the outside."

"I didn't know about them either," Edwin said. "Rosie, Hamlet?"

"No," Hamlet said.

"I dinnae think so," Rosie said. "But there's so much back there. I'd have tae see them tae be certain."

"Do you think that Mallory somehow knew they were there, or her killer knew?" Hamlet asked.

"I have no idea. I didn't sense that Dr. Eban's questions were frivolous; but he was curious, not certain. Maybe Mallory was just curious enough to come looking," I said.

"And someone else too," Rosie said. "Curious enough tae kill her tae get tae them first."

"But they didn't get there first, I don't think," I said as I looked at Edwin. "The warehouse seemed undisturbed? It's impossible to know if she was killed because of something in the warehouse or just because she was at the wrong place at the wrong time. I need to look in the drawer. Should we go do that?"

"No, not until the police tell me it's clear," Edwin said. "It seemed undisturbed."

I nodded and blinked away a swell of tears. I swallowed hard just as the bell above the door jingled way too happily.

A man dressed in the head-to-toe white coveralls came around the corner. He pulled off the hood and down on the face mask, and his eyes landed on me. He wasn't the same officer I'd seen outside the shop.

"You are?" he asked, with not a hint of a Scottish accent.

"Delaney Nichols," I said as I stood. "I was here last night, officer."

"You were?" He lifted his eyebrows. He was a big man, and I guessed he was from my neck of the woods even though he hadn't said very much yet.

"Yes."

"I need your statement. If the rest of you would excuse us."

"She'll not be talking tae the police without an attorney present. We're acquiring one for her as we speak," Edwin said.

This was not what the police officer wanted to hear, but he didn't argue. "All right." He sat in a chair next to me. "I'll wait right here."

It was an awkward half an hour, but fortunately not much longer than that.

FIVE

I'd been right. Inspector Raymond Pierce was originally from Duluth, Minnesota, which happened to be the same place my first college roommate had been born and raised. Our short conversation of small talk, interspersed in between all the awkward, went something like this:

"You're from the States?" he asked.

"I am. Kansas. You?"

"Duluth, Minnesota," he said.

There were a million more questions that should have followed and would have in any other setting, but neither of us asked those questions. The strain (on my part mostly; Inspector Pierce seemed practiced at waiting out uncomfortable moments) went on way too long. I was relieved when Tom and the attorney finally rushed through the bookshop's front door. The attorney moved with a dramatic flourish; Tom followed behind with less flourish and more concern. I sent him a quick smile to tell him I was okay. He seemed to relax a bit.

Gaylord Buchanan didn't look like an attorney. He looked more like a pub owner who'd been awakened too early; I'd seen such a thing before. His messy dark hair and jeans and T-shirt made me wonder where he'd been when Tom had called him.

Introductions were made, and I didn't miss Inspector Pierce's tight eyebrows when he realized I wasn't the only one who'd been in the shop the night before. He looked at us before the formal questioning began and asked, "Anyone else?"

We both shook our heads.

Edwin, Rosie, Hamlet, and Hector removed themselves from the back table and left it to the four of us. My coworkers stepped outside the shop, where more people in white coveralls were gathering, coming out of the close, I thought.

I was given a moment alone with my attorney—a man I, surprisingly, found to be more soft-spoken than any attorney I'd ever met. He listened with intense eyes that made me almost uncomfortable. I was glad he was on my side.

He'd gotten a rundown of the night from Tom. After I told him about my time at the pub with Sophie, Rena, and Mallory, and my version of the events, he said, "Just stick tae the facts and the truth. Do not give your opinion about anything, including what you think the women thought of each other or what they might have truly thought about the doctor. Don't offer up anything about the possible affair, but if you're asked specifically about it, just answer honestly and without putting your own interpretation into it."

These were all things I knew, but I sensed that actually doing them correctly might end up being a challenge.

As the four of us sat down together, the moment suddenly felt over the top. Tom and I had done nothing wrong, and I just wanted the police to know what we knew, or at least that we'd been at the shop and hadn't seen anything suspicious. From a distance, I knew that having an attorney present whenever you talked to the police was the only smart way to go. Up close and in person, it was stressful and seemed unwarranted, even if he was on my side.

"The both of you were here together last night?" Inspector Pierce began.

Tom and I nodded and I added, "And I was at the same pub the victim—if it's who I heard it was—was at last night."

Inspector Pierce sent me a blink.

"You were at the pub too?" Inspector Pierce asked Tom.

"No, I met Delaney here afterward," Tom said.

"All right then, let's start from the beginning," Inspector Pierce said as he looked at me. "How did you know the victim, and what were the two of you doing together last night?"

Doing my best to stick to just the facts, I relayed what had happened at the pub, except for the part about the possible relationship between Sophie and Dr. Eban. I did mention that the women seemed to respect their professor even though they also seemed to be bothered by him being there, in the middle of their night out. Because it would be so out of context without the mention of the alleged possible affair, I also didn't mention Rena's request of me to watch over Sophie if something happened to her.

"And you two searched the . . . warehouse for some scalpels?" Inspector Pierce asked.

"We did," I said.

"Did you find any?"

"We did."

"Where are they now?"

"Still locked inside the warehouse, in a desk drawer, as far as I know. I haven't been over to check."

"You didn't know the victim? We have confirmed that the

deceased's name is Mallory Clacher." He looked at Tom, emphasizing Mallory's name.

"I didn't know her."

"These scalpels, would they be worth killing for?" Pierce asked.

"I don't know their true value. And I don't understand what's behind killers' motives anyway. I'd have to research to put some sort of monetary value on them," I said.

"The warehouse is real, but you told the doctor and the others that it didn't exist?" Pierce said.

"That's correct. We don't advertise it, and it has become somewhat of a legend, I guess."

"Is it a secret because of the value of the items inside?"

"Yes . . ." I answered.

"Delaney?" Inspector Pierce continued.

"Right. Well, kind of. It's Edwin's personal world, a place he created full of things that interest him. He's not about the money so much as he is protective of his passions. As you probably saw, that side isn't as well taken care of. The steps are worn, there's more grime on the windows. It might not be considered safe." It was probably perfectly safe, but that felt like the right thing to say.

However, the attorney, Gaylord, sent me a look that told me to remember to just stick to the facts.

Inspector Pierce nodded. "Are the two of you dating?"

"How is that relevant?" Gaylord interjected.

"I need to understand why they were here, together, in the middle of the night," he said.

"We're together, a couple," Tom said, but Gaylord sent him a frown.

Inspector Pierce nodded. "Maybe there's some sort of connection to what Delaney said at the pub and Mallory being here. She might've been curious, I don't know, but I'm going to figure it out. And she wasn't here alone, obviously. You said," he looked at his notes, "that Sophie went with her. I'll talk to Sophie and the other woman, Rena, but I'll have more questions for the two of you." He looked only at me.

"Have you checked on them, Sophie and Rena, to make sure they're okay?" I asked.

"I know some officers visited the victim's building, but you're the first person to tell me about last night," Inspector Pierce said. "I don't know who has been questioned and who hasn't, but everyone was accounted for."

I hadn't said anything earlier, but it suddenly felt deeply wrong to leave something out. I looked at Gaylord. He wasn't going to be happy with me, but I said, "There's a little more."

"Do tell," Inspector Pierce said.

I shared the details about the favor that Rena had asked of me, still not mentioning the alleged affair. Surprisingly, Gaylord didn't frown at me, and Inspector Pierce called in another officer to go check on the women immediately. He asked to get them both into the station for questioning.

"Well, someone killed Mallory Clacher," he said after he dismissed the other officer and turned his gaze back to only me. "The last person or persons seen with a murder victim is of particular interest. I appreciate your cooperation, but no going back to Kansas or anything for a while."

"No plans at the moment," I said. "I mean, of course not."

"We need fingerprints of everybody here, mostly to rule you out. I need any specifics if any of you have been in the alley—the close—recently." Tom and I said we hadn't, but I wasn't sure about my coworkers. "I've got an officer with a fingerprint machine. He'll be right in."

"You don't have to give him your fingerprints voluntarily. Not yet at least," Gaylord said.

"I don't mind," Tom said.

"I don't mind either," I said.

Gaylord nodded.

Two officers came into the shop. I couldn't make out the words that accompanied their somber tones as Inspector Pierce stood to join them by the front door.

"That was fine," Gaylord said. He turned to me. "Did you and the victim have any harsh words for each other?"

"No," I said. "We barely knew each other."

"I didn't think so, but the inspector didn't ask that specifically and I wanted tae make sure." He frowned. "We might have a conflict I didn't foresee. If the victim was related tae a man named Conn Clacher, I might not be able tae represent you. He's a local thug, and I've represented him a time or two. If there are connections . . . Well, I just don't know."

"Thug?" I asked. "Do you think he could have had something to do with Mallory?"

"I'm going tae make some calls and see if there's any connection. If so, I'll tell the police, but I'm fairly certain Conn isn't in town."

"Do you think Inspector Pierce will ask to see the scalpels in the warehouse?"

"Probably, but that's okay, isn't it?"

"Does he need a warrant?"

"There was a murder. They have full access."

I nodded.

"Listen to me. Do not ever talk tae the police about a crime without an attorney present. Promise me." He handed me his card. "Tom and I went tae university together, but no matter of our friendship, I'm a defense attorney. I'm not leaving until he's done, but do not talk to him without me or one of my colleagues."

"I won't."

A knock sounded from the shop's front window, turning those of us inside silent as we looked that direction.

A young woman was outside and peering in, her face close to the glass, her hand shading the reflection. Lots of blond curly hair framed her pretty features.

"Tom?" Gaylord said.

"I . . . uh," he began. He shrugged. "She works for a newspaper, I guess."

"I forgot," Gaylord said. "Excuse me—I'll go tell her tae go away, and then make those calls."

Gaylord left the bookshop, making his way around the police by the front door. He and the woman obviously recognized each other, and they came together in a brief hug and greeting and then seemed to speak to each other in, by all appearances, a friendly manner.

"You know her?" I said to Tom.

"We were friends at university."

"Oh." I smiled at his discomfort.

Gaylord became distracted by another passerby. I didn't recognize the man he turned to talk to, and the blonde didn't seem to know him either. She stepped away from them and knocked on the window again.

One of the officers looked at her and said something. She hesitated, and then said something to him. He said something else before he turned away from her. Obviously irritated to have been dismissed, she frowned as she peered up toward the sign above the window and chewed on the inside of her cheek. She turned and waved to Gaylord, who sent her a distracted return wave before she walked away from the bookshop.

"I'll have to meet her at another time," I said.

"This is an inappropriate moment tae try tae be clever, but is there any chance you'd like tae move tae Glasgow?" Tom said.

Edinburgh wasn't quite big enough for me and all of Tom's previous girlfriends, or at least women he'd dated long enough that they'd been upset when he didn't want to date them any longer. We'd run into a number of them.

"Long commute," I said.

Tom smiled ruefully.

"Thanks for calling Gaylord. I like him," I said.

"My pleasure. He's still living a young single man's life, out every night, but he's a fine attorney. Don't ever hesitate tae call him if you need him, Delaney. He'll be there for you."

"I appreciate it," I said. If Tom thought I hadn't noticed his slightly disapproving tone with the words "a young single man's life" he was wrong, but that sort of thing was currently the least of our worries.

He looked at me, frowned, and said, "Her name is Bridget, but I'd rather not talk about it."

Bridget, huh? "Sure."

The bustle that took place in the bookshop for the next half an hour or so was surreal. We should not have been moving out of the way of the police; there should not have been blackened marks of fingerprint powder around and on the front door. There should not have been a dead body in the close; someone who, it seemed, was killed while trying to get inside the book-shop. There should not have been a skull carried out in a see-through bag by one of the anonymous crime scene officers. And watching the filled body bag being rolled to the ambulance might have been one of the most soul-aching moments I'd ever experienced. None of this was supposed to happen.

But it had.

She'd been so alive, complaining about her dark roots, even. Life was fleeting. You should enjoy each moment because you just never knew. Were these still clichés when they were such truths?

I tried not to cry, not because I felt like I needed to be strong, but because I felt like I needed to be smart. Something had happened the night before that must point to a killer. It was right there.

I just had to remember what it was.

SIX

Inspector Pierce remained outside a long time, watching, directing, discussing. He was definitely in charge.

Tom and Gaylord sat at the back table with Hamlet. I didn't know what they were talking about, but I noticed they'd been looking at some old maps of Inverness that Hamlet had spread over the table the day before. Rosie sat at the front desk and Hector on the desk's edge watching the goings-on with human-like blinks of curiosity. Edwin watched everything too, but he stood by the front window, his attention sometimes focused inside the shop with the rest of us, sometimes outside the window.

"Edwin," I said as I approached him. "I'm so sorry for all of this."

"Lass, you didn't do anything wrong. None of this is your fault."

"I know we locked the doors, but I can't help but think that if Tom and I hadn't come here last night, this might have not happened. Maybe we were followed, and . . . I don't know."

"I don't think that's true," Edwin said. "I think my secrets are becoming too unruly, Delaney."

It hadn't occurred to me that he might have that interpretation. "No, Edwin, it's not because the warehouse is supposed to be a secret. We don't know all the circumstances yet, but it's definitely not that."

If the secret of the warehouse had led to Mallory's murder, then we were all at fault because of our insistence on keeping the mystery, the secret, going. I didn't want that to be the truth.

Edwin gave a throaty harrumph and then leaned a little closer as he lowered his voice. "You know about the skull room at the university? I believe it's part of the medical school."

I blinked. "No." I looked toward the stairs. Inspector Pierce had gone over to the dark side again, this time with two other investigators.

"Of course not. Why should you? There's a room full of skulls at the university; I think the medical school professors are in charge of it. It's not open tae the public, but there for study and research. It's available tae visit by appointment only."

"And a skull by the body. That's one more reason to suspect Dr. Eban," I said.

"Is it?" Edwin said. "Or does that feel a wee bit like a red herring?"

"The killer put the skull there to keep the police on the scent of the medical school professor, or professors? That's possible. It does feel obvious."

"Aye. Whatever it means, I hope the police will put together where it came from quickly. All of the skulls there have a mark on their inside designating where they're from."

"You've seen the skull room?"

"I've contributed two skulls."

I blinked.

"Well, not . . . I acquired them from medical schools in Germany. It was . . . it's a long story. Aye, I've seen the room. It's spectacular."

"Did you mention it to Inspector Pierce?"

"No. I didn't think about it until a few minutes ago. I'll tell him before he leaves, but if they're any good at their jobs, they already know." Edwin looked back toward the stairs. "He wants you and me tae go with him to the warehouse when he's done with the other officers."

I nodded. "Good. I'd like to look in that drawer."

"Aye." He squinted back toward the stairs. "I'm surprised they haven't insisted already, but they seem methodical. Maybe they feel other things are more important."

"You're thinking something else?"

"Did Mallory have anything tae do with the books the other two brought in? The medical books?"

"I don't think so. They were from Rena's father, according to what she and Sophie said. Why?"

"Offhand, I can't make a connection tae murder, but a couple of strange things have happened since the day they brought them in. I thought it was all coincidence, but now I wonder." He glanced around again. "There was a call after they arrived. Someone was looking for those books specifically."

"Sounds like a good coincidence. Hamlet says stuff like that happens all the time," I said. "Did they want to buy them?"

"He said he was 'interested,' but I told him we didn't have what he was looking for."

"Why?"

"It was too easy, Delaney. It's happened before, aye, but these books are extremely rare. There was a tone tae the gentleman's voice that made me think he was searching for answers, not books—he didn't sound like a typical customer. I began to wonder if the books had been stolen, but I haven't done anything about it because . . . well, the women are your friends and I just didn't know yet."

"You were waiting and watching? You didn't want Sophie or Rena to get caught if they'd done something illegal?"

"Well, I like them, you like them, and . . . it wasn't that I wouldn't want them caught. It was more about me wanting tae know the reason they might steal something if that's in fact what happened. I was just waiting a wee bit tae learn what might have been behind everyone's motivations before I pointed anything out. Does that make sense?"

"Yes." If anyone believed that there might sometimes be a good reason to do something illegal, it was Edwin, but I really hoped my friends hadn't stolen the books. "You said a couple of things have happened. What else?"

"Aye. I was in the kitchen the other day, making some tea, and I noticed something about the window. It seems as if someone might have tried tae break in. Mind you, lass, I can't be sure, but I wondered."

"What made you think that?"

"The glass was cracked and there are scratch marks on the bars."

"The glass was cracked *then*?" I'd been in the kitchen just the day before, and I hadn't noticed, but I might not have looked at the window. "The bars would be impossible to file through."

"I believe someone might have tried, though, but we'll never know. The glass is gone now."

"You think that crack, or whatever you noticed, has something to do with the medical books?"

"I can't be sure, but the timing is odd, and none of us knew about the scalpels before you found them last night."

"Someone suspected the scalpels were there. Dr. Eban."

"Right. All roads seem tae lead tae him. The warehouse didn't look the least bit disturbed, but I'm anxious tae see if the scalpels are still there."

"Me too," I said.

"Mr. MacAlister," Inspector Pierce said as if our wishes had conjured him. He came down the stairs with the other officers behind. "We're done with everything but for one more trip to the warehouse to look in that drawer."

"Did you find any clues?" I said.

Inspector Pierce blinked at me. "I'm not at liberty to discuss that." He turned his attention back to Edwin. "Let's take a look in that warehouse again."

"Delaney will have to come with us," Edwin said.

"I understand, but neither of you touch anything. I'll wear gloves."

"I'll come along too," Gaylord piped up from the back table. I hadn't seen him on the phone again so I guessed he hadn't heard back from his colleagues about Conn Clacher's possible tie to Mallory Clacher. He was still Tom's and my attorney.

Tom remained at the table with Hamlet. In tandem, they both sent me a supportive nod. I nodded back, probably not as confidently as I'd wanted to.

Inspector Pierce frowned at everyone but didn't say anything. The four of us were silent as we marched over, three of us following Edwin and his quick, long steps that led us quickly to the red door.

The doorknob and parts of the frame were covered in black chalky marks.

"You fingerprinted this door?" I asked.

I didn't think Inspector Pierce would answer but he did. "Even though there's no evidence that someone got in this far, the shop's front door was open. Maybe someone came and tried all the doorknobs, and you told us you were in here. Checking other knobs became pertinent. We printed the office doors upstairs too."

I nodded and turned the key three times around to the left before I pushed the door open. "Do you want us to wait out here first?"

"No, just don't touch anything," he repeated. "Point, and I'll do the honors."

Edwin, Gaylord, and I followed him in. I could tell Gaylord was holding back a reaction, but he did send me a moment's wide eyes.

"All right," Inspector Pierce said as he looked at me. "How's it look? A general impression first."

"Fine. The same as last night," I said as I noticed the paper over the surface of the desk and the message that I needed to call Birk.

"This the desk you put the scalpels in?" Inspector Pierce pointed as he walked to it.

"Yes, in the bottom drawer." My eyes skimmed over the box of Rena's books still sitting on one of the shelves. I veered that way as I walked to the desk and confirmed that the books were still inside it, undisturbed from what I could gather. Edwin and I shared a glance. I could tell he was torn as to whether or not he should mention the books to Inspector Pierce. I didn't think he would, and I wondered if I should. I looked at him again. He seemed to tell me to make my own decision. They were Rena's books and Edwin had only been guessing connections. I didn't say anything. Yet.

With gloved hands, Inspector Pierce pulled open the drawer.

"In that small treasure chest," I said.

Inspector Pierce moved all three latches easily, and lifted the lid. The four of us peered inside at the bags with the scalpels and the cases.

"Exactly as they were when we left them," I said, relief washing through me, though I wasn't exactly sure why. Why was it still a good thing that the scalpels hadn't been taken? Maybe it was as simple as the fact that they were part of the story Tom and I had told about our middle-of-the-night adventures, and seeing the scalpels somehow proved we were telling the truth about everything else too.

"Scalpels, huh?" Gaylord said.

"Yes," I said. "They look like barbers' razors."

"I didn't touch anything, didn't even think tae look in the desk, but as I told you I did come in and look in here this morning before you and I had a look. Nothing seemed out of place," Edwin repeated.

Inspector Pierce closed the drawer. "Have you ever had any break-ins before? In here, or in the bookshop in general?"

"Never," Edwin said.

"How long have you been in business? How long has this room been . . . this room?" The impatient look on the inspector's face made it clear what he thought about the warehouse: he didn't like its existence.

"In business since the 1950s, this room since the mid-1960s."

"Only one attempted break-in, if that's what happened here, in all that time?" Inspector Pierce said.

"Aye," Edwin said.

Gaylord lifted his eyebrows in my direction, but didn't say anything.

I didn't understand what Inspector Pierce didn't believe, but it was clear he suspected he wasn't getting the whole truth somewhere.

"I'm going to talk to the other women you were with, as well as Dr. Eban, today. I need you to call me if you remember anything else that might help."

"I will," I said.

"Inspector, do you know about the skull room at the university?" Edwin interjected.

"Yes, and we have confirmed that the skull found next to the victim was from there. The skulls are marked on their insides. That might prove to be the easiest part of the case."

He'd answered quickly. We all looked at him. I wondered if he regretted sharing that bit of information. He didn't appear to.

"Lock this place up," Inspector Pierce said after he'd pulled out his phone and taken pictures of the scalpels in the drawer. "I see no reason to turn it upside down. It looks like no one got in here and the items that were discussed are undisturbed. Let me get some results on the fingerprints and I'll let you know when you can resume as normal."

Inspector Pierce watched me closely as I relocked the door. He had us glance into the kitchen. The window was broken, but there was no glass. I assumed it had been cleaned up by the police. Black fingerprint dust decorated the small window frame.

"You can board up the window from the outside if you'd like," Inspector Pierce said. "I really don't want you on this side for at least the rest of today, at least until I hear if any of the crime scene folks need to come back. If you just want to leave it, those bars will keep anything out; anything larger than a cat or a rat, I suppose."

"I'd rather not tempt any animals. I'll have it taken care of from the other side," Edwin said.

"Suit yourself."

The close wasn't like some alleys I was familiar with back in the States. As with most of them in Edinburgh, it was clean, a space for exploration. It had been named Warden's Close because a prison warden had once lived on it, back in the day when people were packed together in the city and creatures like rats brought fleas that spread the plague, killing off much of the population. Twice. I hadn't see a rat since coming to Edinburgh, other than one time when Tom and I took a walk by the ocean and came upon some docks. A rat, cute enough for a children's book, had peered out at us from under some wooden planks, twitching his whiskers before he disappeared under again.

As cute as that rat had been and despite the fact that I hadn't ever seen one near the bookshop, I was all for boarding up the window, no matter from which side.

We watched as the remaining officers and then Gaylord left the shop, leaving behind them an unexpected silence and sense of discomfort. I hadn't realized that though it was weird having them there, their official capacity had also layered in a sense of protection that they took with them.

"I'll have the shop cleaned," Edwin said. "Everyone please go home and get some rest. We'll begin business as usual tomorrow if the police say it's okay."

The front door swung open. It was the woman with the

blond curly hair. Bridget. It was as if she had been lurking outside and waiting.

Her eyes moved over each of us, but landed on Tom.

"What are you doing here?" she said.

Tom didn't answer as he gave Edwin and then me a strained, apologetic frown.

"How can we help you, lass?" Edwin said.

Reluctantly, she pulled her attention away from my pub owner. "My name is Bridget Carr. I'm with the *Renegade Scot*. I heard there was a murder here," she said. "I'd like tae get the facts straight for an article."

Love goes by haps; Some Cupid kills with arrows, some with traps.

Hello, bookish voice. Hero's words to Ursula from *Much Ado About Nothing* might have come to me because of something I sensed in Tom's attitude toward his old friend. Or maybe she was just so pretty that I wanted to shine some sort of bad light on their previous relationship.

"I'm sorry, we won't be able tae help you with that today. Perhaps you could give us some time and maybe stop by tomorrow," Edwin said.

"It'll be old news by then," she said with a smile and a shrug. "Was there a murder?"

"Lass, I'm sorry. We'll have tae ask you tae leave," Edwin said impatiently.

Unbothered, she stood a moment and stared at Edwin. The strained silence lasted a few beats too long before she sent Tom what might have been a glare, though it was difficult to interpret, and then left the shop.

"A friend of yours?" Edwin asked Tom.

"Used tae be," Tom said.

"Aye," Edwin said as he looked out the front window again.

"Aye," Tom said.

I swallowed the surprise jealousy that blossomed in my chest. I didn't think I had such a thing in me. I was sure I had no reason to be jealous. Tom gave me another apologetic frown.

But then, just after the frown, I was almost certain that he took a brief but real and curious glance out the front window. That couldn't have been what I saw. Could it?

No, it must have been my imagination. Hopefully.

SEVEN

Edwin shooed us out of the bookshop. He locked the door and made it clear we weren't to return until the next day. He would have someone board up the window later in the afternoon, but he didn't want any of us to join him for the task. Rosie, Hamlet, and I argued that we should be there too, but Edwin wasn't to be argued with today.

After everyone else was gone and Tom and I were walking to his pub, he said, "I can take the day off. We can do whatever you'd like."

I looked toward the pub's front window. Rodger was probably already inside multitasking.

"No thanks," I said. "I'm fine."

"Can I drive you home at least?"

"No, I want to walk some. I'll take the bus when I'm ready."

He held me a little tighter and a little longer than normal when we hugged goodbye. I liked it when he did that.

I set off with a plan to go around the block, clear my head, enjoy the temporarily clear skies. But I couldn't help myself. My feet, guided by my curiosity, took me around the block once and back to the close. I wouldn't disobey Edwin's and Inspector Pierce's orders not to go inside the shop, but I needed to see where Mallory's body had been.

I less-than-furtively made my way down the narrow-spaced alleyway. Not all of the closes were narrow, but this one was. If I stretched my arms, I could touch both walls with my fingertips. I hadn't asked my landlords, Elias and Aggie, about the history of this one and only knew about the warden's one-time residence because of what Hamlet had told me that first day. Once word of the murder spread it was sure to become busier with curious tourists and locals.

There was nothing architecturally appealing about this one, like some I'd seen, but it did garner some attention simply because it was located so near the Edinburgh castle, as well as Grassmarket Square.

I'd noticed before that it was clean, but today it was pristine. Not even a random scrap of paper littered the concrete ground. I wondered if the police had removed many items. There was no sign that a dead body and a disembodied skull had been found down here. There was nothing gruesome anywhere.

The close was bordered by the dark side of the bookshop and a small used-furniture shop, and I noticed the different bricks used in each building. The bookshop's were reddish brown, but the furniture store's were lighter gray, darkened around the edges from the passing of time.

The window that had been broken was just above my head, too high for me or someone close to my height, like Mallory had been, to get a good look inside, and there was nothing in sight that she could have stood on.

Tentatively, I put my fingertips up to the grate on the ledge and estimated how hard it would be to hoist myself up. It wouldn't be impossible, but it wouldn't be pretty. Why would anyone break the window after they noticed the security grate anyway? With awkward leverage, I tried to pull on one of the bars. The grate wasn't going anywhere.

I stood back and looked up at it. It did look like someone had taken a file to it. Breaking through would have been almost as impossible as moving it. I didn't know how things were bolted in, but it wouldn't budge; even with some good help and a file it would have taken more days than anyone would have patience for. And even if the grate could somehow be removed, the window was small. Some people could probably make it through, but only narrow people. There was a chance I could make it, but I'd have to squirm and wiggle.

I looked out toward Grassmarket. The view wasn't wide, and someone would have to be purposefully looking this direction to notice anything going on, but it was difficult to picture the scenario of someone thinking they could try to break in or murder someone in daylight without being seen. I frowned back up at the window.

"You know, it's said they buried witches down here," a voice said.

I jumped and made a too-loud noise that was a combination of a curse and a yell.

"Sorry," Bridget said with an unfriendly smile as she sauntered closer. "I really didn't mean tae scare you."

She held something in one of her closed fists. I squinted as I eyed a sharp point. She noticed my look and stopped moving forward. She opened her hand and I saw that the item was indeed sharp, and grayish white.

"I don't know what it is," she said. "I found it earlier, at the opening," she nodded backward toward the square. "I heard there was a skull back here with the body, but this isn't part of a skull. It's plaster. That made me wonder if what I'd heard was a skull was maybe a death mask or something similar. Do you know?"

"Death mask?' I said, though I was pretty sure I knew what she was talking about.

"Aye. A cast of the face of a dead person, done in plaster as far as I know, but maybe other materials were used too. It's not a contemporary tradition."

I cleared my throat. The item could be used as a weapon. Nevertheless, I moved a little closer and looked again. It could have been mistaken for part of a bone, maybe a skull. With a ragged edge, it was only about four inches long and a couple of inches wide at its widest points. It might not have anything at all to do with the murder.

"I don't know what the police found. You should have shown them this, though," I said.

Bridget shrugged. "They should have noticed it themselves." She stuck it out closer to me.

I looked at her and then rubbed my fingertip over it. The ragged edge wasn't sharp like the pointed end. The surface was smooth. "Yes, feels like plaster."

"That's what I thought."

"What are you going to do with it?"

"I don't know."

"Consider giving it to the police." In fact, I wondered if I should call Inspector Pierce and tell him she'd shown it to me. The only reason I didn't had something to do with not trusting her. I wondered if she had just brought it with her as curiosity bait to reel me in. If so, it had worked.

"I'll think about it." She closed her fingers and pulled back her hand.

"What are you doing here?" I asked.

"I need to know what happened." She nodded toward the window. "I hear there was a murder. I saw the body bag coming out of the close, but I need confirmation that someone didn't just keel over on their own." She waited and blinked. When I didn't say anything, she continued, "There's so much mystery around the owner of the shop. And there's that secret room of his, or so I've heard." She nodded at the window again. "Is it right inside that window? The room? Boost me up?"

"I'm not going to answer your questions, but I believe Edwin said he would talk to you tomorrow," I said as I made my way around her. She didn't move to give me any extra space, and the squeeze-through only made me clench my teeth tighter.

"He said I could stop by tomorrow, but he didn't say that he'd talk tae me," she said as she followed behind. "You work there? You sound like you're from America. Where?"

"Look, I have to go," I said. "Stop by and talk to Edwin tomorrow."

"I'll just get the police report today," she said. "Then I'll write a boring, police-facts-only article. Or, maybe I'll add the part about the redhead from America who seems to work at the shop being spotted later, suspiciously trying to look into the window under which the body might have been found. I see the window has been broken out. Aye, that could make it interesting."

I no longer disliked her only because she was so pretty and had dated Tom.

"Print whatever you like. It's your integrity on the line," I said.

"Good one."

I kept walking.

"You don't want to know about the witches buried down there?" she said as she kept pace with me, now outside the close. "Most tourists love the story."

"I'm not a tourist . . ." I said before I realized what she was doing.

"So you *do* work there?"

I kept walking.

"Anyway. Back in the day, they used tae roll accused witches down the hill on the other side of the Royal Mile. There used tae be a loch there right where the Princes Street Gardens are now located. It was where everyone who lived on the Royal Mile dumped their waste; nasty business. If the woman being rolled into the filthy loch drowned, she wasn't a witch. If she didn't drown she was, so she'd be brought over here tae Grassmarket and hanged or burned at the stake. A lose-lose situation, if you ask me. There's legend that there was someone, or perhaps a number of someones, who liked tae steal the hung bodies and bury them down the close, right outside their room. People lived more in rooms down here, not flats, but you know what I mean. I don't know if the legend has any truth tae it, but there's no record of anyone being arrested for the weird behavior. I know because I did a story on it once. Have you heard of the *Renegade Scot*?"

I certainly had heard of the paper. I'd read it frequently, along with any other newspaper I came across. I still didn't know nearly enough about my new home; reading the local newspapers, even those with "renegade" in the masthead, was one way to learn. I didn't admit that to her, though. In fact, I had to force myself to keep ignoring her. She was interesting.

She was not to be deterred. "Really, it's true! It's called Wardens Close now, but it used to be Auld Bane Close until someone higher up in the government found out their ancestor lived there and was an old prison warden."

"Auld Bane?" I said, because I couldn't help myself.

"Right. That's Scots for 'Old Bone.' Clever, huh?"

I'd known about "auld" but not "bane." Seemed obvious now.

"Interesting," I conceded.

"I know lots of interesting things," she said. "I'm always happy to share my stories."

"I'm sure," I said, trying hard not to like any part of her, including her undeniable charm, evident even through her pushiness.

"But just tell me this, yes or no, was there a murder at the bookshop?" she asked just as I spotted the approaching bus.

"Come by the bookshop tomorrow," I said. "I'm sure Edwin will talk to you."

I boarded the bus and took a seat halfway down the aisle. I was glad she didn't board too. I'd escaped her for today, but my relief was short-lived. I looked out the window and watched as she turned away from the bus stop and started marching purposefully toward Tom's pub.

It looked like she wasn't going to "ring" him after all.

EIGHT

I hadn't meant to go to Sophie and Rena's flat, but when the bus stopped near their building I hopped up and joined the others who were disembarking.

I stood outside a long time, looking for a police car or something that might dissuade me from checking on my friends. Neither police cars nor police officers were in the vicinity, so I pushed through the gate and made my way to the front door.

I couldn't see her watching me from inside, but the underclassman I'd recognized at the pub opened the front door. Her eyes were red and puffy.

"Did you hear?" she asked as she sniffed. "Did you hear about the murder?"

"I did, and I'm so sorry," I said. "I'm a friend of Sophie and Rena's. I saw you last night at the pub. My name is Delaney."

"Hi." She sniffed again. "Lola. I didn't see you last night. Were you with Mallory too?"

"I was."

"Do you know what happened to her?"

"I don't. I'm sorry," I said again.

"We're all so distraught. How did this happen? Did you see Mallory with anyone else last night? Dr. Eban was there. Did he talk to her?"

"I'm not sure. Why do you ask?" I said. She spoke about Dr. Eban as if I should know exactly who he was, and that she hadn't noticed him join our table. I didn't correct her assumption that I was a medical student too.

"That's what everyone is talking about today, that Mallory and Dr. Eban were having an affair. Do you think it was true?"

I tried to quickly remove the look of confusion that pulled my eyebrows together. She was too distraught to notice my reaction, but I wanted to know more, wanted to know if wires had gotten crossed, and just who was supposed to be having an affair with whom. However, I didn't want to contribute to something getting further out of hand. Any clarification I tried to seek would only make things worse. "It's never good to listen to rumors." I felt like I should be pointing my finger with the advice. I cleared my throat.

"Of course not," Lola said. Her eyes filled with tears again and she put a tissue to her nose. Without saying anything else, she turned and went back into her flat, closing the door with a half slam behind her. I thought about knocking to see if she needed someone to sit with her, but I didn't. I thought about the gray-haired man she'd watched leave the pub, and I lifted my hand to knock on her door, but questioning her about the man would have been too random and bizarre, and completely unsympathetic to her grief. I lowered my hand.

As I moved down the hallway toward the stairs that led to Sophie and Rena's flat, I passed a makeshift memorial. Flowers and cards were piling up outside the door where Mallory must have lived. I became choked up again myself when I saw the tribute, but I'd pushed away the emotions by the time I knocked on my friends' door. If they needed me at all, they'd need me to be strong.

Sophie opened the door with her own set of red and puffy eyes and nose. "I thought you'd be the police." She blinked. "I'm sorry, Delaney. Come in, come in."

The living room of their shared flat was small and always messy; books, papers, and clothes; jackets and sweaters were everywhere. Most of the time their two laptops were also open and in view, but today they were closed, sitting side by side on the coffee table amid a sea of empty and stained coffee cups. Sophie and Rena sat together on the worn love seat, and I grabbed a stool from under their kitchen counter.

"I just can't believe it," Sophie said. "How could this have happened?"

Rena handed her a tissue. She was sad too, but she handled her grief in a more withdrawn, quiet way that didn't include tears.

"I'm so very sorry," I said. I swallowed hard to keep from joining in with Sophie's contagious tears.

"She brought me home, Delaney!" Sophie said. "I remember that part. She made sure I had some aspirin and a glass of water before she left. I remember."

I nodded.

"She was so sweet!" Sophie continued.

Rena looked up at me. "She was killed outside the bookshop where you work."

It was both a question and a statement.

"Yes, in the close next to the shop."

"We were talking about the bookshop with Dr. Eban. He

said something about scalpels. Do you think he killed her?" Rena said.

"I don't have any idea, but I told the police all about that conversation. You're still waiting for the police to talk to you?"

"They said they'd be here soon," Sophie said.

"Just tell them what happened," I said, though I wondered why Inspector Pierce hadn't arrived yet or had Sophie and Rena go down to the station to give statements. He'd probably gone to talk to Dr. Eban first.

Rena's dry eyes seemed to move too quickly today. They usually sparkled with smooth wit and intelligence, but today they were jerky. "Sophie thinks she might have been the last person tae see Mallory alive, other than the killer."

"Yes! And I was all about me last night. My feelings, my stupid marks!" Sophie said. "I didn't once ask how she was doing, or how she felt she did on the exam. I didn't ask her anything about her."

"It's normal to feel the guilt you're feeling," I said. I was going to add that since she didn't kill Mallory she had nothing to worry about. But I didn't know who killed Mallory. As sweet and kind as Sophie had been to me, I couldn't be one hundred percent sure about anything.

Sophie and Rena *were* sweet and smart women, though perhaps somewhat edgy, with a street savvy I didn't possess. Still, the last person I'd seen Mallory with last night *had* been Sophie, and their cabdriver. It had also occurred to me that I didn't actually know where Rena went after I got into my cab. I wasn't suspicious of them, but it would only be normal to wonder.

"Delaney's correct, Sophie. We'll just tell the police what we know. And you had nothing tae do with Mallory's murder. You couldn't hurt anyone. It's not in you," Rena said.

"No, but I could have at least been a little less selfish," Sophie said.

"Do you remember what Mallory said to you on the ride home last night, maybe before she left your flat?" I said.

"I've been trying!"

"Try again," Rena said.

Rena and I were silent as we waited for Sophie to think. She put her fingers to her temples and closed her eyes tightly, and I remembered that she probably had a terrible headache stunting her thoughts and making her memory sluggish.

She opened her eyes. "I can't remember anything clearly. I wish I could. That's how blootered I was."

Even with my very own pub owner, that's one I hadn't heard before. I held back a smile.

Sophie had had too much to drink last night, but she'd also had coffee and a break before Mallory took her home. It was a stretch for me to think she couldn't remember some things, but she didn't seem to be lying.

But maybe she was.

"Rena, did you get home after or before Mallory left your flat last night?" I asked.

"A few minutes after. Sophie was already fast asleep. I didn't wake her up."

Sophie nodded absently, but she seemed lost in her own thoughts.

As innately suspicious as I was, I could not sense even a tiny bit of murderous guilt in either of them. But I did sense guilt— which was probably normal under the circumstances. Even I felt guilty. I wished I'd done something different that might have prevented Mallory's murder.

"You guys know anything about her family?" I asked.

"Her father, you mean?" Sophie sniffed.

"Is his name Conn Clacher?" If Gaylord had represented Mallory's father, then there was definitely a conflict of interest in him representing me and Tom.

Rena frowned. "No. Boris. Boris Clacher. He's a strategic director at the medical school. Part of the administration."

"Not Conn?"

Rena and Sophie looked at each other. Sophie said, "No. Why?"

"It's not important." I thought a moment. "Mallory lived in this building and she's from here? Her father works in the medical school?"

"Aye. He's well respected. And, I get what you're saying, but it's best not tae live with family while you're going tae medical school, if there are other options," Rena said.

That probably applied to all higher education.

"You suppose Dr. Eban and Boris Clacher had a . . . strained relationship?" I said.

"We were just talking about that. We aren't aware of any problems, but Mallory mentioned that her father and Dr. Eban used tae be such good friends, about ten years ago. We asked her what happened tae make them less friendly. She didn't answer us. We didn't think much about it at the time, but we are going tae tell the police when they come by," Sophie said.

Rena nodded. "The police stopped by this morning, but didn't question us. They just made sure we were okay. I think they talked tae one of the residents on the first floor about

Mallory but I don't know. The news spread from there. We didn't even think tae tell the police ourselves that we were with her last night, but they called not long ago to inform us they were coming over again. We've been waiting. We guessed they figured out we were with her, but we weren't trying tae hide the fact. We've been so stunned about everything."

I nodded again. "I told them. I didn't have a moment to let you know they'd be getting in touch. I thought they would have talked to you by now."

"That makes sense," Sophie said. She and Rena shared a glance. Were they bothered that I told the police about them? They didn't seem to be. Sophie continued, "What else can you tell us? She was killed right next tae where you work. Did you find her?"

"No, Hamlet and Rosie did. You've met them. I don't know much more than that. It was tough." Another well of tears tightened my throat, but I swallowed again.

"That had tae be so terrible," Sophie said.

I pushed forward. "Did anyone not like Mallory? Did she have enemies?"

"No!" they proclaimed at once.

"Everyone loved her," Rena said. "She worked very hard, studied all the time. She rarely went out, even on Fridays after an exam. We had tae beg her last night." Now, her eyes filled with tears, but she blinked them away.

My heart beat even heavier. I sighed and looked at my friends. They were unquestionably distraught. They weren't faking it. But there was something else to their emotions or behavior, or both. I listened hard for my bookish voices, silently beckoning them to say something. Anything. What was I sensing about these two women?

The voices had been so silent lately that I was surprised when one answered. One of my favorites, C.S. Lewis.

Someday you will be old enough to start reading fairy tales again.

Did someone in the room need to grow up, mature? Or was I grasping at so many straws that I'd been making up my own fairy tale? Impossible to interpret at the moment.

"Do you think Dr. Eban might have had something to do with Mallory's murder?" I asked. I hesitated, but only for an instant. "Lola, downstairs, mentioned an affair. Between Mallory and Dr. Eban."

They exchanged another look as I zoned in on Rena.

"We can only speculate," Sophie said, her voice so clear that I did a double take. She didn't sound upset at all.

"Delaney," Rena piped up. She sat forward and looked at Sophie before she turned her attention back to me. "I . . . I made a mistake. There was nothing going on between Sophie and Dr. Eban."

"You were pretty sure last night."

"No, that's not true. I told you that Sophie wasn't sharing this part of her life with me and that I was guessing."

"It was just my marks, Delaney. I'm not doing well, and I've been worried. Rena turned it into something else," Sophie said. And then she changed the subject. "We heard Mallory was suffocated."

Had the police released the cause of death?

"I don't know . . ."

"Burke and Hare," Sophie interjected. "That's how they killed their victims."

"You think it might be a copycat Burke and Hare murder?" I said.

"Not that so much, as . . . well, Dr. Eban, Delaney. We told you about his strange . . . adoration almost for the killers," Sophie said.

"Did they leave a skull behind with their victims?" I asked too quickly.

The two women sat up. "What?" they said together.

"There was a skull there?" Sophie said.

"A skull?" Rena added.

"Sorry. I don't know how much the police are going to share, and my information is spotty at best. But did Burke and Hare leave bones behind?" I'd been caught off guard and I didn't know how to get out of it.

"Not that I know of," Rena said, perplexed. "But there's a skull room on campus, part of the medical school."

"I heard," I said, at least keeping mum about the confirmation from Inspector Pierce that the skull had come from that room.

"I'm sure Dr. Eban has full access tae it. We were given a tour our first year—the same day of our first dissection." Rena fell into thought.

"Dr. Eban is an extraordinary teacher, but he's such an odd man," Sophie said. "He might leave a skull behind at a murder scene."

"Tell the police you think he's an odd man, of course, but they'll want an explanation," I said.

They both nodded.

"What did Mallory think of the books you brought to The Cracked Spine?" I asked.

The two women worked way too hard not to look surprised by the question. Had I hit a sore spot?

"She didn't see them," Rena said with a clipped tone.

"No," Sophie said.

I nodded. "Had Dr. Eban?"

"He didn't see them either. Why?" Rena asked.

"No reason, really. It's just that right after you brought them in, we got a call from someone looking to buy them if we had any."

"Interesting timing," Sophie said.

They wondered why I'd brought up the books. I didn't want to tell them about my entire conversation with Edwin, but I took note of their surprise.

"I know, right?" I said. "Edwin hasn't sold them yet. I'm not sure he'll ever be able to part with them. He wanted me to send you his gratitude again."

"Oh, well, thank him again for buying them," Rena said.

I nodded. "Rena, you were concerned for your own safety last night. I feel like there's more to that."

Their surprise about the books didn't even compare with the surprise, almost shock, that lifted their eyebrows.

Rena frowned at me as Sophie looked at her roommate. "You were concerned for your safety?"

Rena shook her head. "I was being way too dramatic. Too much gin, I suppose."

Sophie opened her mouth to say something else but was silenced by another look from Rena, this one demanding that Sophie stay silent.

Like can happen with longtime, good friends, a silent but forceful communication moved between the two of them. They were in everything together; college, flunking out the first time, trying again, and then medical school. In that moment, they were reaffirmed as a team. It was them against me. I could see it, and I could feel it in the air.

"Okay," I said. There were also lies in the air, but I had no way of knowing which parts were false and which were true. I hoped the police could wade their way through and find some answers. And, I hoped the three of us could get past this icy moment I'd somehow brought on.

Rena stood. "We need . . . tae get back tae things, Delaney. Thanks for coming by."

It was an awkward end to our conversation, but I didn't argue. I realized that maybe my stopping by their flat hadn't been such a good idea. In fact, it might lead to interference with the police investigation of the murder; I'd prepared them for things the police might question them about. They'd probably prepared anyway, but I'd just given them a big heads-up.

They were intelligent women.

There are friendships that can survive moments of strife. The three of us hadn't known each other long enough for sustainability to have become an element of our friendship. I hoped that once the truth about Mallory's murder became clear, we could resume where we left off, but I sensed an obvious shift. I'd said or asked too much, or both.

I hoped they didn't have anything to do with Mallory's murder. I didn't believe they did, but I did think they knew something that might help the police find the killer. They had secrets. Didn't we all?

After rushed words of goodbye, Rena shut the door to the flat with a forced gentleness. I looked down the empty hallway and thought about what I should do next.

One idea came to me immediately.

NINE

About a month ago, sparked by the books Sophie and Rena had brought in, Edwin and I discussed notable University of Edinburgh Medical School alumni. Charles Darwin and Sir Arthur Conan Doyle had both studied and graduated from the esteemed school. Darwin hadn't surprised me, but Sir Arthur had. After learning the news, Sherlock Holmes's bookish voice had been in my head for days.

Once I left my friends' flat with a destination in mind, Mr. Holmes spoke to me again, in his British accent but in a disjointed stream of sentences that overlapped and became convoluted in my head. I could have probably focused enough to stop them if I wanted to, but as the words bobbed up from my subconscious, I molded them into a rhythm that was both comforting and pleasant. When I spotted Professor Eban's name on the small marquis board that listed the office room numbers of the medical school professors, most of the voices fell away, leaving me with a singular sentence.

You know my methods, Watson.

It wasn't appropriate for me to have any "methods" when it

came to seeking answers to a murder, but I couldn't deny my need to search for answers, so there I was, at the university, moving through the front doors of a building full of classrooms and offices, contemplating the best way to conduct myself to get some answers. Though it was Saturday, the building was unlocked, but in the few minutes I'd been there I hadn't seen anyone else.

Like almost every other place I'd seen in Edinburgh, and other parts of Scotland too, the medical school's buildings were beautiful architecturally and sprinkled with a magic that made me think of castles and knights in shining armor. Never mind that knights in shining armor had been in England, not Scotland (Hamlet had reminded me of this more than once when my daydreams were inaccurate), the stone structures took me back to a time of lords and ladies, and discoveries like the earth being round and penicillin.

The university was established in 1726, but the Royal College of Physicians had been teaching medicine in Edinburgh since the early sixteenth century. Between my own research and what I'd found in one of the books Sophie and Rena had brought in, I knew that the history of medicine in Scotland had begun with potions, spells, and amulets many centuries earlier. Somewhere along the way I'd read about Burke and Hare and their horrific crimes and how important, ultimately, the study of corpse anatomy had been to the advancement of all medicine. Fortunately, the methods of obtaining bodies for study had become less murderous over time.

As the centuries had passed, the Edinburgh Medical School had become world-renowned. Studying medicine wasn't in my future, but I had a deep respect for those who had the calling to do so. As I set off down the long hallway toward Dr. Eban's office, I spent a moment already missing what my friendship with Sophie and Rena had become and their sharing of some of the things they learned. If I couldn't find it in me to be a doctor, at least I liked to hear about what future doctors were learning.

I hoped we'd be okay.

Education never ends, Watson. It is a series of lessons, with the greatest for the last.

"Got it, Sherlock. Thank you," I said quietly as I zeroed in on Dr. Eban's office door.

I debated knocking, but didn't. Instead, I put my hand on the knob as I tried to formulate what I would say to him if he was there.

I finally shrugged and decided I'd just go with whatever happened.

But the door was locked.

"Can I help you?" a woman asked from over my shoulder.

"Hello, yes, I'm looking for Dr. Eban," I said as I jumped in my skin and then turned.

"He'll not be in today," she said. "Are you a student?"

"A friend," I said. It was a lie, of course, but this stately woman with importantly styled gray hair was probably a professor. She knew I wasn't a student even as she'd asked the question.

"I see," she said as her eyes bored into mine. Hers were intelligent, inquisitive eyes that matched her hair.

Her scrutiny was uncomfortable, but unwarranted, I thought, so I stood my ground and tried not to back away.

"Aye," she said as she cocked her head. "He'll not be in. In fact, many of our office hours are canceled for the day. We've had a tragedy."

"I'm so sorry. What happened?" I asked.

"A death in the family. Of sorts," she said. "Are you a *new* friend of Dr. Eban's?"

"Well, I suppose, yes. I didn't meet him all that long ago."

"And you're not a student? Or a prospective student?"

"No, neither."

When I didn't go on, and after she'd sized me up some more, she continued, "I'm Dr. Eban's wife."

"Oh!" I said reflexively. Hadn't Sophie and Rena described her as fierce? That would have been one of the words I'd have used too, even before she'd introduced herself. However, they'd been complimentary, I thought, and I was glad to meet this intelligent and fierce woman. A plan came together in my mind. It wasn't a perfect plan, as I would soon find out, but it was better than nothing. "I . . . Yes, we met recently. I'm friends with some medical students. I work at a bookshop, and I was coming by to ask his advice on some old medical books. My boss is looking to sell the books, and since Dr. Eban is the only person I know here, I decided to begin with him. I thought he could direct me appropriately. You know, to an expert who could tell me more about the books."

She relaxed in the way I'd seen other women who didn't trust their husbands relax—after they realized he hadn't been cheating.

"I see," she said again, the now friendly if small smile making her seem younger. "You chose well. He is the one tae speak tae. He knows his books. He's set up many a display from his collections." She half-smiled again. "You might be sorry you asked him, but I'm sure he'll be happy tae share his knowledge, wordy though it will be. Perhaps you could come back another day? And block off a good chunk of time."

"Of course. Thank you. I'll try to call first. I'm sorry about the death in the family."

She nodded, and grief pinched at her eyes. She extended her hand. "I'm Dr. Meg Carson."

"Delaney Nichols."

"You're from the U.S.?"

"I am. I was lucky to be offered the job here in Edinburgh, and I jumped on the opportunity. I've only been here for about a year."

She turned as if to lead me out of the building. I went along as we walked slowly down the hallway.

"An adventure?" she asked in the way everyone did, a tinge of jealousy with the curiosity.

"Yes."

"That's a lovely idea," she said, sounding even more youthful. "I'd like tae do something like that someday. We'll see."

"I recommend it."

"What's the name of the bookshop? You said you wanted tae talk tae Bryon about some books. What kind of shop is it?"

This is where my plan would implode or be the reason that Meg Carson might not be so happy to have met me. I didn't know how much she knew about where Mallory had been killed. But I had to give her an answer.

"The Cracked Spine. Mostly used. We have many rare books and manuscripts we acquire and then resell or trade."

"I have a . . . novel," she said, seemingly embarrassed, but not aware of the connection of the bookshop to Mallory. "It's old. I've thought about selling it."

"We love novels," I said.

I thought back to meeting Dr. Eban at the pub. He seemed almost sixty, but a young almost sixty. Dr. Carson didn't look old either; her hairstyle was so sophisticated that even her gray hair didn't make her seem older. But she had that old-fashioned shame about enjoying novels. I still knew some book snobs who thought fiction wasn't important, but for the most part that was a dated and long-dead attitude.

"What's the book?" I asked as we stopped just this side of the entryway.

"*The Scottish Chiefs* by Jane Porter," she said.

"I've heard of that one. Early nineteenth century?" I said.

"Aye. 1810."

"It's about William Wallace?" I said, having recently been submerged in Wallace's history. Goose bumps rose on my arms as I thought about the dangers of that recent experience. I rubbed my arms, but Dr. Carson didn't seem to notice.

"Aye. My mother read it tae me when I was a wee lass," she said. She smiled. "The language and writing are old-fashioned, but I relished every time she read it tae me. The copy I have isn't something from my youth, but something I found in a bookshop not too long ago. It's in pristine condition."

"I know we'd be happy to take a look at it. I'm not usually the one to determine the value, just authenticity, but I can get you to the right person if that's what you want to know," I said.

"Grassmarket?" she asked.

"Yes." I gave her the address and watched her closely.

"I will try tae stop by soon," she said after a brief hesitation.

I inspected her gray eyes. She'd put the pieces together possibly, but she wasn't completely sure. I smiled.

"Thank you for your time, and we'd love to see you at the shop," I said as I pushed on the door.

"Lass? What are the titles of the books you want to talk to Bryon about?"

"*An Atlas of Illustrations of Clinical Medicine, Surgery and Pathology,* from the early twentieth century."

She didn't hide her surprise. She lifted her eyebrows and blinked as her mouth made an O. She finally spoke, "Hand-drawn illustrations?"

"Yes. You know about the books? Oh, of course you do. I'm sure most medical school professors and doctors would know about them."

She half-smiled once again. I wondered if that was her only smile. "Well, I've heard of them, and Dr. Eban, Bryon, will be very happy tae talk tae you about them. I have your address. I'll have him ring you. It won't be today . . . the death . . . but I'm sure he'll want tae meet with you soon."

"I look forward to it. I'm truly sorry for your loss. Someone in your family or your husband's?"

"Neither. A student." She looked at me, and her eyes hardened. She'd definitely put all the pieces together. I would answer honestly if she asked me any questions, but I held back from offering anything more. I'd dug myself in deep enough. Time to cut myself loose.

"Oh, that's terrible," I said, pushing on the door some more.

"Goodbye, lass."

She nodded once, curtly, and then motioned for me to go, almost swept me away. I did leave, and she locked the door behind me before she turned and walked back toward the hallway. I heard her quick footsteps fade away.

I took the locking door personally and wanted to check it just to make sure. It was definitely locked tight.

It had been a meeting of mixed, and confusing, messages. I hadn't had a plan, and the one I'd improvised had been less than ideal.

However, in a way, I now understood the "fierce" description regarding Dr. Carson's persona, and I wondered how she
might use that fierceness to put her husband in his place, if
that's what she did. Though I'd wanted to talk to Dr. Eban, I
found Dr. Carson just as interesting, if not more so. However,
I didn't know what to make of either of them.

I decided she'd probably still pass along the message about
the books. If she was the type of person I thought she was, she
would use any excuse to question her husband about me, no
matter that we didn't really know each other and that chances
were he'd forgotten all about meeting me.

"Hello." A female voice pulled my concentration away from
the door.

"Lola, hello," I said to the woman I'd only formally met this
morning. I didn't jump in my skin as much this time. She didn't
look any the worse for wear.

"Small world," she said. "I assumed earlier, but are you a
student here?"

"No," I said. I looked back at the office building. "Long
story why I was here today." I looked at her and the backpack
slung over her shoulder. "Are you here to study?"

"On my way to a group project meeting now. Glad to get
my mind off what happened to Mallory, but I'm not a fan of
group projects."

"I remember that feeling," I said.

She was so young that, unfairly in my mind, she seemed on
the opposite end of the spectrum from Dr. Carson. Her dark
ponytail fell all the way to the middle of her back and her large
blue eyes shone even bluer against her matching sweater and her
fair, smooth skin. There were no red eyes, no red splotches, but
she looked tired. It would have taken me a couple of days to

bounce back if I'd been crying as hard as she had been. She had a pixie nose that somehow looked refined, but I imagined it had been cute when she was a little girl.

"What year are you?" I continued as I stepped next to her.

"What year do you think?" she asked.

"Freshman?"

"No. It's my last year. I get mistaken for a new student all the time."

"Nothing wrong with looking young."

"No, I suppose not."

"What are you studying?"

"I have to get to my group, but walk with me if you'd like," she said.

We fell into a comfortable but quick pace.

"I'm studying economics," Lola said. "My mother is from the U.S. and my grandfather is in banking in Virginia. I'm moving there after school, see if I like it."

"An adventure?" I said.

"Yes," she said.

I stopped walking before I said, "I'm sorry to bring this up again, but earlier you mentioned a rumor about Mallory and Dr. Eban."

"Oh. That. I was upset, and I should never have said anything like that," she said quickly. "You were right about rumors and all. I'm sorry." She looked to her left quickly, toward George Square, a patch of short trees and green grass beyond some of the campus buildings, where students passed through, or relaxed when the weather allowed, which wasn't often.

There were no events there today, and only a few students passing through.

I wondered what she'd seen or was looking for, but she

moved her attention back to me before I could notice anything curious.

"You don't think it's true? The rumor?" I said.

"I really don't know, but it was weird and wrong for me to make such a comment at that moment."

"It's okay," I said. I watched her but she didn't look back at George Square. "Do you know much about Dr. Eban?"

"I guess I know his reputation."

"Because you go to school here, or because of where you live?"

She thought a moment. "Both, probably. I don't know if I would know about him if I didn't live in a building with so many medical school students. Since I do, though, I pay more attention to things that might be said about him."

"Like?" I said.

She made a doubtful noise in the back of her throat. "I'm not really sure. I don't want to say anything that's . . . Well, I shouldn't have said what I said in the first place."

She turned and started walking again. I kept pace.

"Do you think you should tell the police about Dr. Eban? Maybe because of Mallory specifically. Even rumors should be considered, maybe. I shouldn't have chastised you. I'm sorry."

"Oh, I already told the police," she said as if it had suddenly become clear to her that that had been my concern all along. "That was the first thing I told them. They showed up not long after you left Sophie and Rena's. I . . . I happened tae see you leave. Oh, yes, I told them."

"Good."

"It's what Rena and I discussed last night. When she said she was as sure as I was that Mallory was with Dr. Eban and that's why she hadn't come home. It seemed like the right thing tae do."

My steps hitched as I processed her words.

"Last night?" I said. "You talked to Rena last night?"

"Sure, when she got in, she stopped by Mallory's door and knocked. I heard her so I peered out, told her I'd seen Mallory leave after coming in with Sophie an hour or so earlier. I'm a light sleeper, and I hear and see almost all of the ins and outs in our building. I wish I could sleep better, or that the walls were thicker, or that I couldn't see most everyone coming and going."

"What time was that?" I asked, holding back on suggesting she could close her blinds.

"One or one-thirty," she said.

Hadn't Rena said that she'd come home shortly after Sophie? Sophie and Mallory had left the pub at around midnight.

"Rena got home that late?" I said.

"Aye, she does sometimes. We all do," Lola said.

"I remember," I said. I was probably reading way too much into Rena's late night and the lie about when she got home. She was a grown-up who'd just taken a big anatomy exam. A late night with whatever activity she desired was well deserved and she didn't owe anyone an explanation. Unless murder had been involved, of course. And, she'd knocked on Mallory's door. Mallory was a grown-up too. Obviously, she had left at some point after dropping Sophie off. She'd been killed in the close. That didn't mean she'd been with Dr. Eban. I wished I'd thought to somehow ask Dr. Carson if she knew where her husband had been all night.

"You remember . . . being at university?" Lola asked.

I smiled. "I do. I worked hard, but I wish I'd had a little more fun."

Lola laughed. "Not a problem for me. In fact, my first couple of years' marks show how I should have held back on the fun a wee bit." She looked toward the small, ornate old building we'd come to. "This is my stop. After seeing you a few times over the past few months, it's nice to have finally met you, Delaney. I'm sure I'll see you around."

"Nice to meet you too," I said as she started up the building's front stairs. "Hey, Lola, did you by chance tell the police what time Rena made it home?"

She turned and shook her head. "I don't think so. Not specifically at least. It didn't seem to matter much. Do you think I should?"

"I do."

"Okay." She looked up to a man waiting for her by the doors. "Gotta go though."

I nodded and watched her greet the man in a knit cap. They hurried inside without looking my way again. Though I'd enjoyed school, I was grateful I wasn't on my way to classes or exams. And especially to group project meetings.

I'd probably already ruined my relationship with Sophie and Rena, but I really wanted to know why Rena had gotten home so late, or had left and then come back.

If I hadn't ruined it yet, it looked like that was next on my agenda.

TEN

"They haven't answered my calls," I said to Tom as I balanced my phone on my shoulder and took the coffeepot from its perch on the machine. I'd tried to call Sophie and Rena a few times since leaving Lola at the university the day before. "I'm not surprised, but I don't want to just stop by their flat again. Yet. I might later today."

"You had a productive day yesterday," he said into his phone. "What do you think Rena was up tae after the pub?"

Saturdays, date nights for many couples, were the evenings Tom and I most often didn't spend together. They were, naturally, one of the pub's busiest nights, and Tom sometimes didn't close in time for us to be together, at least with me still awake enough to be good company. As with this Sunday morning, he was usually back in the pub early to finish any remaining cleaning and do his weekly paperwork. It was a comfortable routine, and we both usually tried to go our own ways with the hope of getting together later in the day. We enjoyed our Sunday afternoons, but for now a phone call would have to do.

"Rena was probably not doing anything that had anything

to do with the murder, but I'm curious. Why did she lie? Except that her personal life is none of my business. I'm aware of that. And maybe it wasn't technically a lie. She probably did come home first and then knock on Mallory's door before she left again."

"The question is where did she go?"

"Yep. Hopefully, the police know."

Tom paused, but not for long. "You're going to call Inspector Winters, aren't you?"

I smiled. I'm sure he heard it in my voice. "I thought I might stop by and see him."

"I'm not surprised. Let me know what he says."

"Okay, so," I paused, but couldn't think of a way to ask him a question any other way than outright, "did that woman stop by and talk to you at the pub yesterday?"

After he paused too, he said, "Bridget? Aye, briefly. I took a call and she got tired of waiting for me tae hang up."

"I thought she might be headed your way. I tried to call your mobile, but no answer. I didn't think of trying the pub phone. She caught me looking around where Mallory's body had been found, and asked me if there had been a murder. I got on the bus as soon as I could without telling her much of anything. At least the fact that it was a murder is in the news now."

Mallory's murder had made the front page of the *Scotsman*. However, no details were given. The article I'd seen said only that she was murdered and an investigation was under way. The reporter didn't even mention where her body had been found. It was a sparse story, making me think the police hadn't shared much of anything yet.

"Aye. She's a persistent reporter, I'm certain. I'm sorry about . . . the past circumstances. She knew I didn't want tae talk tae her either. Delaney, you know you have no need tae worry about me. I'm one hundred percent yours as long as you'll have me around."

He'd said this so matter-of-factly that I wondered if he really understood the ramifications of his words.

"Glad to hear it. I'm in too, for as long as you'll have me around."

The pause went on a little longer this time.

"I'm terribly sorry about the lass, Mallory, and for her family and friends," Tom said.

"It's sad. Mallory's father's name is Boris, not Conn— Sophie and Rena told me, but that was mentioned in the *Scotsman*. I think Gaylord is okay to represent us if we need him."

"Good tae know. He's a good friend, and an even better attorney, though I hope we don't need him."

The crash of glass and curse words from Rodger came through the phone.

"I'll talk to you later," I said before Tom hurriedly ended the call.

It would have been easy to lose myself in a daydream that was all about Scotland and my handsome pub owner, even if it seemed to have turned into more than just a daydream. The edges of my daydreams were less and less fuzzy all the time.

But I had things I wanted to get done and I knew someone else who liked to work early Sunday mornings, and who might be able to answer some of my questions.

———

The National Museum of Scotland wouldn't be open until ten on Sunday and the administrative staff would be a skeleton crew, but my connection would be there early.

I had met Joshua Francois, a young prodigy from Paris, when I'd been roaming the museum one day. He already held a number of degrees, and at the tender age of twenty-three he was working on his PhD as well as in some sort of internship capacity at the museum; he was paid a small sum, and his even smaller office, a onetime supply closet, might not scream status, but he was well respected by everyone at the museum. He and I had hit it off immediately because of that mutual part of us that experienced glee when talking about or even just thinking about the history of things. He knew a little bit about everything.

I called him as I stood in front of the museum's locked main doors. He answered with, "You're here, aren't you? I'll be right there."

I didn't have to wait long.

"Delaney! I'm so glad to see you," he said as he pushed open the door. He spoke English without a hint of any other accent. When he spoke his native French, he sounded perfectly French. The same was true when he spoke the other languages he'd mastered. "I've been missing you."

"I've missed you too," I said as I went through and he shut the door behind me.

He was tall and lanky with glasses too big for his narrow face, but he wore them well.

"I'm sorry I had to bow out of our last lunch, but you're here today. What's going on? Any more murders?" he said with a smile that deflated when he noticed the look on my face. "Really? Oh. Well, come along, let's talk in my office."

He led me through the expanse of the main displays and then down two short hallways to his hidden door. He looked around before he reached for the handle—a ring that pulled outward and that was normally flush with the surface. I hadn't noticed anyone else since coming inside, watching us or not, and I didn't completely understand why the location of his office was such a secret, but I enjoyed playing along.

Once in the office, I took my normal seat that positioned me so my knees were crammed into one side of his desk. The large computer screen was bright with a spreadsheet; he'd never explained to me why he always had a spreadsheet displayed. The ever-present yellow notebook was also there, facedown again as always, and there was nothing else on the desk.

"Tell me what's going on," he said, still with a lowered voice, though it didn't seem likely anyone could hear us, or was trying to.

"I will. But first, your dissertation?"

A smile lit his face. "Done yesterday. I mean, there's more to go, I have to defend it and everything, but for all intents and purposes, it is done."

"Congratulations! The first of many to come, I'm sure."

"Oh gods and goddesses above, I can't do that ever again." He took a deep breath. "At least until the next time, right?"

"You aren't leaving the museum, or leaving Edinburgh now, are you? At least not until you're finished with everything?"

"For now, I'm here. I don't know what tomorrow will bring," he said as the smile faded a bit. He loved his work at the museum. He enjoyed Edinburgh. He and I had a real kinship that we both enjoyed.

"Oh, I hope you stick close by," I said.

"Me too. Let's not worry about tomorrow, all right? Talk to me. What happened and why do you need me?"

It's not easy to begin a conversation about a murder, even if the person you're telling didn't know anyone involved, and even if the person is a friend you can talk to about pretty much anything. To top it off, Joshua was one of the most empathetic people I'd ever met, so I treaded lightly as I relayed the tragic details I was willing to share. He hadn't seen the newspaper yet, said he was just about to read it. I didn't get into the rumored affairs, but just mentioned that the women I was with at the pub thought Dr. Eban was strange, and that though I might have thought him strange, he wasn't off-putting to me at all.

"He's brilliant," Joshua said, his heart heavy over the demise of Mallory, a woman he didn't know. "Odd, but brilliant."

"I'm trying to understand how he's odd."

Joshua bit at his bottom lip a moment. "Creepy. No, not creepy, eerie. Black cape, vampire eerie, but real-life stuff. He comports himself with that kind of an attitude. Does that make sense?"

I nodded. "I heard he's intrigued by and uses Burke and Hare in his teachings."

"I've heard that too. He also has an eye for the pretty women, or, again, so I've heard. He's a flirt."

"More than a flirt maybe? Do you think he's ever been . . . I don't know, forceful toward the women he found attractive?"

Joshua shrugged. "Anything is possible, but that's not the rumor." He thought a moment. "His wife is something else."

Fierce? I thought, but only thought. I wanted his impressions without my interference. "How?"

"She's even more brilliant than him. I think she's been a part of many new drug discoveries that have hit the international market. She's had more articles published than anyone else at the medical school, maybe more than everyone else combined. I think she was even in on a design for a better ultrasound machine. I'd have to do some research to find the details, but I'm happy to look into it."

"Thanks," I said. "Do you know Mrs. Eban, I mean Dr. Carson, personally?"

Joshua laughed. "I've breathed the same air as she has. It has been an honor to hear her speak the few times I've made it to one of her lectures. I adore her, but I'm not in her league."

"You're in everyone's league, Joshua."

"Dr. Carson's . . . not to be messed with. It is a huge mistake to contradict her, or question her in a way that makes her look mistaken about something. I've heard she can reduce students, other professors, and administrators to ash when they've sent a difficult attitude her direction. She's . . . gosh, 'fierce' might be the word."

I held back a nod. "But you like her?"

"What's not to like?" he said sincerely.

"Have you ever talked to Dr. Eban?" I asked.

"No, he's almost as talented as his wife, but only almost. I've never seen him speak, but only because of conflicting schedules. I'd be interested."

"Do you know about the skull room on the medical school campus?"

"Of course. I've seen it."

Though the article in the *Scotsman* hadn't mentioned the skull by the body, I'd already decided to tell Joshua that part of the mystery, though I still wished I hadn't said anything to Sophie and Rena.

"There was a skull by the body. From the skull room. The inspector confirmed that's where it was from by a mark on its inside."

"And Dr. Eban is the professor in charge of the room. He's the keeper of the keys, so to speak."

"He is? Well, that makes him look guilty, huh?"

Joshua thought a moment. "Actually, I think it's too obvious. I think the killer must have planted it."

I nodded.

"What do you know about death masks?" I asked.

"Everything. What do you want to know?"

"They're made of plaster?"

"Sometimes wax. And there are two different definitions. Casts of a face after death; something to keep. However, there's also the death mask left atop the face after death, like the ancient Egyptians."

"I'm talking about in Scotland, the ones kept by the living. Is there a way to date the plaster, or the wax? Know when it was created?"

"Possibly. It would depend on exposure, et cetera. Why?"

"Would the skull room have any of those? Would Dr. Eban have access to any?"

"I wouldn't be surprised if the skull room has them, but I don't remember seeing any in there. I'm sure we'd all be surprised by Dr. Eban's collections. He has a display case right outside his classroom. He probably has the gory stuff hidden. At least that's what he's been asked to do."

"What kind of stuff does he keep in the display case?"

"Gosh, so many different things. Medical instruments, books, historical clothing. He had a brain in there a couple of years ago; that's what he was asked to remove. Even for a medical school hallway, it was a bit much for any chance public viewing."

"Things like old scalpels?"

"Sure." He looked at me.

I hadn't told him about the warehouse, but he'd asked a time or two. I didn't want to say so much that I had to lie to him about its existence once again, but I did wonder.

"Old scalpels would be pretty valuable, I bet," I said.

"Some. Why are you asking about old scalpels?"

I shrugged. "Just curious. I'd like to see the skull room. Would that be possible?"

"I'll see what I can to do this week. Have you heard of Sir William Turner?"

"I feel like I have, but I can't place him."

"He was a professor of anatomy at the university way back in the 1860s. He collected most of the skulls. There are also preserved specimens, mostly of malformed fetuses. No ultrasounds back then. The specimens helped in the study and discovery of why some didn't make it full term, as well as birth defects. If you have a sensitive stomach, it can be tough, but it's undeniably interesting."

Since I tended to be squeamish, I wasn't sure I would be able to find the specimens as interesting as Joshua seemed to, but I was sure I'd find the skulls interesting.

"They had to start somewhere, right?" he said.

"Exactly," I said. "Thanks for trying to get me in. Can I ask you more about Burke and Hare?"

"Of course."

"I know the general story of what happened, but can you tell me more?"

Joshua stood. "Come on."

"Where are we going?"

"We have a whole corner devoted to the killers."

"You do? How have I missed that?"

Joshua smiled. "You and I are slow-goers through this place. I know I've never visited that corner with you. At our rate, we were bound to get there in a couple of months, but we'll veer off course today."

I'd been visiting the museum one section at a time with Joshua. He'd been the most knowledgeable tour guide, sharing small details I never would've picked up on on my own as we lingered over every display case's items. We were museum soul mates. It wasn't easy to find our kind.

We went up a flight of modern steps and then to a corner that transported us back in time. The three wide display cases were only about as high as my shoulders. Framed in ornate black wrought iron, the cases themselves were showpieces. I zoned in on the natural focal point, a black-and-white sketch of the two murderers, front and center in the first case. Their faces had been familiar to me since I'd moved to Scotland.

My first week in Edinburgh, I'd found my way to the Cadies and Witchery Tours; their shop was not far from the bookshop and on the way up to the Royal Mile. The tour group members had been not only fun and interesting, they'd been helpful in pointing me to places in the city I should explore. At that time, a calling card case made with some of Burke's skin had been on display in the shop. It had been one of the strangest things I'd ever seen. I couldn't tear myself away from it for a good long few minutes, and I'd become intrigued enough to later look up the killers' pictures.

"I saw a card holder made with Burke's skin," I said, as Joshua straightened the corner of a plaque describing the display. He nodded. "Why did they make such a thing?"

"Yes, the judge who sentenced Burke to hang also decreed that his body be used for study at the school of anatomy.

Irony—eye-for-an-eye thing, I suppose. His skin was used for a few items, like the card holder. Here, read this." Joshua pointed at a card displayed atop a small easel.

I read aloud: "Your body should be publicly dissected and anatomized. And I trust, that if it is ever customary to preserve skeletons, yours will be preserved, in order that posterity may keep in remembrance of your atrocious crimes. Lord Justice-Clerk, David Boyle." I looked at Joshua. "The judge said this?"

"Yes, and Burke's skeleton is kept at the University of Edinburgh. Hidden away somewhere, though it's sometimes displayed."

"His skull?"

"With his body, I presume, but those would be secrets I'll never be privy to. Post-hanging, his body was dissected at Old College. It's a building at the university that now has administration offices. A note was written in his blood by the man who dissected him. Here." Joshua pointed to another shelf. "Ours is just a copy, though."

I read again: "This is written with the blood of Wm Burke, who was hanged at Edinburgh. This blood was taken from his head." I stood up straight. "Goodness, that's gory."

"Right. Not only was his skin used for the business card holder, I know there's a book made with it along with his death mask, speaking of them, on display at Surgeons' Hall at the university. We've got a replica death mask, though." He pointed again.

"Hare's death mask too?" I noticed there were two.

"This one is said to be Hare from when he was alive," Joshua said. "We don't know what happened to him. He disappeared after he was released from custody after the trial. He's the one who got away, turned king's evidence on Burke. Sad."

"Bizarre, making things from the skin, keeping the skeleton, even the death masks to some extent," I said.

"They were brutal killers." Joshua shrugged. "Too bad they couldn't get rid of them both."

In the next display case, the one mostly about Dr. Robert Knox, I saw a scalpel. I held back a squeal of glee when I recognized it to be just like the ones Tom and I had found in the warehouse, except that the ones in the warehouse were in pristine condition, seemingly never used. There were no signs of blood or skin on the one here in the case, but it was obvious it wasn't in the same great condition.

"Is there a case?" I asked.

"For the scalpel? Not that I'm aware of. That would be quite the find," Joshua said.

For a moment I couldn't take my eyes off the scalpel.

"What's the deal with scalpels?" Joshua asked.

I looked at him. "Nothing really. Are all the death masks and replicas secure somewhere? Have any of the actual ones or copies gone missing?"

"I don't know. I'm truly not aware how many are in existence. Some were found in the cupboard of a former prison, one that neither Burke nor Hare had been incarcerated in. Who knows how many are in existence."

I'd been suspicious that Bridget had made up finding the piece of plaster because she knew she could bait me with the idea of a death mask to get an answer about the skull. I still doubted her story, but I couldn't be sure.

"I'm so sorry for the victim," Joshua said as we moved back and lingered in front of the masks. "Rosie found the body?"

"She and Hamlet."

"That's going to bother her even more. I'm sorry about that too."

"She's tough, but yes, it will," I said.

"I'll take her some cookies, though that sounds a bit jovial."

"She'd like that."

Joshua had fallen in love with the bookshop, and then with Rosie—in a grandmotherly way. They'd hit it off the second they'd met, and I'd begun to think that when he stopped by he was there more to talk to Rosie than to me. I was happy for their friendship, something they'd both seemed to need, even if neither of them had realized it.

"You know," he continued, "though I don't agree with the ways Dr. Eban does it, there's something to what he says about the killers contributing to medical science in important ways. The murders probably would never have happened if the doctors and students had had enough cadavers. Dr. Knox was probably desperate enough to learn what only cadavers could teach him that he didn't ask any questions when Burke and Hare brought him bodies."

"Were there not enough people dying?" I asked.

"No, no, that wasn't it. Mostly it was because before the Anatomy Act was passed in 1832, only condemned prisoners' bodies could be used for scientific study. As more students filled the university's halls, fewer and fewer prisoners were condemned to death. There was a definite want for bodies." He cleared his throat.

I pointed at a plaque that was titled "Body Snatchers." I said, "Grave robbers?"

"Yes, Burke and Hare killed, but others simply stole bodies from graves. That was illegal too, but supply and demand, you know. The money was good. Back then I'm afraid it was a short leap from grave robbing to murder." He fell into thought and shook his head.

"You wish you could have seen that time in person, don't you?" I said.

"Just briefly. Then I could travel on to the time of the dinosaurs for a week or two, and then, of course, I'm sure I could figure out the true identity of Jack the Ripper given a day or two in London."

"I have no doubt."

One of our favorite topics of conversation was about what time period we wish we could visit. Neither of us wanted to live in a different time, just vacation there, for day or weekend trips.

"Imagine the excitement with the deluge of medical discoveries," Joshua said.

"And how particularly awful it was when they didn't know how to save people from what's now considered easily treatable illness."

We looked at each other and, in tandem, said, "Appendicitis."

"So many people died," he said sadly.

"So many," I agreed.

We'd had this conversation more than a few times over the almost-year we'd known each other. Appendicitis had killed many, until it was discovered that the offending organ wasn't of much use anyway and just needed to be removed.

"How did Burke and Hare know each other?" I asked as I looked at the masks again.

"Ah. Burke, a vile man, moved to Edinburgh with his mistress. He had to get out of Ireland because he viciously murdered one of his master's horses. He brought his mistress along and left his wife in Ireland. Ask me, the wife got the better end of the deal. Anyway, Burke had known Hare's wife beforehand. She'd married Hare after her first husband died, and ran a lodging house on Tanner's Close in West Port. Apparently, she insisted that Burke and his mistress move in. Though they both worked on the canal, from what I've read I don't think the men met until they lived in the same lodging house.

"They hit it off. They must have both been horrible men. It was after one of the lodging house customers died that Burke and Hare made the money that was owed to Hare's wife by selling the corpse to pay the bill. From there they decided that robbing graves was too much work; they'd just . . . manufacture the corpses themselves."

"Ugh. Gruesome."

"Yes. They said all their actions came from too much drink. There even came a time when they'd only be able to fall asleep after drinking too much, and they had to sleep with a light on. Their crimes haunted them, or so they said. That's some good news."

We lingered at the display a bit longer, but I didn't learn much more. I didn't take the time to read all the articles propped upon the shelves, but this wasn't a normal museum visit. I'd shown up unannounced, and I knew Joshua hadn't carved out the time to be my tour guide all morning.

As we were walking toward the museum doors, though, I had one more question for Joshua.

"How did Burke and Hare kill their victims? What was their method?"

"Ah, well, mostly by smothering them, or at least that was the conclusion. It was a good way to kill someone back then, because that method of murder couldn't be easily determined.

Many times, after Burke and Hare gave their victims too much to drink, Burke would lay atop their chests as Hare put his hands over their nose and mouth. A couple of terms were even invented for suffocation—'burking,' or 'anatomy murder.' I believe they killed in other ways too, but mostly suffocation. Do you know how Ms. Clacher was killed?"

"Strangled, I think. I'm going to find out for sure. Hamlet said there were bruises on her neck."

"That would do it," he said sadly. "Feel free to call and ask me anything, or share whatever you learn." He pushed open the door for me.

"I will let you know. Thank you for allowing me to interrupt your day. And, Joshua, don't leave Edinburgh if you don't have to. I know I'm being completely selfish, but I would miss you."

"I would miss you too. I'll keep you up to date."

I hurried down the outside stairs and crossed the street to catch a bus that would take me down the Royal Mile.

———

"You're the lass from America." The police officer sitting at the reception desk peered over his reading glasses at me. I didn't remember seeing him before.

"I am," I said. "Here to see . . ."

"Let me guess, Winters?"

"Yes."

"Your reputation precedes you, lass." He picked up a handset and pushed a few buttons.

"My reputation?"

"Aye, we've made jokes about sending you all our old cold cases." He smiled. I hoped the jokes were good-natured.

"I'd take that job," I said.

Right before Christmas, Edwin had received a box of items on his front porch. He'd asked me to see if I could figure out who they belonged to. My explorations had taken me down a strange path that led to a killer back in the 1960s. I hadn't meant to find a killer, but I was glad I had, because as a result at least one of his victims had received some peace, if there was such a thing. My experience made me think there was.

Into the phone, the receptionist said, "Winters," then pulled the phone away from his ear. "The lass from *Kansas,* is it?" I nodded, and he spoke back into the handpiece. "She's here to see you. Uh-huh." He looked at me again. "Another murder?"

"Uhm. I'm afraid so."

"She's done it again," he said back into the phone. "Right, I'll send her." He hung up the phone. "Go on back. Winters said you'd know which room."

"Thank you."

"Good luck."

I did know where to go. I opened the door to the interview room and made my way inside, taking a seat in the chair that I'd sat in a few times now. Inspector Winters was there only a moment later.

"Delaney?" he said as he closed the door behind him. "What's wrong?"

I took a deep breath and let it out slowly. My relationship with Inspector Winters had had a rocky beginning. I'd been in Scotland only a few days when we first met after the murder of Edwin's sister. In the midst of falling in love with this beautiful country and all of its people, I was also trying to figure out who to trust. Initially, Inspector Winters wasn't someone I'd deemed trustworthy. So our transition into what had become a mostly unsuspicious friendship had been a welcome one. But we were still at the "mostly" level.

"Nothing's wrong. I mean . . . well, I wondered if you could answer a question."

"Aye?" He took a seat in the chair across from me. I was glad I didn't see a twinkle of humor in his eyes, something I expected after the greeting I'd received from the receptionist, though murder never really is funny. "How's everyone at the bookshop? After yesterday, I mean."

"We'll be okay. I wasn't sure . . . well, I thought you'd heard, but I just didn't know what you know."

"I was informed early on." He took out the notepad and pen he always carried in his shirt pocket and put them on the table. He didn't lift the cover on the notepad, though, which made the meeting feel unofficial. "I'm kept apprised of some things, particularly when the bookshop is involved. It's in my precinct, but I wasn't in on the early investigation so I'm a wee bit on the fringe of everything here."

I nodded, though I was a tiny bit horrified that any police officer was apprised of the bookshop goings-on. And I really hoped it wasn't because of me. "Have you talked to Inspector Pierce?"

"Not yet. I was hoping to sometime today. Why?"

"I just wondered. Have you heard if the way Mallory was killed has been determined?"

"Aye. Suffocation. In fact, there was residue on her hair from what was probably a plastic bag. It's not a secret. It's been released. The media will have it for tonight's and tomorrow's news."

"That's terrible," I said. "Heartbreaking. Hamlet saw bruises on her neck."

"It wasn't strangulation, it was suffocation, but the bruises could have occurred with the bag being held over her head."

"Oh." I was glad I was sitting down as the room spun for a moment.

"Aye. Was that your question?" He moved the notepad and pen closer together on the table, but he still didn't lift the cover.

"Yes . . . I wondered because. This is going to sound strange."

"Delaney, you telling me something strange is not unexpected."

"I know. All right. You're aware of Burke and Hare?"

Inspector Winters' eyebrows went high. "Of course."

"I think there might be some strange connection," I said.

"Sounds strange, aye, but interesting too." He lifted the cover of the notepad and held the pen at the ready.

"Any chance you could keep a secret?"

"No, typically it's my job tae uncover things, not hide them."

"I know, but maybe you could keep a secret until you couldn't? Keep something to yourself until you *need* to share the information. Until it's necessary."

"No promises. Talk tae me, Delaney."

Since he hadn't talked to Inspector Pierce, he still didn't have confirmation that the warehouse existed. I wasn't sure if Pierce would be obliged to tell him anyway, since it seemed not to have been involved in the murder. Inspector Winters had been asking me about the warehouse's existence since we'd met. He'd first asked about it because it might have had something to do with Edwin's sister's murder. Over time, he'd asked because he was curious, and the legendary reputation made lots of people ask.

"It's about Edwin's treasures. The warehouse," I said.

Now his eyes did light with a twinkle. "I'm listening."

ELEVEN

Though I knew he'd been curious, I couldn't be sure what Inspector Winters would ultimately think of the warehouse. It was a spectacle, sure, but had legend built it into something that it wasn't, couldn't ever be? I knew things were bound to change between Inspector Winters and me when I let him in on the secrets—and between him and my coworkers too—but all indications were that things were going in a good direction.

"So, this is it?" Inspector Winters shone a small flashlight at the red ornate door. The light from the bare bulb hanging from the ceiling and the small amount of daylight that crept in though the grimy windows hadn't been enough illumination for him.

"This is it," I said.

"The door at least lives up tae the reputation."

"Well, to coin a phrase, you ain't seen nothin' yet."

I took the large blue skeleton key from my bag, gave Inspector Winters a small lift of my eyebrows, and inserted the key. I turned it to the left three times, unlatching the heavy bolts, and then pushed it open.

I had made sure that Edwin was okay with my plan, and that whatever cleaning up that needed to be done had been done. The entire bookshop, the close included, was no longer a crime scene and was no longer off-limits, but Edwin had decided to remain closed for business.

Surprisingly, my conversation with him had been rough at first, full of awkward pauses and "oh dear's" but ultimately, he agreed with me that it would be good for Inspector Winters to know about the warehouse, for a couple of reasons. He'd become a friend to me and everyone at the bookshop. There was no need to keep the secret from someone in law enforcement who we also trusted so implicitly.

And now a murder had occurred in a place that was a big part of our world, our home. The police needed to know as much about what might have led up to Mallory's murder as we could supply. Though Inspector Pierce had seen the warehouse, Inspector Winters had a knowledge of the history of the shop and its people. Could that knowledge somehow help? We were about to find out.

Bottom line—ultimately Edwin and I agreed that finding a killer was much more important than keeping the secret of the room filled with treasures.

I could sense Inspector Winters' excitement, though he cloaked it with a wide-eyed silence. I tried not to smile.

I reached around, flipped up the light switch, and led the way inside.

Inspector Winters stood inside the space, put his hands on his hips, and looked around. I moved to the desk and retrieved the treasure chest from inside the drawer.

"This is unbelievable," Inspector Winters said.

"It doesn't disappoint?" I asked.

"It's . . . not what I expected, but, no, it doesn't disappoint. It's a roomful of treasures, just like I'd heard."

"There *are* treasures in here, but there's also some junk. Do you want a tour of some of the shelves?"

He looked around again, slowly. "No, not right now. I want to know why you brought me to see it today."

"I don't know if what I'm going to show you had anything to do with Mallory's murder. Inspector Pierce knows about them too, but you know us. Maybe it would be good for you to know about this room. It was mentioned at the pub the night of the murder. I don't know, there might be important connections."

"Okay." Inspector Winters moved closer to the desk as his eyebrows came together.

I gloved up and showed him the scalpels. I told him most of the details from my evening in the pub with the medical students and professor, emphasizing Dr. Eban's curiosity about Edwin's room, and the scalpels specifically. I told him about Dr. Eban's reputation.

"These are authentic?" he asked about the scalpels.

"I think so, but I will need to do more research. I saw one at the Burke and Hare display at the museum, and it's identical."

"Where did Edwin get them?"

"Like many things in here, he's not sure or he doesn't remember. That's part of the reason I was hired in the first place. More attention needed to be paid."

"It would help tae know where they came from."

"I wish we did know."

His eyebrows came together even more. "People used tae operate with these?"

"It appears so."

"It's a wonder any Scots survived the Black Plague. Twice.

And then the medical experiments that finally led to the miracles that we have." He shook his head. "Amazing."

"Survival of the fittest, I suppose. Will you look more closely at Dr. Eban, or tell Inspector Pierce to?"

He glanced up at me. "It's not my case, Delaney. It's in my jurisdiction, but I wasn't there with the first call, and that automatically gives me a disadvantage. I'll talk to Pierce, but I've heard he's not one tae play well with others. Be sure you tell him everything you've told me, and I'm sure he's looking closely at Dr. Eban. I wouldn't be surprised if he takes the scalpels."

I heard what he was talking around. He was surprised Inspector Pierce hadn't already taken the scalpels, but he didn't want to sound critical.

I nodded. "I don't think he trusts me, since I was with Mallory and she was killed near the shop. He doesn't understand the history of the legend of this room. Between the scalpels, the books Sophie and Rena brought in—let me show them to you. We didn't tell Inspector Pierce about the books yet, but I'm thinking we should now. Or, at least you should tell him. Maybe there's something here that is a clue to Mallory's killer, even if it's just a peripheral clue." I grabbed the box of books and put it on the desk. "You know about the skull that was found?"

"I do."

"Well, everyone I've spoken to—not the police, though; Pierce hasn't told me anything—thinks that the presence of a skull from the skull room at the university, a room that Dr. Eban is somehow in charge of, is either a clue or too obvious to be a clue. To me he seemed charming, but I've heard he's odd. I just hope he's not being overlooked. He's so smart."

"As a rule, Delaney, the police do know that people might be smart enough tae try to fool us. I'm sure Pierce isn't a gump."

"Gump?"

Inspector Winters blinked. "Aye. A fool."

"You used a Scots word?"

"I guess I did. My da uses them frequently."

I smiled. Inspector Winters rolled his eyes.

"I like that word. I'm going to use it someday soon."

When I'd first arrived in Scotland, it seemed that many people felt a need to watch over me: my coworkers, my landlords, Tom to some extent, and Inspector Winters. He was close to my age, but I didn't know him well personally. I knew he had a family, but it had never seemed right to ask about it. No matter that we'd become friends, or at least friendly toward each other—that personal/professional line still existed. I liked his smile and eye-roll; to me, it meant we were becoming even better friends.

He'd also formed relationships with my coworkers. He didn't trust Edwin, but I think he wanted to. He liked my boss, and he could see that Edwin's heart was in the right place—even though it didn't always appear so, and illegal activities occurred because of that place Edwin put his heart. It was as if our cautious affection for each other had a wall in between. But I sensed we were chipping away at it.

"I met Dr. Eban's wife," I continued as I opened the box with the books.

"Aye? How did that happen?"

"I used these books as an excuse to talk to Dr. Eban, but he wasn't in his office. I did meet his wife, Dr. Meg Carson, though."

"What did she say?"

"That talking to her husband about the value of the books was a good idea. She said he knows about these sorts of things."

He nodded and I scooted the box toward him. "You can touch them."

As he lifted one book from the box, I felt a pull of urgency from the bookish voices, though they remained silent. My subconscious was working hard, if not effectively.

"These are extraordinary. Strange, though. The pictures, they're sketches, but they seem so real," Inspector Winters said.

"Hamlet hasn't listed them for sale because Edwin was thinking about donating them to a medical school, maybe Edinburgh, which would be the natural choice, I think. He didn't want to offend Sophie and Rena, though, so he thought we might wait until they were done with school, or at least until summer break. Not sure what we'll do with them now except wait until Mallory's murder is solved. The timing of them coming into the shop is strange and probably has nothing to do with Mallory. Still though, it's strange."

"I agree. They're old, aye?" Inspector Winters said.

"They are. They're both fascinating and gruesome, unless I suppose you're planning on becoming a doctor."

"Oh." Inspector Winters' eyes got big as he looked at something that included blood and pus.

"See what I mean?" I said.

He turned the page, and we looked at a picture of a wartish boil on a leg. A picture of a man's face stretched with concern or pain or both illustrated the top of the page.

"Goodness," Inspector Winters said.

"I know. These were published in 1902. It's a set of twenty-five books. Edwin bought every one of them."

"Did he pay well for them?"

"Probably more than they're worth." I turned to another page that proved to be just as gruesome: a stomach incision.

"They pack quite the punch."

"Think about the work that had to be put into these. Everything done by hand, one drawing at a time."

"I can't imagine. I get impatient if I can't find the proper emoji quickly enough."

I laughed. "Me too." But I stopped immediately when I saw the expression on his face change. "What?"

"Hang on." He put the book back into the box and grabbed his mobile phone. He pushed a button and put it to his ear. "Aye, Winters here. Were some medical books stolen from the university in the last little while? No, I didn't get the call, but I overheard someone talking—I can't remember the details. No? See if you can track something down. Thank you." He ended the call, but the perplexed looked on his face kept me silent a moment.

"These are stolen?" I asked when he looked up at me.

"I'm not sure what I'm remembering, Delaney, but . . . There must be something written down somewhere. A case number, or some notes. I'll figure it out, but something about these books rings a bell."

"That's not good."

"No, but let me figure it out before we get too concerned."

"Should you take them?"

"I don't think so. Not yet. Hang on to them. You were going tae talk tae Dr. Eban about them?"

"That was my excuse. I mean . . ."

"It's okay, Delaney, just tell me what you were going tae do," he said.

"I wanted to talk to him, see him, see how he behaved. There are so many rumors about the man. I guess I just needed to see for myself if he was as bad as I'd heard, because . . . I kind of liked him in the few minutes we talked. That's what I meant earlier. Is he fooling everyone? Is everyone being a gump?"

A twitch of a smile pulled at the corner of his mouth. "You think you misread him?"

I thought a long moment. "No, I'm worried that he left clues to tell the world that he's a killer, but that the police are misreading him like I might be."

Inspector Winters looked at me a long moment.

I continued, "I know the police aren't fools, but I just . . ."

"I get what you're saying. I'll talk tae Pierce. He might want the books and the scalpels."

"Thank you."

I put everything back where it belonged and locked up. As we made our way over to the other side, Inspector Winters said, "Did Dr. Carson say anything else about the books?"

"Like what?"

"Anything."

"No, just that her husband was the one to talk to. Why?"

"I'm not sure."

We paused by the front door as Inspector Winters fell into thought.

"I'll ring you later," he said when he came out of the reverie.

"What did you think of the warehouse?" I asked as I opened the shop's front door for him.

"I think it's overwhelming. I think your boss is daft, but keeping ridiculously valuable items in a back room behind his bookshop is only one of the reasons why. From a security perspective, I think it's fairly secure, but some alarms would be better. Alarms around the entire bookshop would be helpful." He looked over my shoulder and into the shop. "And I think it would be a wonderful place tae explore, perfect for someone like you, Delaney Nichols from Kansas."

"It *is* perfect."

"Good. Thank you for trusting me tae see it. Thanks tae Edwin too."

I sighed. "You might not believe this, but I didn't like keeping it a secret from you."

He looked at me. "Aye? Well, we've come a long way then."

"Since you haven't arrested any of my friends, yes." I smiled.

"Yet, at least. There have been moments. Thank you again for sharing the room with me. I'll tell Edwin the same."

"You're welcome."

I closed the door behind him. After a second's hesitation, I locked it too.

The otherwise empty shop was quiet and shadowed without the lights turned on. I walked over to the switch, but didn't flip it up. Edwin had decided we weren't going to open; no need to make customers think we had. I could get some work done, but things felt off. Perhaps it was natural to sense discontent after such a tragedy, but goose bumps rose on my arms, and the quiet was too loud for comfort.

"Anyone want to chat?" I said to all the books.

No one answered. I decided I didn't need to be there any longer.

For the first time ever, I was a wee bit glad to be leaving the bookshop.

TWELVE

"Och, gracious, this is . . . Oh dear, oh dear," Aggie said as she read the article.

"I know." I shook my head.

I'd taken most of the afternoon the previous day just for me, getting my emotions and head straight again. Tom had been busy, and though it would have been better with him, I'd enjoyed an afternoon to myself. It looked like today wasn't going to be quite the same, though it looked to also be about me.

Hamlet had called extra early, about five in the morning.

"Delaney, sorry tae wake you, but you've made the paper. The *Renegade Scot*, not the *Scotsman*," he'd said. "I thought you'd like tae know as soon as possible."

I'd sprung out of bed and made my way across the tiny courtyard that separated my cottage from Elias and Aggie's, and tapped lightly on their back door. I knew they'd be awake.

"Lass?" Elias had said as he'd opened the door in his undershirt and pants while holding a steaming cup of coffee.

"Any chance you guys have your copy of the *Renegade Scot*?"

"Aye. Aggie's in reading the papers now."

"May I come in and look at it?"

He stepped out of the doorway and went to put a shirt on as I joined Aggie in their small kitchen.

"Lass?" she said over the paper, the *Scotsman*.

"May I see the *Renegade Scot*?"

"Aye."

Aggie hadn't looked at that one yet, but it was easy to find the article, right there on page three, above the fold.

I read through it quickly, and then gave the paper back to her as Elias joined us in the kitchen. He read over Aggie's shoulder. It didn't take long for her "oh dear's" to begin.

"It says here that ye talked tae the reporter," Elias said.

"The only thing I said was that I didn't want to talk to her," I said.

"Says ye were peeking in a window where the victim had been," Aggie said. " 'Sneaking' is the word she used, I believe."

"Technically I was, kind of, but not because I was reliving the crime, like she implies. I wasn't behaving as if I was guilty; I was irritated by her!"

"Weel, she said that ye only looked like ye might be doing such a thing. Not that ye were." Elias was trying to be helpful. He sent me a hesitant smile.

"I know, but she made it sound like . . . oh, my, she made it sound like I could be the killer. The untrustworthy stranger from America!"

"Those werenae the exact words," Elias said.

Aggie sent him an eyebrow lift before she turned to me. "But ye arenae a killer, lass."

"The redheaded American come to Scotland to work at the

bookshop might now be involved in something unsavory." I'd read the words only once but I'd memorized them already.

"Aye, but ye just arenae a killer," Aggie repeated. She cleared her throat. "This will pass."

My phone buzzed in my pocket. I hurried to grab it.

"I'm on my way over," Tom said without a hello. "I'm afraid the article is my fault. I'm so sorry, love."

"How is it your fault?" I said.

"I'll explain when I get there."

"I'm in the McKennas' cottage."

"I'm almost there."

"Tom says the article is his fault," I said as I put my phone on the table. "He's on his way now."

"How is it his fault?" Aggie asked.

"I'm not sure yet, but I suspect it's because he used to date the reporter."

Aggie glanced at the paper. "Bridget Carr?"

"Yes."

"Never heard of her until right now. I read almost all the papers every day. She's not a big-name reporter," Elias said supportively.

"Maybe she's trying to be," I said.

"Aye," Aggie said. "She sees this as her big break or some such nonsense. Did it end badly for her and Tom? That was a silly question. They arenae together. Of course it ended badly for her."

In classic tabloid style, Bridget Carr had taken me down, as well as Edwin and the bookshop. He'd been polite to her, much more polite than I had been, and yet she'd called him the "aloof Edwin MacAlister." I almost felt worse about that than how she'd made me look guilty of murder. The shop had remained closed and he hadn't been available the day he'd told her to return. Had she thrown us under the bus—me under twice—just because of that?

"Ye ken what they say, that all publicity is guid publicity?" Elias said as he poured me a cup of coffee.

"I've heard that expression before, but I wonder if this might be the exception. This is not good news for my job security, let alone the reputation of Edwin's bookshop, a place and a man that don't deserve a bad reputation, by the way."

"No, Edwin does more good than bad," Aggie said. Her eyebrows came together as if she wasn't sure she'd said that the way she intended, but she didn't rephrase it.

A knock sounded on the front door.

"Must be Tom," I said as I stood. Elias and Aggie followed hesitantly behind.

Part of the reason Tom had been busy the day and night before was that his aunt had taken ill and he and his father, Artair, had gone with the elderly woman to the hospital. We'd spoken only briefly, because he'd been pulled away by some doctors who'd come into his aunt's room.

We'd ended the call with a "maybe" we'd see each other later, but I hadn't heard from him again until now. As I opened the door and saw his disheveled state, my priorities realigned.

"How's your aunt?" I said.

"No worse. I'm sorry about the article," he said. "I didn't know . . ."

"It's okay. Whatever it is, it's okay," I said. I looked back at my landlords and then at Tom again.

"Come through here," Aggie said. "Go tae yer hoose, Delaney. Ye need some privacy."

Tom and I hurried through the McKennas' cottage and to mine, which was on the other side of a shared deck. As we closed the door to my cottage, I said, "Really, how is your aunt?"

"She's stable. Along with her dementia, she now has a heart condition, but she's being well taken care of. I'm sorry I didn't call or come over last night; Da and I were at the hospital all night. I grabbed a copy of the paper as I went out to the vending machine for some coffee. I'm . . . I didn't think Bridget would take what I said tae her and twist it so."

He hadn't brushed his curly hair except with his hands, his dark beard was a touch beyond stubble, and his cobalt eyes were shiny from lack of sleep and stress.

"It's okay. Really, I'm sure. Come on, let's get some coffee and toast." I led us into my kitchen.

The air was too charged with emotion. Moving into roles we'd never defined out loud but had become familiar with, Tom made the coffee and I put bread in the toaster and gathered toppings. The familiar activities gave us the time we needed to find our centers again. Before long, we were at the table.

"Okay, me first," I said as Tom ignored his toast but lifted his coffee mug. "I talked to Bridget briefly, as I said. The article wasn't incorrect, but it was misleading. When I talked to her, it was mostly me telling her I didn't want to talk to her. She expounded, and technically much of what she said is true. It's the tone that isn't."

"I suspected as much when she came into the pub tae talk tae me. Yesterday again. I didn't even think tae tell you she came back. I tried tae say the same, however," he smiled ruefully. "I'm a wee bit protective, and I didn't like her accusations when she told me she'd seen and suspected you. I told her you hadn't killed anyone. She wasn't happy the shop was closed. She was . . . she was her normal self, and I wasn't as kind as I should have been."

"Before you go on, just so you know, I love that you're protective, and so far you've not said anything to upset me." I smiled.

It was clear we were both feeling better.

Tom relaxed and continued, "It was when she asked about Edwin . . . She said something about him being mysterious and asked why he would hire someone from America if he didn't want tae make sure his newest employee was kept in the dark about his past."

"I see."

"Aye. Then I defended you and Edwin a wee bit too much. She asked if you and I were dating."

"And she was jealous that we were."

"I'm not sure 'jealous' is the word . . ."

"I am."

"Anyway, it was when I told her how long we'd been together that I think she became determined tae put you in a bad light."

"Your relationship with her didn't last long?"

"Just a few weeks, and then . . . I'm not proud of the way I handled it, but she caught me out with someone else."

"Ouch. Well, that would not be good. I'd have to be on her side on that one."

"Aye. I wish I had a good excuse. I apologized tae her back then, but it wasn't enough. If I'd just ignored her when she came into the pub again yesterday . . ."

"She still would have written something. The shop was closed and Edwin had said he would talk to her. She'd found a good story, made it better, maybe. It's too bad she jumped the gun on the details. She might be able to make something of what it's actually going to become."

"Aye?"

"Well, it's a big story, for sure. All the media are covering it; she's just trying to gain an edge, but she might be digging her own grave. I guess we'll see."

"I don't know," Tom said. He pushed back his messy hair, and my heart, still beating quickly from the adrenaline, seemed to sigh and beat even more quickly for another reason.

I smiled.

He blinked at me, perplexed by my expression, probably. "I'm sorry if I contributed in any way tae any trouble for you or for Edwin," he continued. "I'll ring him later this morning."

"I'm sure he would appreciate that." I put my hand over his around the coffee mug.

My phone buzzed and I looked at the caller ID.

"It looks like you can tell him over the phone if you want. It's Edwin," I said.

It had been a long time—since my first day in the shop, in Edinburgh, in fact—that I'd been so scared to talk to my boss. But I had to answer.

THIRTEEN

"Delaney?" someone said as I stepped off the bus.

I jumped in my skin as I searched for the person attached to the voice coming from my left.

Rena walked purposefully toward me, a copy of this morning's *Renegade Scot* clutched in her hand. For a smallish paper, a lot of people sure did read it.

"Rena," I said. "Hey. How are you?"

"Not good at all. We all read the paper this morning. Is there something you didn't share with us? Did you know Mallory before?"

Edwin had called to send me his support. He'd told Tom not to worry, that he, I, and the shop were all going to be okay. I had the best job in the world, I'd been thinking on the bus ride over, anxious to disembark and get to work.

But amidst the morning traffic, the vehicles and the pedestrians on the sidewalk, I had a sense that we were being watched. It was probably unwarranted, but Bridget Carr had made me paranoid, Rena's words just now even more so. As many times as I'd read the article, I hadn't picked up on anything that sounded as if Mallory and I had known each other before Friday night.

"Can I buy you a coffee? Maybe a muffin?" I said as I started walking toward the bakery next to the bookshop.

"Uh . . ." she said as though she had more to say and my plans had interrupted hers. Nevertheless, she walked with me to the mostly empty bakery.

Once we were inside, I turned to her. "I didn't know Mallory before. That article makes me look guilty, but I'm not. The police don't think I am either." I hoped, but I wasn't so sure. "Have a seat, I'll grab us some breakfast."

I motioned to a small table in the corner and then walked up to the counter for coffee and muffins.

I hoped a small break would help Rena's state of mind. Mine too.

"Delaney! Hello," Bruno said. With his gruff voice and his wide chest and large arms, he was not what you might have expected to find behind the counter of a patisserie, but he was one good baker. "How's the crew next door? I heard about the terrible . . . the tragedy over the weekend. I'm so sorry."

I nodded, waiting for him to say something about the *Renegade Scot* article, but he didn't. "We'll be okay, but we're sorry for the victim and her family."

"Aye. Let me know if any of you need anything at all."

"Thanks, Bruno."

I wasn't hungry and I'd had more than enough coffee, but I ordered coffees and muffins for Rena and me.

"I'm sorry about that article," I said as I put the items on the table. "It happened mostly because I wouldn't talk to the reporter. She's a bulldog, which might be a good trait for a journalist, but to me she has teetered on the edge of unethical with that article. What she said happened didn't happen exactly that way." I sighed. "There was no way to talk this through without sounding defensive, but basically I told her that I didn't want to talk to her."

Rena ignored the muffin but took a shaky sip from the coffee. "You didn't know her? Mallory?"

"No," I said. "What made you think I might have?"

"It just . . . This article makes you sound so suspect. I wondered if you . . . I wondered if Sophie and I set her up by bringing her to the pub that night. You two acted like you didn't know each other, but I wondered if we put her in harm's way."

I took a slow sip of coffee. There was something—or there were a number of somethings—wrong with what Rena had just said. Of course, I could've chalked it up to the trauma and tragedy that she'd been through, but something told me that wasn't it.

There will be time, there will be time
To prepare a face to meet the faces that you meet.

I was glad for the bookish voice's words. They'd come from poetry this time. T. S. Eliot's "The Love Song of J. Alfred Prufrock"—a poem, oddly for the moment, about seduction and intellectualism, though I interpreted the words I'd heard to mean something about creating an illusion for the world to see. What illusion was Rena working on?

"I didn't know Mallory," I said. "Why would it matter anyway? What are you afraid she told me, Rena?"

She blinked and then moved her shaking hands under the table to her lap.

"Okay," I said. I took another sip of my coffee, stalling.

"Nothing," she said a long moment later. "It's not that,

Delaney. It's just that a fellow student was killed and the reporter talked to you."

"Just because I was there, Rena. I was looking in the window—not like Ms. Carr made it sound, but, nevertheless, I was there. I didn't tell her anything because I didn't know anything."

Rena looked around. There was no one sitting near us, but she slunk in her chair.

"Do you feel threatened?" I asked.

"Yes. I mean, not really . . . I'm just upset. When I read this article, I felt like you didn't tell me something. Like Mallory didn't tell me something. I guess I just wanted to know what I was missing."

I nodded, feeling the same way she said she did. "Did you tell the police everything?"

"Yes."

"What time did you tell them you got home?"

"Right after Sophie. I told you that already."

"But you left again. Where did you go?"

She didn't know how I knew, but she wasn't going to back away. "None of your business."

"It's the police's business. I hope you told them."

She shrugged. She wasn't going to tell me one way or the other. However, she was correct—it was not my business. I could only hope that me knowing she had left was enough to make her worried I'd tell the police before she did.

I shook my head. "Look, I'm . . . I just want the killer found too."

"The police are doing their jobs, surely," she said quietly.

"It's been my experience that everyone has so many secrets

that the police aren't ever really able to do their jobs thoroughly. I hope you did tell them what you were doing Friday night after the pub."

She looked at her coffee cup on the table in front of her.

"Rena, has Dr. Eban ever asked anyone to do anything . . . do something to get a grade?"

Her features relaxed. I thought she was going to shake her head, but she didn't.

"It's a tough go, you know? Medical school is really hard," she said.

"Right, but students should never be asked to do things against their will. I know you know that, but I'm beginning to wonder if there's something happening that's made you, and possibly others, lose sight of it. I understand you being upset about the murder, but I wonder if there's more going on. Things happening behind the scenes that might not cause murder directly, but might lead to it indirectly."

"Nothing's happening," she said only somewhat unconvincingly.

I looked at the newspaper she'd set on the table, its fold wrinkled from her grip.

"Rena, you can talk to me if you need to," I said. And then I followed up with my own lie. "You know what? You can tell me anything, and if you want me to keep it from the police I will. Just tell me, if that's what you want."

She looked at me, and tears filled her eyes. For a moment, I saw relief and gratitude, but then she thought too long, or she realized I was lying too, and she blinked away the tears and the moment.

"Thank you, Delaney," she said too politely. "I'll keep that in mind." She stood. "And thank you for the breakfast."

She stood and took the newspaper with her, but left behind the mostly full coffee cup and the completely untouched muffin.

I knew how she felt. I wasn't hungry either.

I cleaned up the table and then bade Bruno a distracted goodbye.

"Take care of yourself, Delaney," he said as I left.

Feeling much different than I had during my time alone in the shop yesterday, I was glad to finally be heading back to work.

———

"It's best tae just ignore it all," Rosie said right as I came through the bookshop's front door. "It will pass."

She stood behind the desk holding the newspaper. Her reading glasses were perched on the end of her nose and Hector was in the crook of her arm. He sent me a tiny bark of support.

"I see you've read it," I said.

"Aye." She shrugged and put the dog on the ground.

He ran to me, and I grabbed him, then lifted him to my face.

"I can't believe she twisted our brief encounter into something like this," I said as I let the dog kiss away some of my stress.

"She's an irksome one tae be sure, but it will pass, Delaney."

"Oh, Rosie, I hope so," I said.

"It'll be fine, lass," Rosie said as Hector pushed himself a little harder into me.

I was grateful for Edwin's call earlier. I'd spent too many moments over the last year wondering about my job security—not because I'd done a poor job, but because I'd overstepped my bounds or discovered secrets that weren't meant to be discovered. I didn't think the article was in itself something I might be sacked for, but it was just another piece of straw to be thrown on the haystack.

Even my secretive boss might someday have his limits.

The shop's phone rang. In the quiet, the sound was extra shrill and ominous. I wondered if we'd get calls or complaints all day because of the article.

"The Cracked Spine, how can we help you? . . . Aye." Rosie's eyebrows came together over her nose-tipped glasses. "One moment please."

Rosie covered the mouthpiece and quietly said, "It's for ye. A gentleman who says he works at the medical school. Says ye talked tae his wife on Saturday."

"Dr. Eban?" I said as I placed Hector onto the desk and reached for the phone.

"He didn't give his name, but ye might want tae think a wee bit before taking calls this morning."

She was correct, of course, but I couldn't resist.

"I'll talk to him." I cleared my throat and took the phone. "Dr. Eban?"

"Aye. I heard you stopped by my office on Saturday tae ask me about some books. My wife told me."

"I did." Had he put together the facts that we'd met Friday night and that I was standing in the bookshop next to where one of his medical students had been killed?

"I'm in my office this morning if you'd like tae come by. I'd love tae see the books. She said they were some of the illustrated volumes from the Sydal Society."

"That's correct."

"I'd be intrigued. I can come tae you if that would be easier," he said.

It would have been much easier, but I didn't want Dr. Eban inside the bookshop, particularly today.

"No, I can bring a couple of them to you. Anytime this morning okay?"

"Fine. I'll be in all morning. If I'm not in my office, I've just run tae grab some tea and will return shortly."

"I'll be by soon."

As I hung up the phone I wondered: Had he put the pieces together in his head? How would he react when he saw me?

There was only one real way to find out.

"I'm running an errand," I said. "I'm sorry, but I think this is important."

"Um. Okay," Rosie said as Hector sat and whined at me. "Where are ye going?"

"The medical school—Dr. Eban's office specifically," I said as I made my way to the stairs. "Don't worry—I won't talk to anyone without leaving the door open."

I hurried over to the dark side, happy for the distraction from another wave of nerves and self-pity.

The warehouse was cold, but comforting in its homey way. I spied the message from Birk and said aloud, "I'll call this afternoon," before I grabbed the box with the books, took the top one on the stack, and placed it into a transparent protective sleeve. One would be plenty for him to look at.

I double-checked the scalpels, and the treasure chest. Everything was where I expected. As I locked the door, my cell phone buzzed in my pocket.

I dug for it as I made my way up the stairs, but didn't see who was calling until I'd walked through the doorway to the other side.

"Hey," I said to Rosie, "I'm—"

But I didn't finish telling her I was back where she could talk to me in person before I noticed the small crowd of three, if you included Hector, looking up at me from the bottom of the stairs.

"Oh, there she is," Rosie said as she hung up the phone. "She was here after all. My mistake."

"Ms. Nichols," Inspector Pierce said. "You have a minute?"

I wanted to tell him no, but of course I couldn't.

FOURTEEN

"You're famous," Inspector Pierce said as he scooted the paper toward me.

We sat at the back corner table. Rosie made it her business to have something to do at the bookshelves opposite us. The shop wasn't big enough for privacy, and I didn't suggest that we go over to the other side. I didn't want to be alone with Inspector Pierce, but I didn't call Gaylord either. I hoped that wouldn't prove to be a mistake.

"I didn't mean to be. She used some creative license with that story."

"She's a journalist, not a creative writer."

Rosie sniffed.

Inspector Pierce and I glanced over. She kept her back to us, so he and I resumed looking at each other.

"At least she—they—should be journalists," I said. "She struck me as hungry, out to find a big story. If she couldn't find one, she was going to make one up."

"Were you looking in the window?"

"I was," I said. I squelched an urge to explain further.

"What were you looking for?"

"I was deeply curious, and it wasn't off-limits. Seemed like a natural thing to do, considering the circumstances. The fact that she said I was suspiciously looking in the window . . . well, either that was just her opinion or the creative license I was talking about."

Inspector Pierce leaned closer, moving his arms across the table. I squelched an urge to scoot backward. "Did you know the victim before you claimed to have met her on Friday night?"

I blinked. Like Rena, he'd read that into the article. I was perplexed and wanted to read it again.

"No, Inspector Pierce. I didn't. May I ask why you think so?"

"The tone of the article."

"Are journalistic articles supposed to have tone?"

"Maybe."

"I thought they were just supposed to state the facts."

Inspector Pierce sat back and nodded slowly as he continued to squint at me.

Rosie turned and interjected, "Edwin closed the shop." She walked toward us. "He told us specifically not tae come back tae work until the morning, *inside* the building. Ye'd already said the outside was clear. None of us were here or I'm sure one of us would have explored with Delaney. The reporter just wanted a story."

"Everyone left but Delaney?" Inspector Pierce asked.

"Aye," Rosie said, though she had no idea that I'd walked around the block before coming back to the close.

"Did you know about the burial site that's back there?" I said, so out of the blue that I had to force myself not to apologize.

"No," Rosie said with a blink.

"No," Inspector Pierce said, but I could tell he was intrigued.

"When I wouldn't tell Bridget anything she told me that there's a legend that women who were accused of witchcraft were buried in that same area. She thought that would intrigue me into a conversation. Any other setting, time or place, even person probably, it would have, but I didn't talk to her except to tell her I wouldn't talk to her."

Inspector Pierce nodded again. "I hear stuff like that all the time. Scotland's history . . . anyway. Tell me more about the legend of the warehouse. What am I missing? It just seemed like a room with a lot of junk. And you said nothing was out of place."

"Nothing was out of place, and yes," I said, "it is legendary, though I don't know on what scale. Almost every person I tell where I work mentions it. We don't advertise it, and we don't invite many people over to see it."

Rosie shrugged. "We're not going tae let customers traipse over tae the other side without an escort. Ye saw the bad lighting, the dirty conditions. It wouldnae be safe, nor good for business. People like a good mystery. Ye should ken that. Since we dinnae allow explorations, people have made it into something it isnae."

Rosie was very good at this.

However, Inspector Pierce didn't hide his skepticism.

"You're an officer of the law," Rosie continued. "I'll happily escort ye back over there if ye'd like tae see more, but I'm not going tae allow tours tae the general public."

I nodded along.

"I don't need to see it again right now," Inspector Pierce said.

I couldn't tell if he was convinced or not as Rosie and I watched him. I didn't know why it mattered, except this was exactly why I'd shown the room to Inspector Winters—because

I'd felt that Pierce hadn't quite understood what it was, so I doubted he could find a possible connection. I didn't want there to be a connection, but I did want Mallory's killer found.

"I'd like to take another look at the window, both from the outside and the inside," he said. "I think we checked from the inside and didn't find a breach, but I'd like to make sure, from both directions, just one more time."

"Have you talked to the reporter?" I asked.

"No, not yet. I thought I'd come see you first."

"You might want to talk to her."

"And why is that?"

"She claims to have found something in the close that day," I said. "I don't know if she was making it up or not, but you should ask her about it."

Take that, Bridget Carr. The zip of revenge I felt was immature, but I didn't care.

"What did she find?"

"I think it would be best if you just asked her."

"I will. Right after I look at the window. Let's go."

I'd been holding on to the book, and I set it on the table as I stood.

"What's the book?" Inspector Pierce asked as he stood too.

"An old medical book." I slipped it out of the protective sleeve and opened to a middle page. "Illustrated, from the early 1900s. Here's a picture of a compound fracture. This was drawn a long time ago."

At first he scowled, but then he seemed genuinely interested.

"Hand-drawn?" he said.

"No computers back then," I said. I wanted to tell him more about the books, where they came from, but not without Gaylord present. I was probably already talking too much.

"Must be worth a fortune."

"We've had more valuable books in the shop, but this one and its companion volumes are worth at least a few thousand."

"Sounds pretty valuable to me. What's the value of this shop's inventory?"

"It would be impossible tae put a number tae it," Rosie said.

"That's what Mr. MacAlister said," Inspector Pierce said as he looked at the book again. He'd been testing us, or confirming.

I thought about telling him that we kept all the really valuable books locked up in the warehouse, but that wasn't true. We did keep some back there, but not all of them. We had no alarms, and if someone wanted to break a window and take something from the shelves, they could probably get away with it. I'd pointed those issues out to Edwin more than once, and he'd taken my comments under consideration. But I didn't think he'd ever secure the shop the way Inspectors Pierce and Winters thought it should be secured.

I cleared my throat. "Did you hear from an Inspector Winters?"

Inspector Pierce blinked at me. "I have a message to call him. Friend of yours?"

"Yes."

"Delaney, did you tell him something you didn't tell me because he's a friend?"

"No, I told him that I wasn't sure you were making a connection between the legendary reputation of the warehouse, the scalpels, and Dr. Eban's fooling you. He told me I would be incorrect in my assumption and that the police were used to people attempting to fool them." It was almost the whole truth.

He blinked again, and shook his head this time. "How do you think he's fooling me?"

"The skull maybe."

"Because he has access to the skull room on campus and placing a skull next to the victim would seem too obvious, so someone *must* have planted it there?"

I nodded.

"I appreciate your concern regarding my methods, but your friend is correct: I'm working hard not to let anyone fool me."

"Good."

"Let's look at the kitchen window from the inside first," he said.

Rosie and I shared a glance as I followed behind Inspector Pierce. She put her finger up to her lips as if to tell me to remain as mum as I could. She was probably more concerned about Gaylord not being there than I was. I nodded. I could tell she tried not to look doubtful, but she didn't pull it off.

I was as curious as Inspector Pierce. Would we find something no one had noticed before?

But there was nothing new to see. The window hadn't been opened from the inside in so many years that Inspector Pierce and I both speculated on the number of paint layers that were keeping the frame from moving even if the security grate hadn't been in place. From the inside, there was no indication that anyone might have jimmied or tampered with it.

Per my idea, Inspector Pierce carried a chair outside to the close. We both started to hurry when we spied something colorful and unexpected under the window.

"Flowers," I said as we got closer.

"Don't touch them," Inspector Pierce said as he set the chair to the side and then crouched.

"I don't see any cards or anything that might indicate who left them," I said.

"They could be from anyone." Inspector Pierce stood and looked up and down the close. "I already noticed there are no cameras around."

It wasn't a question, but I said, "Not that I'm aware of."

"After all the media coverage, this might turn into some sort of shrine, which is fine, but I'd like to have a look at anyone who wants to pay their respects. I'm going to get in touch with the city and put some closed-circuit cameras around here."

"You must think I'm innocent, or you wouldn't have just told me your plan," I said with a small smile.

"Oh, I don't think you're innocent," he said far too seriously. "But I also don't think you killed Mallory Clacher."

"I'm guilty of something else?"

"I don't know. You're too involved and I wonder if you're trying to hide something."

I wanted to defend myself. But Gaylord would have thought that a bad idea, so I didn't respond.

Inspector Pierce didn't seem to care. He moved the chair under the window and climbed atop it. "Still looks like a file was taken to it, but I have a hard time believing anyone would hold out much hope that that would work." He climbed down and grabbed the chair. "It looks no different down here than when I first saw it, except for the flowers. I don't think you tampered with anything."

"Of course not."

He sent me a stern look, the likes of which I hadn't seen since my father caught me trying a cigarette when I was fourteen. One cough-riddled puff had been the extent of my bad-girl ways. Dad's stern look had thwarted that method of rebellion, but not as much as the burn in my chest and throat had.

Inspector Pierce carried the chair as we headed back down the close toward the bookshop.

"Delaney, have you ever heard of Dr. Glenn?" he asked as we came out of the close and into Grassmarket.

"Sounds like a name I've heard, but I can't place when," I said.

"Okay, so have you ever heard of the *murderer* Dr. Glenn?"

"No."

"Look him up. He was friends with Dr. Eban and Dr. Carson. Ten years ago, he was accused of killing some patients at the hospital. He was also a professor at the medical school." He stopped walking and put the chair down. He pulled out his phone and called up a website. He held the phone toward me. "Have you ever seen this man?"

I looked at the picture a long time because, in fact, he did look familiar, but only slightly.

"I'm not sure if I've ever seen him, but his face is so . . . normal."

"Right, average in every way, except murder, apparently," Inspector Pierce said. "This picture is ten years old. Can you imagine him with ten more years?"

"Not really. What happened? He's a killer?"

"Yes. Look up the stories, look up more pictures. I'd like you to keep aware, and keep a look out for someone who might look like him. Run the other way if you see him, and then call me. Do not approach him, no matter what. In fact, stay away from all of them."

I nodded, and didn't tell him I was going over to see Dr. Eban just as soon as he left.

"All right. I want one of those scalpels. Will you get it for me?"

"Of course."

He picked up the chair again and resumed walking back into the bookshop.

I looked around one more time before I followed him. There was nothing out of place. The flowers were a bittersweet reminder of the tragedy that had occurred, but the infrequently walked through close was not very notable, considering that according to Bridget Carr it was covering up old witch bones. It seemed like there should be more to it, but it was one of the plainest closes I'd seen in Edinburgh.

Nevertheless, I reminded myself, women may have been killed and then buried there as alleged witches, and a terrible murder had just occurred there. The close may have looked plain enough, but the feeling in the air was anything but.

I shivered and followed Inspector Pierce inside. He took the scalpel and left.

FIFTEEN

I didn't always make the best decisions. I knew this, but as I knocked softly on the door I took a deep breath and told myself it would all be okay. My concerns had nothing to do with meeting Dr. Eban in his office. There was plenty of foot traffic in the building today, and I'd leave the door open. I'd set something else in motion, and no matter that I already regretted doing it, there was no turning back now.

"Come in," Dr. Eban said.

I pushed through.

"Oh! I know you," he said after he stood and looked at me with thoughtful consideration.

"Yes, from the pub Friday night." I set the book, back in the sleeve, on my side of his desk and extended my hand. "Delaney Nichols. I'm sorry to bother you so soon after such a tragedy for the medical school, but my boss is very interested in understanding these books' value, and after meeting you, I thought you'd be the perfect appraiser. I ran into your wife and she confirmed my idea."

He shook my hand slowly, his eyes angling with more than

curiosity. "I see. I'm not an appraiser, though; you do understand that, don't you?"

"Of course." I waved it off. "But you're a medical professional, the first one I've met here in town on a personal level . . . and Dr. Carson said you know your books."

He nodded. "That's right: Kansas, in the States." He smiled as if the pieces had come together in an appealing way. But then he frowned. "Hang on. Mallory was killed near the bookshop where you work? Meg didn't say . . . I . . ."

"Yes, she was killed near there. I'm not sure your wife made the connection either after I told her where I worked." I wasn't sure what else to say.

He lifted his eyebrows, and I wondered if he was trying to tell me that his wife wouldn't have missed the connection. But all he said was, "All right."

"We've given full access to the police, and they've cleared the shop." I didn't want to sound unsympathetic, but I also wanted to divert Dr. Eban away from thinking that someone who worked there might have had something to do with the murder.

If he knew about the article in the *Renegade Scot* I didn't want to give him time to remember it. I forged on, "My timing is insensitive. If you'd like for me to come back another day . . . I'm sorry about Mallory, but my boss really would like me to find out more about these books. I . . . well, I heard some books were stolen from the university, maybe from the medical school, recently I think. My boss heard that too. We thought you might know if that was real or just a rumor. I guess I'm also making sure these aren't the stolen items. You know, before we get the police involved. If we have to, I mean." It was all improvised, but not too far from the truth.

It was difficult to interpret what was going on behind

Dr. Eban's bright, intelligent eyes. No matter that I liked him, I couldn't deny that he was odd in a way I still couldn't pinpoint, smart beyond ways I could imagine. I'd yet to see his macabre side, but I would have liked to. I couldn't help but speculate that he didn't think like the rest of us normal, not-genius-type people did.

Finally, he said, "Have a seat, and let me see what you've brought."

I left the door open, and he didn't ask me to shut it.

"Sure. I only brought one, but we do have the whole set."

His eyes widened as I pulled the book out of the sleeve and scooted it in his direction.

"May I touch it?" he said.

"Only if you don't have chocolate on your hands."

He didn't smile, but he did check his hands. "They look clean." He held them out for me to inspect.

I cleared my throat. "I'm sorry. Of course, please look through it. It isn't fragile enough to be destroyed with a careful look-through."

He was slow and meticulous, though there was a moment as he turned a page that I thought I saw expectation, followed by confirmation.

"Have you seen this book before?" I asked.

"Not this one specifically, but I have looked through other copies. We have a couple in the library. This copy is magnificent, though. Pristine."

I was silent as he fell under the book's spell again, and I resisted checking my watch or phone for the time. That something else that I was worried about depended upon timing. I'd know in about thirty seconds, I thought, if I'd planned well.

"Lovely." He closed the book.

"So, this doesn't look like something stolen from the university?"

"No. I would have been aware of that."

"That's good news. Any idea what a whole set would be worth?"

"I could only venture a guess, but I imagine the medical school would pay handsomely."

"That's good to know," I said as the phone on his desk rang.

"Excuse me." He picked up the receiver. "Dr. Eban," he said in a clipped tone. "I don't understand . . . Call security . . ." He turned his chair and looked out the window. "I don't see anything. Where? All right, one moment. I'll be right out."

He hung up the phone and stood. "I apologize. There's something going on outside the building. Excuse me a moment, but I'll be right back."

I held my breath as he left the office.

I felt terrible for the trick, and surprised he'd fallen for one of the oldest ones in the book, but extra grateful that Joshua had agreed to help, that he had access to Dr. Eban's direct office number, and that he knew how to make the call look like it came from an unassigned number. I'd thought maybe Dr. Eban wouldn't answer, but he had.

I had disembarked the bus briefly. I'd stopped by the museum on the way to the medical school and asked Joshua for some help. He'd been more than willing to play the part. He'd called Dr. Eban and said there seemed to be some sort of issue outside the building and that those involved said they wanted to speak only to him. Joshua was outside now, presumably watching Dr. Eban and hiding behind a tree.

It was a terrible and probably somehow illegal thing to do, and the fact that I'd gotten a young person involved was making me feel awful.

Nevertheless, I hurried around the desk and touched the mouse pad sitting on Dr. Eban's laptop, bringing the machine to life. As I'd hoped, his email was open and easy to see.

I didn't want to read any of the emails. I just wanted to see who they were from; at least that was what I kept telling myself.

I held my phone at the ready. Joshua was going to text me the second he saw Dr. Eban come back into the building, but our quick calculations had led us to think he'd be away from his office for about three minutes.

I quickly scrolled through the in-box list, seeing many names, most of them female (though that wasn't what I was looking for, and I didn't think it mattered), but not one that looked familiar. Most of the names were followed by @edinmed.org.

But then, about twenty emails down, I saw one that didn't seem to be from a university account. There was another reason it caught my attention. The moniker was Glasgowgirl50, and the server wasn't part of the school's network. And I knew this address.

I didn't have a lot of time to think about what I was doing. I knew it was bad enough that I'd done this much. I didn't know where in the spectrum of lawbreaking my actions fell, but I was at least invading privacy.

The email from Glasgowgirl50 was in the group of already read emails. He'd never know if I opened it.

I opened it.

Dr. Eban, I need to talk to you about our deal. Meet me Friday night, after pub hours. Same place.–R

It was dated the day before Mallory had been killed. My

heart sank. The email was from Rena, or at least from the address she'd used to send me a few emails.

My phone dinged.

He's back in the building.

I closed everything I'd opened and scrolled everything back into position. But when I got to the top a new email appeared, lit blue as it bumped the rest of the emails down a line.

It was from Bridget.Carr@erenegade.com.

I only had about twenty seconds, and he would know the email had been opened if I clicked on it. As tempting as it was, I took my hand off the mouse and hurried around to the other side of the desk, taking my seat a mere moment before he came into the office.

I noticed two things as the door opened. I'd left my phone on the other side of the desk, and Dr. Eban's chair was still turning as a result of my rushed exit from it.

I stood just as he came into the room and made a move toward the door, hoping to make our dance look like awkward bad timing.

"Oh, excuse me, I was just coming out to check on you," I said. I hoped I'd hid the moving chair. It had stopped when I turned around and leaned over for the book, grabbing my phone as I did so, but I didn't know what he'd seen. "I've taken up too much of your time. You have work to do."

We danced around each other another moment before he stepped around the desk and sat down again.

"I apologize for the interruption. I have no idea what was going on out there, but it was over by the time I could observe."

"No problem," I said with a smile. I knew my face was flushed with guilt, but I hoped he interpreted it as me just being flustered over the awkward moment.

He didn't look at his laptop screen. He didn't behave as if he was even a tiny bit suspicious.

"Please sit again. I still have some time," he said.

I sat and silently told my heart to quiet down.

"All right, back tae the books. Do you think your boss would allow the school tae purchase them? I have authority tae do such things, and could offer this." He took a small notepad out of a desk drawer and wrote down a sum.

"Oh my. That's quite generous. I'd be happy to ask him," I said.

"Excellent." He paused. "Do you think I should up the sum just tae make sure we get them?"

I didn't think he should. In fact, I knew that Edwin would probably donate the books to the library or medical school at some point if he felt that was the best home for them. But I didn't tell Dr. Eban that yet.

"I'll let you know what he says."

"Between you and me, I'd be happy tae go higher." He looked longingly at the book, which I was probably holding a bit too tightly.

"Want to look through it again before I go?"

"May I? I promise only tae take a wee bit more of your time."

"Sure." I slid the book back to him.

He didn't look at it much longer, but I tried to observe what I could. He wasn't creepy, at least not to me. He'd been friendly, but not too. He hadn't leered at me. His interest in the books was genuine, as well as professional. The very bad idea that I should try to proposition him just to see what he did danced through my thoughts, but fortunately it fell flat. I'd done enough.

We bid each other polite goodbyes with the promise that I'd get back to him soon.

It was impossible not to feel terrible about my intrusion as I made my way out of the building.

Joshua met me as I turned the corner.

"How'd it go?" he asked.

"There wasn't much to see," I said. "But I did what I wanted to do. Thank you for being my partner in crime, though I feel bad for asking you."

"Don't! That was exciting," he said.

I cringed. "No, that was terrible. And, again, I'm sorry I asked you to participate. Thank you again."

"Are you kidding? That was the most fun I've had in ages. Have you forgotten, I've just finished a dissertation? I deserved a little adventure."

Oh geez.

"Come on. I'll buy you lunch and talk you out of a further life of crime," I said.

"Good luck with that." He smiled, way too big.

SIXTEEN

After a hurried lunch (Joshua did have to get back to work), as I made my way to the offices of the *Renegade Scot*, I wondered if Dr. Eban had seen the article and was just being polite about not bringing it up, or if he hadn't seen it yet.

What did Bridget Carr want from him? Was it just because he was a professor at the medical school, or had she found out that he'd sat at the same table in a pub with Mallory the night she'd been killed? Had she also found out that I'd been a part of that group?

Though I was glad I hadn't opened the unopened email, I felt a tiny bit of regret over not having read it. I wondered if I could steer a conversation with her in that direction.

However, I had something else I wanted to talk to her about first.

As I peered inside the window of the small newspaper office, I remembered a friend's story. She told me that the best way to figure out if a newspaper is getting readers is for a business to advertise something in it they'll give away free of charge, then see how long the line grows. Not a technical method, but reliable.

I'd called Rosie to see if the bookshop had had any other calls. She said no and that there hadn't been an unusual rush of customers. I hoped the article wouldn't cause people to stay away, but the fact that there hadn't been more curiosity made me wonder just how many people really had read it. I knew that the people in my circle had, but that would be expected.

I didn't know the circulation of the *Renegade Scot*, but it had a small staff. Bridget sat at a desk in the back of the room, her concentrated focus on the computer screen in front of her and not on the guy who was peering over her shoulder, staring at the same screen.

Two other desks were manned with people also concentrating on their screens, and three other people were up and moving around, all of them carrying things like papers, pens, and smart phones.

I opened the door, but didn't hear any sort of ding to announce my arrival. For a long few moments, nobody noticed I was there.

"Help you?" one of the young men walking by asked. He tried to look friendly, but I could tell he was frazzled.

"I was hoping to talk to Bridget." I nodded toward her desk.

She looked up, lifted her eyebrows, and forced a confidence into her expression before she scooted herself away from the desk.

"Hello," she said as she approached. "What can I do for you, Delaney?"

I shrugged. "You got my name right, but you made up the rest."

"I didn't make anything up."

"You intimated."

"That's not making things up."

I sighed. "Can we talk somewhere?"

"Now you want tae talk?"

I glared at her—I could feel the heat in my eyes—before I turned to leave. I hadn't come to her office for a friendly conversation, but this wasn't going in a good direction at all.

"Wait!" she said as she followed me out the door and to the sidewalk. "Hang on."

I turned around slowly.

"Look, there was a murder right outside your bookshop. No one would talk tae me. It's my job tae write the truth. That's what I wrote, even if there might have been a few unclear things."

"Those unclear things have put me in a bad light. I did nothing wrong," I said as we sidled over to an out-of-the-way spot of the sidewalk.

"You wouldn't talk tae me."

I sighed again. We were going to keep going around in circles.

Before I could turn to leave again, though, she said, "All right, maybe I stretched things a bit. I'm sorry about that, but I didn't write untruths."

She'd apologized. It was a wimpy apology, but I'd take it if I could manage to get any other information out of her.

"Okay," I said.

"Okay. So, are you here tae tell me more about what happened?" she asked.

"I don't know much more. I was looking in the window of the bookshop to see if I could tell if it had been tampered with. Yes, there was a murder, and the body was found in the close not far from that window." The police report had said that much. "From neither side—I've now looked—has that window been tampered with, other than the glass having been broken out the night of the murder and some marks on the grate that might be file marks. Might. Anyone who would try to get in that way, though, would be there a long time. That's what I was doing. That's all I have."

"I see. I don't understand why you couldn't tell me that."

"Because I'm just an employee at the bookshop, Bridget. I didn't find the body. I didn't know anything. I don't know you. The police had been there and we'd been asked to close the shop for the day. I felt like it was all none of your business, none of anybody's business at that moment."

"You knew the victim though, right?"

"I'd only met her that night. She was a student at the medical school and I'm friends with two other students. She was at the pub with them. That's it. I didn't *get to know* her at all, but she seemed like a sweet person."

"Yeah, the medical school," she said.

"What about it?" I tried to make my pounce sound like normal conversation.

"I'm not sure." She looked at me. "You know anything about a professor there named Dr. Eban?"

"I know who he is." I paused. "Is he involved somehow?"

Distractedly she shook her head. "I don't know, but I'm trying to get an interview with him. He was friends with Dr. Glenn."

"I've only recently heard about him. He was a murderer?"

She was perplexed. "You don't know who Dr. Glenn is?"

"No idea."

"God, I hope the police do."

I didn't tell her that it was from an officer that I'd recently heard Dr. Glenn's name. "Tell me about him."

"There's too much tae tell. Look him up. He was friends with all of them: Dr. Eban, his wife, who is also a doctor and a professor at the university, as well as Mallory Clacher's father. They worked together back in the day, until . . . Well, it's hard tae think that Dr. Glenn has resurfaced, but if he has," she shook her head, "we're all in danger."

Dr. Glenn had gone from being a mere curiosity in my mind to being someone who could feasibly have been involved in Mallory Clacher's murder. "Tell me more about Dr. Glenn, Bridget."

She looked at her watch. "I would if I had the time, but I don't right now. You'll find all you want on the Web. If you want tae meet later, I could."

The urge to say "yes" was strong, but I pushed it away. I'd look him up on my own. "Mallory's dad's name isn't Conn, is it?"

She smiled. "You know more than you're ever going tae tell me. No, her father's name is Boris. Boris has a brother, a real troublemaker for the family. That's Conn Clacher. He's not a killer, but he's trouble nonetheless. Oh, hell, are the police looking at Conn as the killer?"

"No! Not that I'm aware of at least." I paused, and then decided to be straight with her so she wouldn't bother the Clachers. "Gaylord has represented a Conn Clacher. He was at the bookshop the day you saw him so Tom and I could talk to the police with an attorney present. There could be a conflict in him representing us, that's all."

She nodded slowly. "You a suspect? Anyone at the shop a suspect?"

"No, we just needed to give statements of our whereabouts the night of Mallory's murder. We aren't suspects."

We were two people avoiding telling each other everything, and both of us probably knew it. Briefly, I thought again about meeting her later, but decided not to.

I said, "I don't know who the police suspect."

"You know that her father, Boris, is part of the medical school administration?"

"Do you think that matters? I'm sure many students throughout the school have ties to the university."

"Aye. Something's going on at that medical school, but I can't figure out what or how it's connected to your bookshop. There has tae be something."

"I don't know what to say. I know nothing about any connection."

"I'd appreciate it if you'd help me figure out what it is," she said.

I swallowed hard. "How?"

"Get me an interview with your boss, Edwin MacAlister. He's a mystery himself. I'd be curious as tae what he has tae say."

I didn't want to try to get her an interview with Edwin, but I was just anxious enough about the murder that I might consider asking him.

"I'll try," I said with a sigh. "But he has no ties to the medical school."

"Right. Edwin MacAlister has ties tae everyone and everything in Edinburgh." She smiled and stepped toward the *Renegade Scot*'s doors.

"I will try," I said.

"Thanks. Hey, I'm sorry," she said.

Two apologies.

"Thanks," I said.

"I know you're dating Tom," she added as she reached for the door handle.

"I am."

"You guys have been together almost a year?"

I nodded. I really didn't want to talk about Tom with her.

She squinted and cocked her head. "You're not his type."

Ouch. I laughed.

"But I think that must be why he's so taken with you. For the first time ever, I think he fell for the inside before the outside."

"Well, that's an interesting backhanded compliment, but I'll take it."

"It's true that he's smitten and you're pretty enough, but . . . well, lots of women would have liked that kind of attention directed toward them, and he could get prettier."

Fair point.

She continued, "I would have liked his attention long-term, because he's a lovely man, but he's not good with breaking things off. He's not so lovely then."

"I'll deal with that it if happens."

"Aye. You'll have no choice."

I nodded again. And bit back words that might make me sound as bitter as she did.

"I want you tae know that I don't resent your relationship with him at all. I imagine he thinks I do and that's why I wrote . . . well, that that's why I wrote things the way I wrote them. Not true. I'm a journalist first."

"Okay," I said. I didn't believe her, but I didn't want to argue.

"Oh, thanks for sending the police after me. That was fun," she said with forced joviality.

"I'm trying to be honest with them," I said.

She laughed. "And you think I'm not? Not even close tae true. I showed him the piece of plaster and told him where I found it. He didn't think it was important. But, I do concede that I should have done it sooner."

Two apologies and an admission that she'd been wrong. I needed to keep up with all this good behavior.

"Well, good." I wasn't sure what else to say. If the police had thought the plaster piece was important, they would have taken it from her. Probably at least.

"Right." She looked at me a long moment, a surprise ray of sunshine breaking through the clouds and twinkling in her pretty eyes. They were also honest eyes, even if I didn't want to believe that. "Thanks for coming tae talk tae me. I know you came because you were looking for more information too"—she held up her hand as I began to protest—"but I'm not sure what it was. About Tom?"

"I came to talk to you because I felt I'd been treated unfairly by your article. I hoped that you might clear that up in future articles."

"I'm not sure about that. I can't make any promises. I'll just report the facts."

"Without a slant?"

I'd pushed too far. She smiled, but it wasn't as pretty as her eyes. "I'll talk tae you later, Delaney." She turned and abruptly walked back into the newspaper office.

"I guess that could have been worse," I muttered to myself before I headed back to my own job.

I did pull out my phone on the way and google "Dr. Glenn."

It didn't take me long to figure out who'd killed Mallory Clacher.

SEVENTEEN

"Edwin, it seems so obvious. Dr. Jack Glenn has resurfaced, and he killed Mallory. He needs to be caught before he kills again," I said.

Edwin looked up from his desk and brought his eyebrows together. "*The* Dr. Glenn?"

"Yes, Dr. Jack Glenn: killer, former colleague and friend of Doctors Eban, Carson, and Clacher. They were friends—good friends from what I could find."

Between the walk and the bus ride back to the bookshop, I'd had enough time to research on my phone. I'd learned exactly who Dr. Glenn was, and there was no doubt in my mind that he'd been Mallory's killer. It made so much sense. I moved to the chair in Edwin's office as he closed the book he'd been looking at. In fact, there were a few short stacks of books on his desk. Normally, that was something that would interest me, because he so rarely worked in his own office. Even one stack of books would be curious. But not today.

"You mean, it's obvious Glenn was the killer like it seemed so obvious that Dr. Eban was the killer?" he said.

"I know what you're saying. But Dr. Glenn is a proven killer! And the police are curious about him. They must have found something."

Edwin thought a moment. "He went missing, is that correct?"

"Yes! Here, let me just read a few things to you." I fired up my phone again and went to one of the Web pages I'd found. "Dr. Jack Glenn arrived at the medical school in 1998. He'd come to the school with all the right paperwork that proved he was a highly educated and well-trained surgeon. All that later proved to be false. He was not educated, trained, or experienced as a doctor of any kind."

"Of course, 'Dr. Glenn' became what he was called even after it was proved that he wasn't truly one," Edwin said.

I nodded and then continued. "He worked as a surgeon, researcher, and professor at the university until 2005, when one of his patients died as the result of a botched appendectomy." I paused and cleared my throat, remembering that Joshua and I had just been speaking about the miracle appendectomy procedures had been. "Things became more mysterious when the victim's body disappeared from the hospital's morgue, only to be found in the medical school's anatomy morgue. Dr. Glenn claimed he hadn't been the one who moved the body from one morgue to the other, but no one else seemed to have been near the right place at the right time to do such a thing."

"It's coming back tae me," Edwin said. "Go on."

"In the subsequent two weeks, two more patients died in Dr. Glenn's surgery, and his hospital privileges were suspended. He disappeared three days after the imposed suspension and didn't surface again until his wife called the police from a phone in Inverness.

"The botched surgeries had been kept under wraps pending

investigations, so she hadn't known about them when they left Edinburgh. Everything came to light when, while having her breakfast one morning, she read a small article in the *Scotsman* stating that the police and the university officials were searching for Dr. Glenn, who had gone missing shortly after three people had suspiciously died at his hand. It was thought she didn't have a clue regarding what her husband had been up to, or why they had to leave Edinburgh so quickly, but that was never confirmed."

"Oh, Delaney, she called Dr. Eban, didn't she?" Edwin interjected.

"Yes! It says it right here. Her first call was to Dr. Bryon Eban, someone she knew as a respected colleague and a friend to her husband. He told her to stay where she was, and that he would meet them in Inverness. But she'd felt uncomfortable waiting and then placed a call to the local police, who, apparently, didn't believe her when she'd told them who she and her husband were.

"Dr. Glenn overheard the call and then proceeded to suffocate her with a bag. He got away, and hasn't been seen since."

I had to clear my throat to push away the surge of emotion the article sent through me. "I didn't know anything about him, Edwin. I don't ever remember hearing about him back home."

"I'm sure we don't know about many of your country's killers either, Delaney. Did the police arrest Dr. Eban back then?"

"He was picked up when he arrived at the Glenns' place. He was brought in for questioning as well, but was never a suspect in the murder. He was released."

"Though I remember the case, even many of the details, I didn't know any of the people involved. You say both Inspector Pierce and Ms. Carr mentioned him tae you?"

I nodded again. "Yes. Oh, and she would like an interview with you. I told her I'd ask. Now I've asked."

"I know. She left a message or two here. I'm sure she thinks knowing more about the bookshop is somehow integral in finding that poor lass's killer."

"That's exactly what she thinks."

"I know Mallory's father, Boris, but not well, and I only met him a couple of years ago. I don't know anyone else at the medical school anymore. If Mallory came tae explore the warehouse for either the books her friends brought or the scalpels, I'm not going tae share that with any reporter. Not while a killer is being sought."

"I doubt Bridget will give up trying to talk to you."

Edwin frowned. "Aye."

"Edwin, Mallory was suffocated. The preferred method of Burke and Hare. It sounds like Dr. Glenn used the same method, at least once, on his wife. He brought the body of a man he'd killed to the medical school's morgue, just like the historical killers did with their victims."

"Do you think the murderer is Dr. Eban or Dr. Glenn?" Edwin asked.

"What if they're in on it together? Some sort of vendetta against Boris Clacher?"

"Oh, Delaney. That sounds like something so big, with so many pieces. You said the police are looking at this angle?"

"Inspector Pierce told me to look up Dr. Glenn. I'm sure—"

"Delaney!" Edwin exclaimed as he pounded his hand on his desk.

I jumped in my seat and my hand went to my heart. "What?"

"Come with me."

I followed Edwin down to the warehouse, where we gathered the treasure chest with the remaining scalpels and then hurried over to the light side.

Rosie and Hector watched us with matching wide eyes as we closed in on the front desk.

"Rosie," Edwin said. "Weren't you neighbors with Dr. Glenn?"

"Och, aye, 'twas a terrible time, wasnae it?" she said.

"Yes." Edwin set the chest down on the desk and opened it. He signaled that I was to take out the scalpels and the two cases. I did.

"Aye!" Rosie said. "I forgot all about those razors."

Edwin and I looked at each other.

"These are the scalpels, Rosie," I said.

Horror overtook her features. "The eetems that Dr. Eban asked aboot the night ye were all with the lass?"

I was afraid the news would topple her over, so I nodded, gently.

Rosie gasped. Hector barked in response.

"Call the police, lass, we need tae tell them where I got those razors . . . scalpels," Rosie said.

"Where did you get them?" I asked.

"From that killer, Dr. Glenn."

Oh boy, I thought. "Let's start from the beginning. What happened?"

Rosie nodded.

"I purchased them at a jumble sale," she said.

"Like a garage sale or a rummage sale?" I asked.

"Sounds aboot right," Rosie said.

I looked at Edwin.

"Rosie used tae live next door tae Dr. Glenn and his wife in West Port. It was back when he first came tae Edinburgh. She got them at the jumble sale and brought them to me," Edwin said. "It was a long time ago and I don't remember much about it except that we didn't think they were anything."

We looked at Rosie. She nodded.

"Aye," she said. "Ye were just beginning Fleshmarket. Fifteen years anon. Always busy. Dr. Glenn said they were just wee trinkets, souvenirs, and we didnae think any differently. We put them in the warehouse and didnae think aboot them again. Weel, I didnae."

"That's right," Edwin said. "And when Dr. Glenn committed his murders and then disappeared, we talked about looking for the items you got from him."

"But we didnae," Rosie said. "That was when my dear Paulie passed."

"Paulie?" I said.

"My husband." Rosie's eyes pooled with tears, but she blinked them away quickly.

"I had no idea you were married," I said. "I'm sorry, Rosie."

"It was a sad time," Edwin said. "Of course, we all paid attention tae the news about Dr. Glenn, but we were much more focused on Paulie and Rosie."

"That makes sense," I said, knocked off my center a little by the news that Rosie had been married. I should have known about that.

Rosie looked at the scalpels. "Even when ye first talked aboot these, lass, I didnae put it all together. I should have. I'm sairy."

"Don't be," I said as I regathered the scalpels. "This is going to help the police, I know." I looked at her. "What was he like? Dr. Glenn?"

"He was a nice man, tae me. His wife was lovely. Their daughter adorable."

Reactively, I put my hand up in a halt motion. "Hang on. Daughter?"

"Aye."

"Oh, I forgot about her too," Edwin said. "She was skirted away after her mother was killed, moved into foster care."

"I didn't read anything about a daughter," I said, further shocked by this additional news.

"Aye," Edwin said.

"How old was she?" I asked.

"Thirteen or fourteen," Rosie said.

"What was her name?"

"I remember exactly, because I'm a flower name too," Rosie said. "Lily. 'Twas Lily."

I wanted to look her up. I wanted to find a picture. But I also wanted to call Inspector Pierce and give him the news of where the scalpels had come from.

The door opened and three customers came in. The women were all about my age, and from my neck of the woods.

"Is it okay to bring our drinks in? They're just iced coffees," one of the women said as she held up her cup.

"If ye dinnae spill on anything," Rosie said with a friendly smile.

"Listen to that accent! Is that a real dog?" another woman said. "We'll be careful, I promise."

"Aye," Rosie said, and Hector, knowing his role well, smiled.

The women fell under The Cracked Spine's spell. They would enjoy their time in the shop, and Hector would enjoy their attention.

"Come along, lass, let's go back tae my office and make some calls. Do a little more research," Edwin said quietly.

Any other time, I would have approached and talked to the three women. Not today, though. Today, we had a killer to catch.

EIGHTEEN

"They all worked with Doctors Without Borders. Doctors Eban, Carson, Clacher, and Glenn, though he wasn't a real doctor. The title stuck, even through all the horror he inflicted. They were friends and did a lot of good," I said to Tom.

He slid a glass of water over the bar. There were only a few other customers in the pub. It had been a long and late evening at the bookshop and it was good to be with my pub owner.

"I remember Dr. Glenn's murders, but I didn't pay attention tae his life."

"Do you remember his daughter?"

"No," he said sadly.

"Lily. I couldn't find a picture. The Internet was going strong ten years ago, but the media must've respected her youthful age and her privacy and kept her picture out of the stories."

"That's good, and probably wouldn't happen now."

"Probably not. I did see pictures of all of the doctors when they were younger. I'm sure Dr. Glenn's murders were devastating in so many ways. In fact, I wonder if the fierceness and mistrust I saw in Dr. Carson came more from that time than

any other. The pictures I saw of her from back then were . . .
she was so naturally happy, with big smiles."

"You think she's not that way anymore?"

"I only talked to her briefly, and she might have just not liked
me or suspected me of something, but she's not like the pictures
I saw. Not anymore."

"Do you think she was just sad about Mallory?"

"I'm sure she was sad, but no, I was seeing something different."

"What did the police say?"

"I talked to both Inspectors Pierce and Winters, though Pierce
had already started putting things about Dr. Glenn together.
They were very glad to have the information, and Inspector
Pierce came to the bookshop, talked to Rosie—and she insisted
that no attorney be present. I don't know where it will go from
here, but he was there a long time. We all talked about Dr. Glenn,
what was either remembered or whatever research we found."

"Did Winters come in?" Tom asked.

"No, it's not his case. They are part of the same precinct, but
Pierce works from a satellite office up by the castle. Winters
wasn't in on the case at the beginning. He's brought himself up
to speed, but I sense that he doesn't want to get in Pierce's way. I
talked to him on the phone. He told me he can't find anything
about a case of missing books from the university either."

"Something must be ringing a bell for him."

"That's what he said. Now, he thinks he overheard another
officer on a phone call, just answering some questions, not filing
any official report. He's trying to remember which officer, and
then that officer has to remember the call. He's not giving up."

"He'll figure it out."

I took a drink of the water. "I have another thought."

Tom leaned toward me, his elbows on the bar, his eyes locked on mine. He knew that what I wanted to say was important; he was giving me his full attention.

Would his full attention ever not disarm me? Despite being tired to the bone, and off-kilter because of the many terrible circumstances surrounding me, I swooned a tiny bit.

I cleared my throat. "So. Lily. She was thirteen when her father killed her mother. She was placed into foster care. In Glasgow."

"Okay."

"Sophie and Rena are from Glasgow."

"Do you think that they might know Lily, or do you think one of them is Lily?" Tom asked.

"I don't know exactly. They're too old to be her if they've told me their true ages. I just don't know. Rena said the books came from her father. Maybe . . . I just don't know."

Tom thought a long moment. "Goodness, if Glenn has resurfaced. Wow."

"Exactly. I think it's a possibility."

"I hope not."

"Me too."

Tom stood up straight again. "I can't believe Rosie bought the scalpels at a jumble sale."

"I know. Did you know her husband, Paulie?"

"Aye, Paulie was sweet and kind, as you might imagine would be perfect for Rosie."

"I can't believe I didn't know about him."

"It wouldn't be like Rosie tae talk about him. Too sad for her. She and Regg are happy."

"I don't think they're talking marriage, but yes, they're happy."

"Good."

"Tom, lad, another one?" one of the customers said as he lumbered up to the bar.

"Sorry, Mel, last call's a while ago."

"Aw," Mel said.

Tom whistled. I didn't think I'd ever heard him whistle before, and a smile pulled at my lips. "You're not driving tonight, are you, Mel?" he said.

"No sir. Cab all the way."

"Coffee first?" Tom reached around to the coffeepot and poured Mel what I knew was a cup of extra-strong coffee. After he made sure Mel took a sip, he moved back toward me.

"Do me a favor," he said.

"Anything."

"Don't go visit Dr. Eban alone again, even if you meet him somewhere on campus."

"I promise I won't."

"Thank you."

Tom eyed Mel as he took the coffee to a table by the front window.

I couldn't resist any longer. "Whistle again. Please."

He looked at me with that smile and those cobalt eyes before he sent me a brief whistle. All the time I'd been in Kansas living a good life, this guy had been here, living an equally good life. Though the moments were fleeting, every once in a while I was sure I felt the presence of fate, or destiny. This was one of those moments.

And then it was mostly gone, except for a tiny piece of it. This had been happening more and more frequently: pieces of fate and destiny taking up residence in my heart.

I sighed, but didn't want to say out loud what I thought was happening or had happened. We'd expressed our feelings. And I still believed in jinxes.

"No more murder talk tonight?" I said.

"Sounds good tae me."

NINETEEN

"Delaney, hey," Lola said as she opened the door.

She'd seen me step out of Elias's cab and approach the building. We'd waved to her through her window, but I wondered if she'd open the door. The look on her face had been more perturbed than welcoming.

"Thanks," I said as I came through and she shut the door behind me.

"You here to see Sophie and Rena?"

"I am." That had been my plan. I hoped they would talk to me.

"They aren't here, but I know where you can find them. They were dressed up when they left so I asked what the special occasion was."

"Where did they go?"

"Church. A memorial service."

"For Mallory?"

"No, that's not today. This one is for the medical school corpses."

"The corpses! I forgot."

"They invited you?"

"Yes, kind of. Where is it again?"

"Greyfriars Kirk."

"Want to come with me?"

Her eyes slanted once quickly back toward her flat.

"Oh, did I disturb company? Sorry," I said.

"No, I'm just working on a project. I need to quit watching the door so much."

She looked down at the ground as I looked at her.

"You okay?" I asked.

She looked up and forced a smile. "Sure. I just let schoolwork get piled up again."

"Okay." I hesitated, but she didn't jump in with anything. "Thanks for letting me in, and for the reminder. I would have forgotten about the service."

"Sure." She turned and went back into her flat.

I hurried out of the building, but by the time I could see her window, the curtain was closing. Was she just tired of watching the door, or was there someone else in there she didn't want to be seen?

None of my business, but her eye slant had set off some internal alarms. Had I sensed she was scared? I hesitated, but decided I was probably working too hard to read something that wasn't there, into *everything*. I hurried back out to the cab. Elias had waited, because I wasn't sure if Rena and Sophie would welcome my visit.

"That was quick," Elias said as I opened the cab door. "They didnae want tae talk tae ye?"

"Do you have time to take me to Greyfriars Kirk?"

"We're going tae church?" he said doubtfully. Aggie made him go to church much more than he would have liked.

"A service for the corpses the medical school uses."

"Aye? Will the corpses be there?"

"Oh. I hope not. No, no, that wouldn't be feasible. It's a service to honor them and their families."

"Awright. Let's go."

I'd been to the church and the graveyard and past Greyfriars Bobby a number of times. A statue honoring a famous dog had been placed in front of the church on Candlemaker Row. Rosie passed it every day, either on the bus or if she exited the bus early and walked the rest of the way to work. She frequently mentioned that she and Hector had stopped to have "a wee bit of the blather" with Bobby, the statue.

The most popular story about the once stray Skye terrier begins with his faithful companion John, a gardener who came to Edinburgh but couldn't find a job and had to switch careers. John became a night watchman with the police force, and he and the stray dog would patrol the cobblestoned streets together. When John died of tuberculosis he was buried in Greyfriars Kirkyard, the graveyard next to the church. Bobby, ever faithful, refused to leave his master's grave. Even after the dog had been thrown out of the graveyard, he snuck back in. He would leave the gravesite only when the one o'clock bell rang at the Edinburgh Castle. Then Bobby would trot to the coffeehouse he and John had frequented, where he was fed a meal. The dog was taken care of for the rest of his life—locals continued to feed him and the Lord Provost paid for his license fee when a law was passed that all unlicensed dogs were to be destroyed. The engraved tag is in the Museum of Edinburgh; I've seen it. Baroness Angelia Georgina Burdett-Coutts had the statue and fountain erected in 1873. I learned all this from Joshua.

There were other less popular versions of the story that cast Bobby as a stray who was well loved by everyone, but didn't patrol the night streets with John. I, like everyone else, liked the version that included the night watchman much better, but no matter which story was true, it seemed the dog was certainly adored.

"There's someone pulling out now." I nodded toward the small car that had been parked not far from the church.

"What do ye call it? Parking karma?" Elias said.

I laughed. "Yes."

"We have guid parking karma today."

"I'll take it wherever I can get it."

"Aye." Elias angled the cab perfectly into the spot. "Are we here tae pay our respects or spy on people?"

"Both, I suppose. I think it's a lovely gesture, and anyone who donates his or her body to science is worthy of respect."

"But ye actually want tae just spy on folks?"

"Right."

Elias laughed. "Awright, I can handle that."

The ghosts of Edinburgh and I had developed an interesting relationship. I wasn't completely sure I'd had a haunted Scottish adventure, but all my friends were convinced that I'd met a few ghosts last Christmas. I wasn't ready to accept that version as truth, but it was difficult to explain it any other way. There'd been other moments too, though less vivid than my Christmas experience.

I'd visited the graveyard a few times since moving to Edinburgh, always with the hope I'd sense something ethereal. One of the oldest buildings to survive from Old Town, Edinburgh, the church and its graveyard were undeniably spooky, and many had claimed to have seen a ghost or two there.

I wasn't one of them. My time there had been peaceful and calm. I enjoyed the setting, but I'd yet to be haunted in or by it. However, I'd always let any listening spirits know that I was open to the idea.

Elias and I hurried through the front wrought-iron gate and toward the church's entrance. We slowed as we opened the wide double doors, and I looked toward the cemetery, green and peaceful with rows of a variety of old gravestones, but no ghosts to be seen.

The church building was used for more than just religious services, so there were no pews. Instead, purple-cushioned folding chairs had been set up in even rows, leaving an aisle down the middle. Massive organ pipes had been attached to the wall above the doors, and were vibrating with a quiet but not overly melancholy tune.

The light streaming in from the stained-glass windows above the sanctuary gave the space a warm glow without casting shadows or giving off glare. Tall archways ran along the length of the building and a magnificent redwood ceiling made the acoustics perfect for today, or for the occasional loud concert.

"Do ye ken that the town council once used this place for gunpowder storage?" Elias whispered as we stalled inside the doors.

"I did not know that."

"Aye." He shrugged. "Of course, the inevitable happened and the place blew, but it was nicely rebuilt."

"I agree."

"Should we sit?"

"Sure."

From the rear of the church it was difficult to recognize anyone, so I just picked a side and led Elias to some back-row seats. Once there, I noticed who was at the pulpit. Dr. Eban. If the police suspected him of anything, they hadn't arrested him yet.

"It is with honor and deep gratitude that we bid farewell tae those who have helped us learn their most hidden mysteries. They have served their country and their countrymen, and that cannot be minimalized. Thank you tae them and tae their families. We honor them today."

"We havenae missed much," Elias said.

"No."

Dr. Eban continued to speak as I looked around. It didn't take me long to spot Rena and Sophie. They were two of the more emotional attendees, dabbing at their eyes and noses with tissues.

I also spotted Dr. Carson, front and center, her straight back and regal gray hairstyle giving me the impression that she was at full attention as she listened to her husband.

Though most attendees were dressed in nice clothes, I spotted only a few here and there dressed in black.

"And, if you'll all indulge me, I'd like tae take one extra moment. The medical school experienced a terrible tragedy earlier this week." Dr. Eban paused and cleared his throat. I zeroed in on him and studied his body language. "Mallory Clacher, a fine student, was brutally murdered." He paused again as sniffles moved through the church, the acoustics giving them an eerie tone. Dr. Eban's emotion sounded genuine. He looked truly upset by the murder; I didn't think he was faking it. In fact, as I looked closer, I saw that he was shaken much more deeply than I would have guessed he'd have been. I wished he'd quit doing things that made me like him. "We would be remiss if we didn't take this moment tae bid her goodbye as well."

I pulled my gaze off him as he paused to gather his emotions, and I leaned forward to better see Rena and Sophie. They were both still dabbing and sniffing, but now with deeper emotion. Their pain was unquestionably genuine. I felt like I was intruding, so I sat back again and looked at Dr. Carson. Her back was still stick-straight, but her attention was no longer focused forward, toward her husband. Instead, she looked down and to the side, as if she couldn't bear to look at him as he spoke. I couldn't tell if she was crying, but I watched as her shoulders shook twice before she steeled her posture again.

I did a quick estimation and thought there were at least a hundred people in attendance. Many of them weren't emotional, but stoic. I saw a few sad smiles when Dr. Eban read through the names of those who were being laid to rest.

"Leuks like he's wrapping up," Elias said when the list was finished. "Do ye want tae talk tae anyone or get out before they see ye?"

"Perhaps just to give condolences. I'd actually like to talk to them about other things, but I think the timing is bad."

"I've got yer back."

"Thanks."

We stalled by the doors as people filed out. Dr. Carson was one of the first toward the door. She stopped when she saw me.

"I know who you are," she said.

I opened my mouth to say something, though I wasn't sure what, but she continued before I could speak.

"There's no need tae have lied. I know you met Bryon at the pub the night Mallory was killed. Why didn't you just say that?"

I couldn't immediately figure out why that was an important thing to know.

"I wasn't trying to lie," I said. "I was treading lightly. I shouldn't have bothered you at all that day, but my boss really was curious about the books. I apologize if I offended or bothered you in any way."

She scowled so fiercely at me that I thought Elias might become protective and defensive. She moved along, though, before he could say something volatile, or make fists and show her his muscles.

"She's a peach," he said after she was out of the building.

"I did have bad timing that day," I said.

Elias grumbled.

I'd just witnessed the "fierce" I'd heard about, and I was again convinced she'd changed over the years. In the pictures I'd seen of her from ten or fifteen years earlier, she looked jovial and happy. What had happened? Dr. Glenn's murders? Dr. Eban's wandering eye? I felt sorry for her.

When the dispersing crowd started to dwindle, I thought I might have missed Sophie and Rena's exit, but I saw them when I looked back toward the pulpit again.

They were there, with Dr. Eban. From a distance I got the impression that there was no contention amid the group. They seemed to be speaking in hushed tones, and from the way they all stood they appeared to be strained with grief.

"Do ye want tae walk up there?" Elias said when he noticed where I was looking.

"Maybe just walk that direction. I don't want to be too intrusive."

"Aye," he said, doubtfully.

I ignored his tone. Slowly, we moved toward them, but didn't go far before Sophie eyed us. She said something to Dr. Eban and Rena, who both turned and looked at us with furrowed eyebrows.

"Hi," Sophie said as she approached. "I'm sorry we didn't look for you. I forgot you were coming."

"No problem. It was a lovely service. This is my friend Elias."

After the introductions, she said, "Thank you for being here."

Her eyes were heavy with dark circles underneath. I put my hand on her arm.

"You doing okay?" I asked.

"Sure. I mean, as well as can be expected." She stole a glance back toward Dr. Eban and Rena, who were glancing curiously at us.

"Is there a problem?" I asked.

Sophie looked at me a long moment. She wasn't the same slightly anxious but happy person she'd been before Friday night. I guessed that she was evaluating whether she could trust me. Elias sensed it too, and seemed to pull backward a tiny bit, just enough to give Sophie the impression that he wasn't listening. I saw a wavering begin in her eyes, and I sensed I was losing her.

Mostly just to keep her there, I said, "I think I upset Rena the last time I talked to her."

She nodded. "Aye. She's been upset."

"I mean when she came to Grassmarket. The article . . . She was upset, maybe rightfully so. But I didn't know Mallory before Friday night, Sophie."

She brought her eyebrows together. "I have no idea what you're talking about. Article? Rena came to see you?"

"Oh. I'm sorry. A reporter from the *Renegade Scot* approached me as I was looking in a window at the bookshop. I wouldn't talk to her, but she wrote an article that had a suspicious slant in my direction. The police don't suspect me," again, I hoped, "but Rena was bothered, rightfully so. You two and Mallory were pretty good friends, and she wondered if I somehow knew Mallory before. I didn't." Hadn't Rena said they were all upset by the article? Who had she meant by "all" if Sophie wasn't part of that group?

"I guess I don't understand, but I never did think you killed Mallory." She sent another curious glance back to Rena and Dr. Eban. Their three-way silent communication was growing awkward, but Rena and Dr. Eban didn't approach us. Sophie turned her attention back to Elias and me.

I nodded. "Dr. Eban said lovely words about Mallory too."

"Aye," she said as more tears welled.

I looked around, and saw that there weren't many people left in the church. "Did Mallory's family attend the service?"

"I don't think so. Dr. Eban just added that part about Mallory. This wasn't a scheduled service for her. Why?" Sophie asked.

"I was hoping to give them my condolences," I said, thinking that all of us on The Cracked Spine staff should have done so already.

Sophie nodded. "Well . . ."

"Hey, Sophie," I reached for her arm as she turned, but I stopped myself from grabbing it, "do you know when Rena made it home Friday night?"

"Shortly after I did." She must have seen the look on my face. "Didn't we talk about this?"

"Lola saw her come in later."

"Lola? The young woman who opens the door for everyone?"

"Yes."

"Well, I don't know how you know her, but she's a strange one. I'm not sure you can trust much of what she says. She twists things sometimes."

"Strange how?"

"Aye. There are . . . This is unkind, but there are some people who would like tae go tae medical school but just don't have what it takes. They sometimes hang around us students or just the school. We call them groupies. Lola finds . . . found Mallory, Rena, and me even more interesting, because we're a wee bit older than the norm. She sees us as motivation. We see her as a wee bit delusional."

"Really? She was at the pub Friday night," I said.

"I didn't notice her, but I'm not surprised she was there. Did you tell the police?"

"I didn't see any reason why I should."

"You should."

"That she was at the pub?"

"Maybe." Sophie shrugged.

"Okay. Sure, that might be important." I looked at Elias and then back at Sophie. Elias got my cue and excused himself, stepping back and feigning interest in some organ pipes on the wall.

"You're okay? Rena's okay?"

"No, we're distraught over Mallory, but I don't think that's why you're curious."

I didn't have time to tread lightly. "Is Dr. Eban holding something over you two? I don't know, do you have some deal with him?" I used the word "deal" on purpose, because I'd seen it in the email from Rena to him.

"What?" Sophie said. "I have no idea what you're talking about. 'Deal'?"

I would bet she was lying, but I wouldn't bet a lot. I couldn't be certain; we just weren't that good of friends.

"Dr. Eban really thought there were scalpels in some warehouse that my boss is supposed to have."

"He probably still does. He's obsessive sometimes."

"Do you know who Dr. Glenn is?" I asked.

Her eyes widened briefly. I'd surprised her, and she tried to hide it quickly.

"Who?" she asked.

"Dr. Glenn. He worked at the medical school and the hospital. He wasn't a real doctor, alleged to have killed some patients, killed his wife. He and Dr. Eban knew each other."

"I've never heard of him."

Now I knew she was lying. Mostly because everyone in Scotland would probably find his name and his deeds familiar, but, also, she wasn't working hard to hide the lie.

Dr. Eban and Rena finally approached. I wondered if they'd seen Sophie become uncomfortable and had decided it was time to save her from whatever questions I might be asking her.

"Hello, Delaney," Rena said.

"Lass," Dr. Eban said.

I suspected they all knew about the books; the fact that Rena had brought them into the shop as well as the fact that I'd taken one to show Dr. Eban. I didn't know what I would say if they brought them up, but I told myself to somehow be prepared.

"That was lovely. Thank you for inviting me," I said.

Elias rejoined us.

"Dr. Eban," he extended his hand, "Elias McKenna. I'm a friend of Delaney's. Yer service gave me a curiosity. Do ye have a moment that I could ask ye a question in private?"

"Of course. Let's step this way."

"Did Delaney tell you I accosted her?" Rena asked Sophie.

"She mentioned that you went tae talk tae her."

"I'm sorry, Delaney. I was just so upset. But I've got my wits about me again," Rena said. "Forgive me?"

"Of course," I said as I looked closely at Rena. Was she being sincere? "How are you doing?"

"I'm not exactly sure how I'm supposed tae be doing, but it's all a wee bit difficult right now." She looked at Sophie. "We've considered withdrawing from school for the rest of the semester, but I just don't know."

"You're pretty far into it for withdrawal, aren't you?" I asked.

Rena shrugged as she and Sophie shared a frown.

"Well, I didn't know Mallory all that well, and you have to do what you have to do, but I do think she would like to see the two of you become doctors as soon as is feasibly possible." If they didn't have anything to do with her murder, I had no doubt that was true. I had been around the three of them together for only a short time, but I could see their friendly support of each other, void of envy but perhaps fueled by a little professional competition; the good kind that made them each strive to be better, not behave spitefully.

Sophie and Rena looked at each other, and I was pretty sure they both had to work hard to hold it together.

"Aye," Rena said.

"Aye," Sophie said.

Elias and Dr. Eban finished their brief conversation and approached us. The two men shook hands, and then Dr. Eban turned and left without telling any of the rest of us goodbye.

Sophie and Rena shared another look and then abruptly told us goodbye before they left too.

A few seconds later, other than a few people still sitting in the purple chairs, Elias and I were the only ones remaining in the church.

"What did you talk about?" I asked him.

"I wondered how one went aboot donating their body tae medicine."

"Really?"

"Aye. I'll talk tae Aggie tonight, but it makes sense tae me."

"Okay." I blinked. I had questions, but figured Aggie should ask them first.

"Where tae now, lass?"

"Any chance you'd like to try to see a roomful of skulls?"

"I havenae ever had such an offer, but I suppose it could be interesting."

"I don't know if we can get in, but let's try. I just need to make a phone call."

"I'll drive."

TWENTY

"Delaney, always good tae see ye," Artair said as he greeted us outside the university's skull room. "Ye too, Elias."

Though Joshua had offered to set up an appointment to show me the skull room, he hadn't been available today. I'd called Tom to let him know my plans had been thwarted, and he said he would call his father, Artair. I protested because I knew Artair had been busy with his sister, but Tom thought it would be good to give his father something else to focus on.

Artair shook both of our hands and hugged me. A librarian at the University of Edinburgh library, to me he was more than Tom's dad. He was a friend, someone I'd come to admire and care for. He was also someone who had helped me when I'd needed information I thought might lead to the discovery of a killer.

"How's your sister?" I asked.

"Same," Artair said with a sad smile. "I'm glad Tom called tae see if I was available tae show you the room. Good tae get my mind on something else."

"Aye," Elias said.

"I'm sorry she's not well," I said.

"She's auld," he said, as if trying to convince himself as well as tell us.

The skull room was off-limits to the public; however, as Joshua had said, visits could be arranged if research was involved. I didn't think I could qualify on my own, and I was in a hurry. If anyone could get us in, Artair had the connections. He hadn't even needed connections; he was able to go into the skull room anytime he wanted. Dr. Eban was the keeper of the keys, and had given one to Artair a long time ago.

"Thanks for doing this," I said.

"Och, my pleasure. I haven't been inside in some tiem, but last year when I was helping put together some book lists for the medical school, one of them was about genetic deformations. A horrifying subject, but one that I found utterly fascinating. I ended up in here. There are more than skulls inside. Ye'll see."

I'd heard as much, but Elias raised his eyebrows at me.

Artair pushed open the door and signaled us to go in ahead of him.

"Wow! It's exactly as advertised. A roomful of skulls."

"Aye," Elias said.

"Aye," Artair said. "It was built specifically for the wee things."

The space we stepped into wasn't vast, but it felt stately and not gruesome, despite the rows of skulls surrounding us. The skulls were in glass-front display cases against the walls on the main floor as well as on the upper level, which also had a walkway balcony around it. We were greeted by three skulls in their perpetual death smiles perched on a small table in the middle of the room. Beyond the greeters, rows of vacant eyes appraised us, toothy smiles sending their forever approval.

"The wood-paneled ceiling and the tile floor are original, built back in the 1880s. The only additions since then are the smoke detector and the fluorescent lights," Artair said.

A large window curved around a wall that didn't have display cases. The light from the windowpanes was shaded with fabric blinds, but I was sure that at one time the natural light must have been more than enough to study the items in the room, during the daytime at least.

"There are so many," I said.

"Aye," Artair said. "Sixteen hundred and eighty-eight complete skulls tae be exact, but only a small portion from Edinburgh. Most of them were sent tae the school from former students as they began practicing medicine all throughout the world."

"The skulls were all used in the medical school?" Elias said.

"Aye," Artair responded. "It's a nasty history sometimes, figuring oot how the body works, trying tae understand how tae fix things. We have our share of horror stories, but it cannae be denied that we've a wonderful medical school that probably only benefited from the terrible things that happened in the past," Artair said. "Not that I condone those terrible things."

"Burke and Hare?" I said.

Artair cringed. "Aye, a bad lot, the two of them. It would be difficult tae give them any credit, but dead bodies were needed. Supply and demand. Och, a bad history, no matter."

"I've gotten to know Dr. Eban a little bit." I knew Artair wasn't all the way up to speed on what had been happening regarding Mallory's murder, but Tom said his father did know about it.

"Aye?"

"Don't like him?" I asked, based on his tone.

"It's not that. I do like him. He's a brilliant teacher, but he's . . . obsessive might be the word for it."

"What about his wife, Dr. Carson?" I asked. "Do you get along with her?"

"She's even more brilliant," Artair said.

When he didn't say anything else, Elias and I looked at him expectantly, but he just rubbed his finger under his nose.

"Do you like her?" I asked.

"I don't know her personally at all. She's not an easy one tae get tae know, but she is brilliant."

"Artair, is it okay to ask you if you knew them back during the Dr. Glenn days?"

"It's fine. I didn't know any of them any better personally, but they were an admired group of people. They were considered kind, even . . . even Dr. Glenn. They helped the community; they helped the world with their studies."

"Was Dr. Carson different back then? Nicer, maybe?" I asked.

Artair thought a long moment. "No, not nicer. She's always been aloof. But she was happier, with less of an edge. Lass, Dr. Glenn's activities changed all of us at the university, but perhaps what he did changed her most of all. I hadn't ever thought about that before, but that's a possibility. She might have changed the most. Why did you bring up Dr. Glenn?"

I looked at Elias before looking back at Artair. "I don't know for sure, but I think the police are considering—considering only—that Dr. Glenn might in some way have been a part of Mallory Clacher's murder."

I thought he'd be surprised, maybe even gasp, but Artair

only fell into thought for another moment, and then said, "Well, that would be terrible, lass, but considering everything, it would not be a surprise."

"Really?" I said.

"You would have had tae live it tae understand it maybe, but the four doctors were together all the time, did everything as a group, and as far as I know none of them suspected Dr. Glenn was a fake. He's been in hiding, or so that was assumed. Perhaps he thought it was time tae show himself, in the way he knows how. It's just not a surprise. It's devastating, aye, but not a surprise."

"I bet that's how the police are looking at it," I said.

Elias nodded.

We walked to another display case, one without skulls.

"Oh. I heard about these," I said.

"Aye. The other items," Artair said. "Abnormal embryonic development."

"Oh. I see," I said as I looked closer. "Fascinating."

"We have ultrasounds now," Artair said.

"Goodness," Elias said as he bent over and looked more closely too.

"If we'd been able to see inside us like we can now, we might have been able tae save them, and in some cases the mothers lost their lives too. Birthing babies might be something that's been done since the beginning of tiem, but it's a dangerous and risky business, and was particularly so before so many medical advancements."

It sounded like Artair was quoting from a script.

"You give many tours?" I asked.

"I used tae. Not so much lately. There hasn't been as much interest over the last few years. I blame the Internet. Many of these skulls are from the collection of Sir William Turner. He was an anatomist here in the early 1900s, and very well respected. I read a book aboot him not long ago that told me something I hadn't learned yet. He knew Charles Darwin. Can ye even imagine the discussions the two of them must have had?"

"I can *only* imagine," I said.

"Is the room what ye expected?" Artair asked.

"More, probably. Do you know if any skulls have gone missing? Or pieces of skulls?"

"No, I don't think so. Have ye found one?"

"One was left by Mallory Clacher's body," I said.

"Och, poor lass. I hadn't heard about the skull," Artair said.

"It's not been made public."

"I see. Well, nothing has been stolen from here, at least that I've been made aware of. The collection is well guarded, and I've not heard of any thefts or damage. I'll ask around tae make sure, though."

I noticed something on the end of one of the shelves. I became so focused on it that Elias had to quickly step out of my way as I approached it.

"Is that a scalpel?" I said as I pointed.

There was no question that it was exactly that, and there was no question that it looked like the others I'd seen lately.

"Aye. One of Dr. Robert Knox's, if the small sign there is tae be believed," Artair said.

"But you don't know for sure that it was his?"

"Well, I cannae be sure, but I doubt the folks who set up these displays would mark it that way if it wasn't. Interesting, huh? They remind me of barbers' razors."

"Me too," I said.

"They would be pretty valuable, wouldn't they?" I asked.

"Aye," Artair said.

"Who would be most interested in this sort of thing? I mean, here or any other collector?"

"Dr. Eban, certainly. He's our resident collector of most of the medical history items. I know other collectors, but the list isn't top of my mind."

I wasn't surprised by his answer.

"Dr. Eban's filled a whole display case right outside his anatomy room. I catalogued a few items last year. No scalpels, though, I think. This is the only one I know about that's on campus."

I blinked at Artair and then at Elias.

"Ah, ye'd like tae see the display case?" Elias said.

"I would, when we're done here," I said.

"Awright," Elias said. "I'll drive again."

TWENTY-ONE

There's not much that compares with the smells of education. Though some of them change as you move through the years, there's that lingering scent of dusty books and linoleum floor wax, mixed with a little fear and panic. Sometimes there's a layer of cafeteria scents too, but not today, not in this building.

"This must be the room," I said to Elias as we stopped outside the room marked "Anatomical Theatre."

"That's quite the display case," he said as he peered inside the case, which was almost as crowded with stuff as Edwin's warehouse shelves.

"Do you see any scalpels?" I said as I dodged a few students entering the theater. I noticed the plaque Mallory had mentioned, about the theater being set up up like Dr. Knox's.

"That wee thing?" Elias pointed.

I leaned over and looked where he was looking. "I'll be. Yes, that looks exactly like the ones I found. Artair must not have known about it."

Elias slipped on his glasses. "The card next tae it says that it was a scalpel that belonged tae Dr. Robert Knox."

"Anything mentioning other scalpels that might be missing?"

"Not that I see."

The hallway had emptied, doors to rooms and halls closing as the last of the students disappeared inside. I wanted to look more closely at the items in the display case, but I also didn't want to miss my chance.

"Let's go in. If we can hide in the back, I'd like to observe," I said as I moved to the door.

"I'm right behind ye."

I was sure Elias expected the same sort of setup that I did—a tiered, circular room with a table in the middle where dissections could be observed. We hadn't taken any time to think about what we were walking into, but the reality of the room, set up as I'd visualized, was much more discombobulating than I'd imagined it would be.

The theater walls were painted light blue, a hue that seemed somehow frigid as well as comforting. Everything else in the seating area seemed to be made of old, dark wood: the curved desktops, the stools, and the panels that lined the outside of each tier. One staging area with a chrome body table was at the bottom of the tiers in the center. Another staging area that looked just like a small stage took up the back of the room. There were even industrial-gray curtains, currently wide open, showing the two doors where Dr. Eban must enter and exit. There was no body table on the stage. There was only a stool and a microphone, the microphone off to the side, the stool front and center. There was no cadaver in sight. Yet.

We found two empty stools amid the only half-populated room. We could probably blend in. As I watched Elias rearrange his cap, I realized that I'd led us—mostly him—into maybe our strangest situation yet.

"Hey, I'm sorry. This isn't right," I said. "Let's go."

A door at the back of the stage opened with a flourish, and Dr. Eban walked in.

I sensed that by that point it would have been weirder to leave than just to sit there and observe. Elias must have sensed the same thing, and we lowered a little on our stools. However, neither of us were hidden; it would have been impossible to hide. I did take a moment to wonder if Dr. Knox had taught in this room. It wouldn't have surprised me, but I doubted it. Surely, his theater hadn't survived the passing of time. And, fire took out so many things in those days. If it hadn't become di-lapidated, it might have burned.

Or, this could be the very room Dr. Knox used.

Dr. Eban didn't notice us right off. Instead, he launched into an announcement about the service he'd given at the church.

"Of course, the first-year students were required tae attend the service this morning, but I know that some of you had other obligations. Let's please take a moment of silence for those who have helped us over the years."

Before the moment of silence was a full moment, a hand shot up on the other side of the large room.

"Question?" Dr. Eban asked with one raised eyebrow.

"Aye. Did ye honor our Mallory, Dr. Eban?"

"Aye, we did."

"Guid."

The student's tone drew everyone's attention his direction. Like my friends, this man wasn't of a traditional age. He wasn't in his twenties or even his thirties. His salt-and-pepper short hair and beard were only the first things that aged him into at least his forties. He wore thick glasses and a wrinkled forehead very well, and his voice didn't ring with youth. If there was such a thing as a traditional medical student, he wasn't it.

"I don't believe I've had the honor," Dr. Eban said. "Are you new to this class?"

"I'm just visiting today," the man said. "I'm here for Mallory. The police willnae listen tae me, and I wanted tae make sure everyone knew who killed her."

"We're listening," Dr. Eban said.

Sometimes in life there are collective moments when things seem to be going a certain direction, but you and others around you sense that the path is about to get diverted. I knew I wasn't the only one in the room to sense that one of those diversions was about to take place. Elias and I shared a brief look that told me he did too. I was sure that, along with everyone else in the room, I knew what the man was going to say. Well, everyone with the possible exception of Dr. Eban. When that inkling came on me, and after looking at Elias, I turned my attention to Dr. Eban. I would always remember this moment and how he seemed genuinely surprised by the man's answer. Either he was a very good actor or he hadn't expected to be accused of murder.

"You did, Dr. Eban," the man said.

A rumble filled the room.

"That is not true," Dr. Eban responded coolly. "And I don't appreciate the accusation. Please leave our class."

The man stood but he didn't leave. He looked around the room and then brought his arm slowly up to point at the doctor below.

"This man is a killer. If you put your trust in him, he will ruin your career and then your life. When that's not enough, he will kill you."

The rumble grew. I didn't see a weapon on him, but a hum of violence filled the air along with his accusation. I watched as a few of the students stood to leave and Dr. Eban reached for his mobile.

The man left his chair and began walking along the back wall toward the door.

"Let's follow him," I said to Elias.

"Aye," he said with his own violent glimmer.

"I don't want to pick a fight, I just want to talk to him," I said, hoping to diffuse Elias's obvious anger.

"We'll see."

Elias led us out of the room. We were followed by a couple of students who'd felt the need to escape even after the man and his anger were gone. Dr. Eban didn't try to stop anyone.

I looked at the doctor before I went through the doorway, and his eyes caught mine briefly. He blinked in confusion, but I didn't stick around long enough to see if he finally recognized me.

"He went this way," Elias said from halfway down the hallway.

We set off at a quick jog.

TWENTY-TWO

Elias pushed through a door at the end of the hallway that led to a stairway. By the time I followed through he'd already traveled up one flight and was turning to go up another.

"How do you know he went up here?" I called to him.

"Only reasonable place. He's hiding from security now."

Elias and I both took the stairs two at a time, but with his head start and determination, he easily beat me up the four flights.

At the top, he pushed through another doorway. I reached it just before it closed. I held the door open and tried to catch my breath as I looked out to the roof.

"Hey!" Elias said to the man, who had indeed gone where Elias thought he would. He stood a few feet back from the ledge and his chest rose and fell quickly with his breathing.

"Who are you?" he said to Elias.

It was at that moment that I knew I was dealing with two similar people. They were both toward the far end of middle age, both with minds and hearts that desired to set things right. The man who'd accused Dr. Eban thought he was doing the right thing, and Elias thought he was doing the right thing by chasing down this man who'd seemed dangerous to a roomful of people. Doing the right thing can get people in so much trouble sometimes.

Hurriedly, I grabbed the rock that had been set outside the door and put it where it would keep it open.

"Hi!" I said a bit too cheerily as I jogged toward them. I held up one hand toward the man and put my other one on Elias's arm. "I knew Mallory. We just want to talk to you."

"How did you know Mallory?" he said as if he was certain he should know me too.

"I got to know some of the medical students. I met her," I said. I swallowed and looked back and forth between him and Elias. "I was with her the evening before she got killed. I work at the bookshop where . . . where it happened."

There was no sense of goodwill coming from the man as he took one step closer to the ledge. I really didn't think he would jump, but that might have just been denial.

"My name's Delaney. This is my friend Elias. What's your name?"

"Why did you chase me up here?"

"Why do you think Dr. Eban killed Mallory?"

"Are you students?" he asked.

"No, we were there to spy on Dr. Eban. Well, kind of spy. We wanted to see him work. Just curious about him."

"Do you suspect him too?"

I shook my head. No need to add to this man's suspicions. "Not until you accused him. Well, I just don't know, but I'd really like to find out. Will you talk to us?"

"I can't leave the roof for a while. I'm sure security is looking for me."

Elias huffed. "They'll look up here too."

"If you'd just close the door on your way back down, they might not think about it."

"It will lock. How will you get off the roof?" I asked.

"I've got someone coming tae get me later."

Elias and I looked at each other. He squinted and then turned toward the door. I wasn't sure what he did, but it included a piece of a receipt he pulled from his pocket and the gum he'd been chewing. A short few moments later, the door was shut, but Elias illustrated how it opened easily. It was a trick I hoped to learn some other day.

While Elias had been working on the door, the man and I hadn't moved from our spots. My breathing normalized, and I noticed that his chest wasn't moving up and down as quickly either.

"What's yer name, man?" Elias said as he walked back to my side.

"Conn Clatcher."

"You're Conn?" I asked. Yes, he and Elias were similar, but I didn't think Elias was as extreme as I'd heard Conn was. "Mallory's uncle?"

"Aye," he said hesitantly.

I sighed. "Can we sit down a minute, Conn? We can move over to the other side where we might not be seen if someone opens the door."

Though there wasn't a lot of space on the roof, the HVAC unit gave us some cover as we moved over to the other side and sat on the ledge, legs inward. The view of the campus was too pretty not to notice, but it wasn't the foremost thing on my mind as I peered over the side, relieved to find a subroof a few feet below. I suspected that Conn's plan to escape had included hiding on it. Dangerous, but apparently worth it, in his mind at least. We sat in a line; me, Conn, and then Elias, who leaned more than sat, obviously tense and ready to intervene in whatever way might be required.

"Does Boris know you're here?" I asked.

Conn shrugged. I took that as a negative. It wasn't fair to peg Conn's personality based solely upon what I'd heard about him, but I suspected that he was doing his brother's dirty work, based solely upon Conn's determination of what that dirty work should be. Though I hadn't met Boris Clacher either, the covert operation was not something I would have thought someone in the medical school's administration would approve of.

"Why do you think Dr. Eban killed your niece?" I asked.

"He's a wicked sort of a man. Manipulative, cruel."

This sort of thing kept happening—people saying bad things about him. I thought he was a little odd, but not murderous. I'd seen Sophie and Rena hanging out with him at the church. I'd heard about his past affiliation with Dr. Glenn. Nothing seemed to jibe all the way. I needed much more information.

"How was he cruel to Mallory?" I asked.

"He had her do unsavory things for her grades."

I was pretty sure that's what he was going to say. "What? Can you tell me specifically?"

"Lass, they're not things I would say tae a lady," Conn said.

"Pretend I'm not one," I said impatiently. More than once I'd been told I'd approached something from an American point of view that just wasn't the same thing in the Scottish world. Maybe I didn't understand the culture.

And sure enough, Elias huffed.

Conn thought a moment as he scratched at his beard. "Things done in the bedroom."

Maybe I did understand. Still. "I mean this like I've never meant anything else before, Mr. Clacher. Tell me specifically the things that Mallory said. The specific things."

Again, he thought as he scratched at the beard and then rubbed under his nose.

"She didn't tell me specifics," he finally said. "She didn't tell her father specifics either. She just said he pushed her to do things."

" 'Do things.' Those were her words? Did she ever say what that was? Or if it included specific sexual acts?"

"No, lass!"

"Then how do you know that's what happened?"

"Because she wouldn't say! I think that's clue enough. She wasn't a liar, she was just modest."

Or she was a willing participant and didn't want to look like one. However, there was a certain general truth to what he was saying. Mallory was in her late twenties at least, but some people of any age would be embarrassed to talk about such things, maybe more so in Scotland. My parents were ultraconservative farm folks. If someone had taken advantage of me in such a way, would I have told them the specifics?

It was hard to know for sure. It was impossible to know what went on in someone else's life.

"She would have told someone what happened. If not the police—and I can see why that would scare her—a friend, or a relative," I said as I thought through what I would do. "Who was her closest female relative, or perhaps a good friend?"

"Her mother, I suppose, but her mother knows as much as Boris and I do."

"A friend?"

"I don't know her friends."

"Has Boris told the police these things?" I said. "Why are you here instead of talking to the police?"

"We did go tae the police. They weren't interested in our interpretations either. But Boris knows his daughter. He understood what she'd tried to communicate to him."

"He did. Are you sure?" I said.

"Aye," Conn said hesitantly.

"Conn, if I promise not to do anything to contribute to your being arrested for anything, will you tell me the truth? Does Boris feel the same way you do about this?"

Conn looked at me a long time. "Lass, how would I really know? He's devastated, that's what I know. He brought up Mallory's . . . issues tae me not too long ago. I know my brother. I'm sure he feels the same way."

"But he didn't come out and say that to you?"

Conn didn't answer.

"What did ye think ye would accomplish in that classroom?" Elias asked, his anger still evident.

"I wanted tae rattle him."

"Ye rattled everyone. Did ye not think of that? Ye were a nuisance and ye scared people, innocent people. Ye disrupted important learning!"

"I don't care."

Elias grumbled.

"Think about it," Conn said. "Would you care what ye had tae do if it meant justice for a loved one?"

"I wouldnae disrupt a bunch of innocent people, but I would find a way tae talk tae the wee man on my own," Elias said.

There would be more than talking during that conversation.

"Well. That's you, and it sounds more violent than what I

did. I just scared people, got them all talking maybe. That was the plan."

It wasn't the worst plan—though I got where Elias was coming from—but it had been poorly executed.

"Look, she had to have told someone what was going on," I jumped in. "Did you or her father spend any time talking to the women who live in the same building she did?"

Conn shook his head. "You have tae understand that Boris can't do that sort of thing. He has a position here. And, frankly, think about it, we're older men, and though I didn't mind scaring a classroom full of people, it would be worse to scare a building full of lasses."

I wasn't sure I would have reacted the way Conn had, but grief does unexpected things to people.

"You don't think Mallory talked to the police?"

"Not about this. I'm sure she didn't."

"I'll talk to her friends," I said. "Maybe they know, and maybe they'll be honest with me."

In fact, I'd given them plenty of opportunities to tell me anything they wanted. I hoped I could figure out a way to get some real answers from them.

"You will?" Conn said. "Why?"

"I know them." I looked back and forth between the men. "I know the women in the building. I can say I heard about what happened today in Dr. Eban's classroom, and see what they tell me. It will be fine."

"That might be helpful. Thank you, lass," Conn said.

Elias grumbled again.

I wasn't sure I'd learn anything helpful or fine, but I tried to hide my sigh and my uncertain eyes before Elias and I made our escape.

TWENTY-THREE

Leaving the roof and the building proved to be an easy, if guilt-ridden, adventure. Elias and I left before Conn—I didn't want to abandon him, but Elias was fine with it. We ventured back down the stairs and then the hallway that led to Dr. Eban's room. We strolled by a man dressed as a security officer, but he didn't give us a second look. I peered into the display case as we passed and was disappointed we didn't have time to take another look at all the items inside, but by then I just wanted to get out of the building without further incident.

"Well," I said when we were safely ensconced in the cab. "I didn't think any of that would happen."

"I'm sorry I took off in a chase. I couldnae help myself," Elias said.

"I'm glad we caught up with him. He's handling his grief poorly, but I'm sure he's very upset."

"A strange way for a man tae handle something."

"The whole family is distraught, I'm sure." I was silently pleased that Elias didn't agree with Conn's coping methods, and I didn't point out how much alike they truly were. However, from what I knew, Conn had crossed over the line separating legal from illegal a time or two; Elias might have done the same, or have done the same more often if he didn't have Aggie. "You know, if Mallory only hinted about things that Dr. Eban did, someone needs to get the specifics. Sophie and Rena might be too scared to tell the police, but maybe they'll tell me. I don't know. I might have overstayed my welcome with them, but at least I hope to make them understand how important it is that the police know the facts if Mallory was truly pushed to do something she didn't want to do."

"Ye sound doubtful."

I shook my head. "I shouldn't, because no one should. These sorts of accusations should always be taken seriously, and explored completely. It's just that . . . I'm not seeing it. However, my intuition could be off." I listened for the bookish voices, and heard only the noise of crickets chirping, or maybe I imagined it.

Elias grumbled. He was thinking. I could read some of his thoughts, but not all of them.

"Want to drive me over to their apartment building again?" I said.

"We're already on the way."

———

The curtain over her window was open and Lola let me inside again, but this time I saw her differently. I'd thought her behavior of always opening the door was friendly, if quirky, but now I wondered if it wasn't some sort of obsessive way to spy and garner information. She seemed happier than the last time, or maybe only less sad.

"Hey, Lola," I said to her as we stood in the entryway.

"Is the cab waiting for you?" she said as she peered out the narrow window next to the door.

"The driver's a friend."

"Okay."

Elias leaned against the cab with his arms crossed in front of his chest.

"Do you know if Sophie and Rena are up there?" I asked.

"I saw them come in earlier and haven't seen them leave again."

"Great. Thanks." I stepped toward the hallway as she went to her door.

I happened to catch sight of her flat as she opened the door wide to go inside. The messy space reminded me of college and Sophie and Rena's place. Coffee cups and a few empty takeaway containers littered the space around books and one laptop. Nothing strange about her flat, except maybe one thing.

"Lola," I said, turning to face her. "Do you think Mallory would have confided in Sophie and Rena?"

"Sure," she said as if she hadn't thought about it much.

"Did she ever have a roommate?" I asked.

Lola sent me an impatient look. "Delaney, you obviously know."

"No, I don't," I said.

"Mallory was my roommate. She moved out last semester and into her own room."

"Lola, I promise you that I didn't know. I didn't even guess. I'm just trying to understand who she might have been closest to. You were so upset. You were closer than I thought?"

She studied me suspiciously. "No, we weren't close. She lived here," she nodded to her own flat, "but her study hours were too strenuous and mine just weren't. She said I was too much of a distraction, what with the way I look out the window all the time. It's just . . . it's just what I like to do."

I nodded. "Makes sense to me. Did she make you mad when she moved?"

Lola laughed this time. "You mean, did I kill her just because she wanted her own space? No, Delaney, I didn't take it that personally."

"Must be hard to live in a building with mostly med students. Why did you do that to yourself?"

She shrugged. "I thought I wanted to be a doctor too. I thought this would motivate me to work harder. In answer to your next question, no, it didn't motivate me, but then who wants to move? Look at this mess. Just folding the clothes I'd need to pack would take too long. I like it here. Mallory was not only more studious, she was neater, too. Her move was easy."

"I understand."

I did understand not wanting to move, but I didn't completely get Lola. I wanted to ask if the police knew they were once roommates, but there was no nonaccusatory way to form the question. I'd ask the police myself.

"Shoot, Lola, Mallory's death has to be extra hard on you. I'm sorry."

Her eyes flashed briefly with teary gratitude. Had she just been waiting for someone to extend some sympathy her way?

"Thank you." She sniffed. "Well, I wish my semester living with Mallory had given me some insight as to why someone might want her dead, but I've got nothing. She was a sweet, hardworking person who didn't share much of herself, her inner self, you know. She was studious and quiet. Never talked about family or friends. I was shocked when I saw her dad coming over for a visit one day. I had no idea her father was such a big deal at the university. The rumors about her and Dr. Eban have been swirling for a while. I just don't know. Dr. Eban and Dr. Clacher work together. The day I saw her father, I wondered if he knew about the rumors and how he felt, and I guess that Dr. Eban would be fired if Dr. Clacher found any truth to them."

I couldn't have told you one member of the administration of the university I attended, but maybe medical school and Scotland were different. Well, I remembered the president's name, but that was it.

"How long ago did you see Mallory's father come by?" I asked.

"A few months, I think. Look, I have some work to do." She smiled stiffly again.

"Sure. Thanks, and thanks for getting the door all the time."

"You're welcome."

She was distracted as she told me goodbye and then shut her door.

I walked down the hallway, past Mallory's door, now devoid of tributes, up the stairs, and knocked on Sophie and Rena's door, but just with a few gentle raps. Somehow, in my mind that seemed less intrusive.

"Delaney, come in," Rena said as she opened the door. She didn't smile, but her tone wasn't unwelcoming.

"Thanks," I said.

Sophie was right inside, sitting on the end of the couch.

"Delaney," she said.

"Hi," I said. "I'm sorry to intrude, and I know we just saw each other, but . . ."

"Have a seat. Believe it or not, we were kind of expecting you," Rena said.

"Rena told me more about the article," Sophie interjected.

"Oh, good, that's why I came over," I lied easily. "I wanted to explain that to you both. The church didn't feel like the right place, and . . . I didn't know Mallory before Friday night, and I certainly didn't kill her."

They looked at me with calm, expectant eyes. I didn't know how to interpret their nonreactions. Did I need to explain more or were they not actually waiting to hear an explanation?

I went through the sequence of events of my explorations down the close, but as I told the story this time a new light was shed. Now, I could see myself through Bridget's eyes, not as Tom's girlfriend but as someone a bit too curious about the view through a window at the place she worked, the place near which someone had just been killed. I didn't want to ponder the revelation in front of my friends, but I knew I would later. Though it seemed natural to be curious, I might be willing to feel a little less angry, resentful, and maybe even violent toward Bridget.

"But still," I said, "there's a killer on the loose, and I'm having a hard time thinking it was a random murder. She was at the bookshop, a place we'd talked about with Dr. Eban only a short time earlier. I can't believe that either of you two were the killer either." I still wasn't sure, but I hoped I sounded like I was. "Do you two think Dr. Eban could have killed her?"

They shared a look.

Rena was the first to move her attention back to me. "Look, Delaney, we don't think we owe you an explanation, but we'd like tae tell you something nevertheless. We haven't told the police, but we are going tae, planned on calling them right before you knocked."

"Okay."

"We saw something," Sophie began.

She paused for so long I thought she was going to change her mind and not tell me. I kept as steady and patient as I could and hoped she'd keep talking.

She resumed, "I saw a man sneaking out of Mallory's flat a few months ago. Late."

"Dr. Eban?" I asked.

"No, at first I thought so, but . . ."

"Sophie?"

"I think it was Dr. Jack Glenn."

I looked at the women. "I'm . . . Did you recognize him? Hasn't he been missing for ten years or so?"

"I didn't recognize him at first. Mallory told us later who he was," Sophie said.

"And you didn't call the police?" I said, holding back firmly on a general sense of aghast.

Sophie looked at Rena. "We wanted to, but Mallory asked us not to."

"Oh boy, you two, I don't understand that one bit."

"Delaney," Rena said, "Dr. Glenn has been in Edinburgh for a few years. He befriended Mallory about six months ago. She didn't know who he was, but kept their relationship hidden because he was so much older. It wasn't until recently that she put the pieces together herself, after looking at pictures of him with her father from ten years ago."

"That had to be a terrible discovery. Didn't know who he was? He and her father were friends ten years ago. She didn't recognize him?"

Rena shrugged. "She mentioned that she didn't recognize him and then she fell in love with him. He with her, too. She said he wasn't the same man he used tae be." Rena shrugged again, but more stiffly this time. "We should have called the police a long time ago, but Mallory asked us not tae. We need tae tell them now. Surely, that's who killed her."

What they were saying both made sense and didn't make sense. Words ran through my mind, but I didn't think they were from a bookish voice. I think it was just something I'd heard in many different places, in one form or another.

Two half-truths don't make a truth.

In fact, even three don't.

"Why did he kill her outside the bookshop?" I asked.

"We don't know, of course," Sophie said. "Maybe she was just curious about the scalpels that Dr. Eban mentioned, and Dr. Glenn followed her."

Dr. Glenn had come back to murder—to seduce first, this time around—family members from his previous circle of friends. Sadly, I could imagine something like that happening. However, it was still far-fetched.

"You need to call the police right away," I said.

"We were just about to," Sophie said.

"You didn't call them because you told Mallory you'd keep the secret?" I said, my aghast beginning to show.

"Not really," Sophie said. "We were scared. Plain and simple scared."

"Oh," I said. "Of course you were. Should we get you some protection?" I reached for my phone. I didn't know what else to do, but I didn't know who to call.

"No," Rena said as she put her hand up. "No, Delaney. We'll be fine, but we *were* scared."

"Makes sense," I said, though it didn't make complete sense.

There was something wrong with the way they were acting—for one thing, they seemed so calm now. And why hadn't they contacted the police? I could only chalk that up to their fear, and perhaps their grief. So much had happened that I couldn't possibly understand.

Sophie stood. "If you don't mind, we'd like tae call the police now."

"I can stay," I said.

"We'd rather not put you in that position," Rena said.

I didn't mind, but I didn't say so. They wanted me to leave. I stood and Sophie saw me to the door. As she opened it, I looked back into their flat.

"Does he look the same?" I asked. "Dr. Glenn?"

"Aye," Sophie said.

"Gray hair," Rena said. She looked at Sophie. "You said he had gray hair."

"Right. Yes, gray hair," she said.

I nodded.

"See you later, Delaney," Sophie said.

"Yes, later," I said, as the door closed.

I'd originally wanted to ask if Mallory had told them anything about Dr. Eban. I'd wanted to find out what Rena was up to Friday night after she'd gone back out, or maybe hadn't come home at all.

But other things were now more important. I didn't believe them about Mallory and Dr. Glenn, I didn't know why exactly. But he certainly made for a convenient place to point an accusatory finger. I decided the police should hear from me too—about the alleged relationship between Mallory and the elusive killer from ten years ago, about Mallory's former roommate, and also about my weird feelings regarding the gray-haired man I'd seen at the pub.

I pulled out my phone and hurried back out to Elias.

TWENTY-FOUR

The Royal Mile was busy today. It was busy almost every day, with tourists from all over the world walking up the hill to the castle, and all the way down to the sea. Maybe it was the comfortable temperature and the clear blue sky, but today it seemed busier than normal as Elias steered the cab slowly and we searched for a parking spot. Inspector Winters' office was at the bottom, by the sea, but Inspector Pierce's satellite office was closer to the castle at the top.

"There it is," I said as I pointed to the narrow space with a sign above it: POLICE. "The window is painted blue."

"Aye. I guess they dinnae want people looking in at their business."

"Let me out here. I'm close to the bookshop. Go ahead and get back to Aggie. I'll get home later."

"Lass."

"I promise I won't go talking to people, asking questions without you or someone else with me. Seriously, I just want to talk to Inspector Pierce."

"Without your attorney?"

"Yes, but it will be okay."

"I dinnae like any of this," he said.

"It's okay. I really just want to make sure the police have all the information I think they should have."

He wasn't happy about it, but part of our relationship's growing pains was him letting me be the adult I was. He finally conceded and stopped the cab.

I watched him turn right at the next intersection down the hill. I dodged some pockets of pedestrians as I hurried across the sidewalk to the blue door. I noticed a narrow gap in it, and wondered if they could see out through the blue or if the view was blocked from both directions.

I pulled on the door handle, but it was locked tight. I had the urge to move closer and peer in, but I still wouldn't have been able to see inside. I knocked, but no one answered immediately.

I stepped back and searched for a business hours sign, but didn't see anything. I had Inspector Pierce's number programmed into my phone, but he hadn't answered the three times I'd tried to reach him on the way over.

I'd have to hope he called me back soon. But as I turned to head down the hill the door to the police station opened.

"Delaney?" Inspector Pierce said as he leaned out. "What's up?"

"Hi. Yes. I called."

"I've been busy. What can I do for you?"

I looked around. "Can I come in there?"

At first I thought he'd say no, but he didn't. "Come on in."

It was a closet of a police station with two facing desks that left a narrow vertical pathway in between them. Beyond was probably a storage closet and maybe a toilet, but the focal point was unquestionably the coffee machine perched on a chrome cart with wheels that probably had to be moved from one side to the other when someone needed to get into the supply closet or the toilet.

"Have a seat." Inspector Pierce nodded to the one ragged chair that wasn't behind one of the desks. "Coffee?"

"Thanks."

I took a seat and wondered what to do with my knees. I would have to swerve them out of the way if Inspector Pierce sat at the nearby desk. Scotland seemed to specialize in indoor tight spaces.

Inspector Pierce handed me the coffee and then sat at the desk across from me, so I didn't have to scrunch my knees at all.

"What's going on, Delaney?" he asked.

"Have you . . . Did you know?" I took a deep breath. "Did you know that Mallory used to be roommates with Lola, a woman who lives in the same apartment building?"

"Yes, we did. Why?"

"I don't know. I just hoped you knew."

He nodded.

"Friday night at the pub, I saw a gray-haired man . . ."

"Delaney . . ."

"No, please listen."

"All right."

I told Inspector Pierce about the wonky sensation I'd gotten when I saw the gray-haired man, and then I told him that I'd heard that Dr. Glenn now had gray hair. He became more interested in what I had to say.

"I don't understand. You looked him up?"

"More than that, I've heard about him a couple of times now."

"Right. Well, it's feasible that he has gray hair, but we don't have a current picture, of course. You think that was him at the pub?"

"I'm not sure. But, did Sophie and Rena call you in the last half hour?"

"I've been on the phone, talking to the police in Inverness, learning about their experiences with Glenn." He looked at his mobile. "I see your calls." He turned his attention back to the phone on his desk, lifting the handpiece and then punching some numbers. "Yes, Rena called. Asked me to call her back."

"You might want to go see them in person."

"What's up?"

"I was just at their flat, and they told me something. Do you want me to tell you or do you want to talk to them in person?"

"I think you should tell me whatever is on your mind."

I told him what they'd said, everything. He was less doubtful than I'd predicted he would be.

"I need to get to their flat, Delaney." He stood up. "Is there anything else?"

"No."

Though he was in a hurry, he did thank me for the information. Nonetheless, we were out of the office with the blue door in record time. I watched him drive away in an unmarked car that was parked on the street. I hoped he was about to zero in on a killer.

As I made my way back to The Cracked Spine, I pulled out my phone and called Conn Clacher. I didn't get the answers from Sophie and Rena he was looking for, but I wasn't going to tell him about Mallory and Dr. Glenn. Hopefully I could say something that would stop him from creating another scene.

Or doing something even worse.

TWENTY-FIVE

"He was a lovely man... Weel, tae me, he was. That's what I ken of him, until he went sae coorse." Rosie lifted Hector to her lap as I looked at her with raised eyebrows. My translator, Hamlet, was in class. "Och. Coorse means bad, wicked." I nodded. "I feel terrible saying such things now, but he was kind tae me. We were friendly neighbors is all, not friends. I didnae have one deep conversation with the man or his lovely wife or wee daughter; neither did Paulie. If Dr. Glenn was putting on an act, something tae hide his evil side, he was guid at it."

I'd completely forgotten to ask Inspector Pierce if he'd learned anything new regarding the scalpels. However, I'd called Inspector Winters and filled him in on everything, including Rosie's connection to Dr. Glenn. He'd been grateful for the update, and in just as much of a hurry to follow up on all the new information as Pierce had been. I'd also left a message for Conn. I hoped he'd call me back soon. I hoped he wasn't making bad decisions.

"Any sense of if Dr. Glenn would ever come back to town?" I asked.

"Do I think he kil't that poor lass?"

I shrugged.

She tapped her lips with her finger as she thought. Hector whined from his position on her lap. "I didnae ken."

"Do you think you'd recognize him?"

"Aye. He's a tall man, and he always had a tilt tae his head. I don't think he could do anything aboot it." She cocked her head slightly. "I'd recognize his figure tae be sure."

The police should maybe be looking for a tall man with a funny tilt to his head, possibly with gray hair. I guessed that narrowed it down a little bit, but not much.

I sighed and was glad to have the distraction of the front doorbell jingle.

"Joshua, hello!" I said.

Joshua bowed as he said, "Ladies."

He greeted Rosie with a hug and a box of cookies and Hector with an ear scratch and a jerky dog treat. They would have both been happy to see him anyway, but hugs and treats were always appreciated.

I directed him to the back table as he declined Rosie's offer of coffee or tea.

"What's up?" I asked, having sensed immediately that he hadn't come by only for a social visit.

He glanced in the direction of the front desk. I didn't tell him that Rosie wouldn't be listening, because she probably would be.

"I found something on old scalpels," he said quietly. "You tried to be sly about asking me about them, but you weren't. I decided to see if I could find anything else out."

"Well, thanks for seeing through my act. What did you find?"

"Did you already know that some scalpels were stolen from the university?"

"No, when?"

"The museum gets special communication from the local police," he began. "Well, it's more that if artifacts, or things that might be suspected to be valuable in a historical way, I suppose, get reported as stolen or lost, we, and other museums probably, receive a communication. So we're on the lookout."

"That's interesting, and makes sense."

"Sometimes inquiries alone are supposed to be reported back to the police." His eyebrows came together.

"You had to report me, didn't you?"

He half-smiled. "I would never do that."

"But you were supposed to?"

"I was, but when you asked, I hadn't remembered where the old report was yet."

"I'm sorry to put you in that position. I didn't even think about it."

"Please don't be concerned about that. I wanted to let you know, though, before you went around talking to other museums about the scalpels." He looked at me, and I told him I hadn't. He seemed relieved. "Anyway, when you told me about them, a memory of something I'd read once did ping in the back of my mind, but I knew it was from some old documents. I had to dig a little to find the report from almost eleven years ago, mind you, that mentioned that scalpels were on a stolen items list from the university."

He reached into his pocket and pulled out a folded piece of paper.

"This is a copy of the report, complete with pictures," he said.

The two pictures at the top of the page held familiar items: scalpels and two display cases.

The report was brief but descriptive:

"Missing from the University of Edinburgh medical school: a set of scalpels (circa 1828 or thereabouts) alleged to have been used by Dr. Robert Knox, the doctor to whom murderers William Burke and William Hare sold their victims. The scalpels were owned by the university. Dr. Bryon Eban had been given charge of the artifacts and he had displayed them in a case outside his classroom. There are two locks on the case. The glass was broken. The scalpels were the only items taken. They fold with a circular hinge and have blue handles. They look like a barber's razor. Only one of the two cases on display was stolen."

"The police need this report," I said.

"Sure, if you think so."

"I do." I looked at the report again. "This was right before Dr. Glenn murdered everyone."

"Excuse me?" Joshua said. "Dr. Glenn?"

"You know who I'm talking about?"

"Of course, but how did he become a part of this?"

I didn't tell him the truth. I just said that the police had brought up Glenn's name, mostly because of his connection to Dr. Eban. Joshua was very doubtful of the possibility that the killer had resurfaced.

"That can't be," he said. "He hasn't come back . . . Wait, I thought he'd died. No, that was just a rumor. Or something. No, that just doesn't sound right. I think it's a stretch to think Dr. Glenn has come back to town with murder on his mind."

"Where is he then? Where has he been?"

Joshua struggled through some thoughts. His eyebrows moved and his lips pursed shut tight. One eye squinted, and then the other. "I guess I wouldn't know, but . . . the thing the police need to know is what might have been his relationship with the victim. Why would Mallory have known him well enough to, for whatever reason, be in that close with him? That's what they need to look at, and at the relationship between the Clachers and the Glenns, maybe back then too. For sure back then."

"I agree, and I think they're looking at all of the relationships." I hoped I was better hiding what I knew about Mallory and Dr. Glenn than I had been with the scalpels.

"But still, Glenn coming back to kill? How terrible. This needs more research. Maybe check old newspaper articles. At a library?"

I knew someone who could help. Artair would microfiche an afternoon away with me anytime I wanted. But I also knew someone at a newspaper, and though I didn't expect us to ever be best friends, I had come to see her side of things a little more.

"Maybe," I said. "Joshua, what about some missing books in your records? Have you received any notice that some books from the medical school were taken? Published in the early 1900s, hand-drawn, gruesome sketches?"

"Recently or a while ago?"

"Recently, I think. Look, there, I did it again. Now you need to report me for two things."

"Never," Joshua said. "I think you're giving me the rebellion I was never allowed to have. I don't know about any books, though. I'll have to check."

"Your parents won't be pleased with me."

"They'll never have to know."

As we moved toward the front door, Joshua bid Rosie and a sleepy Hector goodbye. I followed behind and enjoyed the warmish spring breeze that came inside as he walked out, but he didn't get far.

"Oh, oops," he said as his foot hit something.

An open shoebox was on the ground, impossible for whoever walked out of the shop first to have missed it.

"What in the world?" I said.

Though Grassmarket was a busy place, there were not-so-busy moments too, particularly along our small stretch of the sidewalk. This was, fortunately, one of those moments. We didn't have to get out of anyone's way as we crouched and peered inside the box.

"Uh-oh," I said.

"Is that what I think it is?" he said,

"It looks like a jawbone to me. Don't touch it." I pulled out my phone and silently debated who to call first.

"I'm not planning on touching it. Do you think it's human?"

"I would bet so, but we'd need an expert to tell us."

I found Inspector Pierce's number first, but immediately after I talked to him, I called Inspector Winters again. I knew they'd both be here quickly.

"Someone will be here soon," I said.

"Looks like someone already has," Joshua said as he looked up and around.

From our crouching vantage point and with the cars parked on the street in front of us, at that instant it seemed like we were the only two people left in the world.

Well, us and what remained of the person in the box.

TWENTY-SIX

They hadn't met in person, but had talked over the phone. Apparently, Inspector Pierce had only recently joined the precinct. I was surprised, but I introduced them and they went to work, Inspector Winters taking on the role of assisting Inspector Pierce in whatever ways he instructed.

I hadn't put much forethought into what they might do with the jawbone, but it turned out to be a really big deal. Not as many people showed up as had with the murder, but crime scene people in their white coveralls and a forensic pathologist arrived not long after the police inspectors and other officers. Joshua was excused to go after he gave a brief statement. In his statement, he didn't include sharing the scalpel discovery he'd made as his reason for stopping by the shop. I didn't ask him not to mention the scalpels, but I was glad I didn't have to explain to the police why I'd been asking the brilliant young man from the museum about things perhaps pertinent to the murder. An officer took Joshua's phone number, but dismissed him quickly.

When they were inside the shop and it was crowded with more people than usual, I was curious enough about the pathologist that I moved close and listened in as she talked to Inspector Pierce.

"I'd go with human jawbone," she said.

"Can you guess anything more about it? Age, how long it's been exposed, et cetera?" Inspector Pierce asked.

"No. I'll take it back to the lab for some tests, but it's not a recently . . . exposed bone. It's been some time. It wouldn't be the color it is if it came from someone recently deceased," she said.

"Did it come from the skull room at the university?"

"I don't see a marking, but the jawbone isn't the area that's usually marked."

"I'll look into it," Inspector Pierce said.

Just another day in an old bookshop in Edinburgh.

"We don't have anything but the bone," Inspector Winters said as he came from the back corner of the shop where he'd been talking to a crime scene tech and sidled up next to me as I tried to look like I wasn't eavesdropping. "You're sure you didn't see anything, anyone who you might suspect of leaving such a thing behind?"

"One hundred percent. Rosie didn't either, and she and Hector were up front the whole time," I said. "I didn't see anyone carrying the box, but I'm not sure it would have registered as suspicious anyway."

"I don't know the brand of shoe the shoebox is from, but they will, of course, try to look that direction too. Do you know the brand?"

"I've never seen it before."

"I have," Rosie piped up as she joined us too. "It's a women's shoe line, not expensive, easy tae find in most department stores."

"So someone might have grabbed one of their own shoeboxes, put a jawbone in it, and then dropped it in front of the shop? At least I'd use someone else's shoebox," I said.

"You'd be surprised," Inspector Winters said. "People don't think these things through sometimes. In fact, it's very hard tae get away with a crime. Between cameras and criminals' egos, we usually catch the bad guy."

I looked at him and remembered. "Inspector Pierce said he was going to try to get some CC cameras around here, in the close at least."

"I heard him complaining that it hadn't happened yet," Inspector Winters said.

"Darn it."

The bell above the door jingled.

"Oh boy," I said quietly when I saw Bridget Carr leaning in.

"She's an annoying lass," Rosie said. Hector agreed.

"Who's that?" Inspector Winters asked.

"Bridget Carr. She's a reporter,"

"The one who wrote the article about you?"

"Yes."

"You want me tae send her away?"

"No. Actually, I want to talk to her. Excuse me."

I guided her out of the bookshop and around one of the crime scene technicians who seemed to be doing nothing more than standing in the space where the box had been. We walked to the corner, away from most of the activity.

"Delaney," Bridget said with a sly smile. "You've been holding out on me."

"How's that?"

"Bones. Someone's leaving bones all around the city. That's an odd turn of events, don't you think? And, remember when I told you all about the bones supposedly buried over there in the close? What about that plaster-like piece I found?"

"This just happened. I wasn't holding out, and this doesn't feel like 'all around the city.'" I held up my hand to stop her next argument. "Bridget, I'm bothered by this, and I agree with you that it's strange. What do you want to know?"

I'd surprised her. She wasn't expecting my cooperation. She worked to recover. "Look, I'm all about the story. ALL about it. It's what makes me a decent reporter but a less-than-ideal friend." She blinked at me. "I wish you'd called me."

"The police have been here. They were the first ones I called." I paused. "But I see your side a little. I understand you want a story."

"You see my side?" she said doubtfully.

"I do," I said convincingly.

"Okay," she said, seemingly at a loss for any other response.

I continued, "I don't know about bones all over the city. I know that there was part of a jawbone, human, in a shoebox right over there," I nodded toward the crime scene tech who was keeping his position, "and I called the police. Finding a bone in a shoebox is weird. I would have called the police even if a murder hadn't occurred near the shop."

"Just a jawbone in a shoebox? No other bones in there?" she asked, her demeanor snapping back to professional.

"That was it. Well, it was just half of one. I did overhear the pathologist confirm that it didn't belong to someone who'd died recently, but you should confirm that before you print it. I didn't hear an exact age, or even a real guess at one."

"I will. Thanks." With a blue-ink pen, she wrote the word "jawbone" on the palm of her hand.

"You don't have a notebook?"

"I do. Sometimes I just write on my hand or arm, though."

"Huh."

She shrugged and said, "I heard there was a bone found outside the building where the murder victim, Mallory, lived."

"You mean just now, recently?"

"Yes, but no, now I think it was a mistake. I think it was supposed to mean this bone. The message got muddled, and nothing was going on over there. Do you know people who live in her building?"

"Some. Acquaintances."

"That's not exactly what I heard, but that's okay."

"You continue to try to find ways for me to be involved in this. I guess I am friends with a couple of the women, but we've only known each other a few months. 'Acquaintances' seems like a more accurate description of our relationship."

"If it's any consolation," she said a second later, "I don't think you're a killer. But I do think that like me, though for different reasons, you are looking for the killer. I also bet you will have known the killer when they're exposed. There's something wonky about that building and the medical school. I think you're more exposed to what's going on than you're telling me."

"Bridget."

"Okay, okay, let me rephrase. I think you're more exposed than you even realize. If you're friends with them, I bet you've seen things that you haven't put together yet."

"I don't know," I said as I thought about the gray-haired man. I wasn't going to tell her about him. She and I would never be that good of friends.

My motives for talking to her and being more forthcoming were twofold. I wanted her to let up on Edwin and keep him out of any of her future stories, and I'd thought about asking her to explore old newspaper articles with me. But I changed my mind as I talked to her. No matter that we weren't going to forge a friendship, she would always be writing a story, and I didn't want to unknowingly contribute something that might hurt someone I cared about—or myself, frankly. I'd given her enough.

"All right, I'll talk tae the officers. Ring me if you've anything else tae share. Thank you for the information about the bone. And, if I were you, I'd watch my back, Delaney."

She sent me some lifted eyebrows and then turned and walked toward Inspector Pierce. She tapped his shoulder, and he looked at her with nothing but irritation.

She hadn't scared me by telling me to watch my back, but she had a point.

It was impossible to ignore how many strange and horrible things seemed to be happening so close to home.

TWENTY-SEVEN

"Interesting perspective," Tom said as he handed Elias a cup of coffee. It had to be his first of the morning, since I'd asked him to give me a ride so early. "She might be right, but I don't think you should let that scare you."

"No, lass, she's oot for a story. Ye cannae let her scare ye," Elias said as he rested his arms on the bar. "But ye should be careful. Aye an on."

I looked at him. I didn't know what "aye an on" meant.

"Always," Elias translated. He'd come with me this morning, driving me back to Grassmarket. I hadn't seen Tom in person for too long, and morning coffee at his pub seemed to be the only currently available option. When he heard Elias was driving me, he invited him for coffee too. I'd waited until we were all together to tell them both everything I'd found out and discovered. They'd shown some interest, and some great restraint, as I shared my foray into Dr. Eban's email and the fact that Sophie and Rena thought Mallory was having an affair with Dr. Glenn. Not only had their eyes shown unbelievable a time or two, they'd said it a few times. I'd saved Bridget's words of warnings for last.

"Of course—and I'm not worried." I looked back and forth between them.

Telling them what Bridget had said might have been a bad idea, because it had gotten them thinking about my safety. But I really wasn't worried. I did think her more important point though was about the killer being someone I'd met.

I continued, "No, I'm not worried. I just want to figure it out."

"Aye," they both said, but I caught the quickly raised eyebrows they shared with each other. They would rather I didn't continue to search for an answer to Mallory's murder, but I appreciated them keeping their protests limited to their eyebrows.

"I don't think Rena is telling the truth—to anyone—about what happened the night Mallory was killed," I said. "It doesn't matter what she's told me, and even if she and Sophie told the police about Dr. Glenn and Mallory, I would still like to know what Rena was up to, and what that email meant. As Inspector Pierce was leaving the shop yesterday, I asked if he talked to Sophie and Rena. He said he did, so I asked if he believed the story about Mallory and Dr. Glenn. He gave me no indication either way."

"It's convenient to try to pin a murder on an already proven killer, one who might or might not have gray hair and be in the vicinity," Tom said.

"Do you think Rena kil't Mallory?" Elias asked.

"I hope not," I said. "No idea, but what deal did she and Dr. Eban have . . . and a planned meeting that night? Strange."

"And you havenae told the police about the email?" Elias said. "Och, of course, ye havenae."

"I should not have read it, and I really shouldn't have gotten Joshua involved."

Tom smiled, surprising me. "No harm done, and that kid deserves a little fun. He's worked hard for a long time."

I smiled at him, grateful my pub owner wasn't bothered by that bad decision.

He continued, "I don't know either Sophie or Rena well, but they seem like sweet women, though they've had some tough times. Which one had a rough home life when they were a child?"

"Rena. Moved around a lot before her family landed in Glasgow," I said. "She and Sophie met when they were young and became fast and, I believe, lifelong friends."

"You 'believe'?" Tom said.

"Too soon to tell."

"Aye." Tom's smile turned wry.

I did a double take, not understanding how to interpret the expression. He looked away before I could ask.

"Do you think Dr. Eban saw the wee scalpels in the warehouse somehow?" Elias asked.

"I would have no idea how."

"It's been a decade. Maybe Edwin let people in and he just doesnae remember," Elias said.

"Maybe, but I doubt it."

My phone buzzed from atop the bar.

"Edwin?" I said as I answered.

"Lass, where are you?"

"At Tom's pub."

"Birk rang me in a full-on panic. He said you've not returned his call and he needs tae see us right away. May I pick you up in front of the bookshop in about fifteen minutes?"

"Oh shoot," I said. "He's right. I haven't returned the call. What's going on?"

"He's acquired something he wants us tae see. He heard about the jawbone and now he really wants us tae see what he has."

"What is it?"

"I don't know. Be in front of the bookshop in fifteen if you can."

"I can." I ended the call. "Edwin's picking me up at the bookshop. I'm sorry." I looked at Tom, hoping to relay with my eyes that we needed some time with just us soon. He relayed that he agreed.

"I shall escort ye tae the shop," Elias said.

Sometimes Elias stopped by the pub and visited Tom without me. I wondered what they talked about. Aggie thought it was probably football and whisky.

With a brisk pace, the walk to the shop would take about two minutes. Since we weren't in any hurry, Elias and I took it slow, and talked about football and whisky. I'd come to like football, but still couldn't acquire a taste for whisky. I thought this was a big disappointment in my landlord's eyes, but he pretended it was no big deal.

Edwin's Citroën was there when he said it would be, and I told Elias I'd see him later.

"What do you think it is?" I asked Edwin as I belted in.

"We'll see," he said as he steered the car deftly and with too much speed to Birk's house.

———

I knew the way to Birk's house, though I'd only been there once before. I liked Birk, and had come to know him better when I'd

helped him validate a letter he had from the real Rob Roy Mac-
Gregor. Before we'd worked together one-on-one, I'd thought
he was somewhat phony. But I'd come to realize that Birk was
a different person when Edwin was around. He'd make his personality bigger, which was something I didn't understand,
but I'd become fairly certain that he didn't even know he was
doing it.

His neighborhood was filled with big houses and big yards
and gardens. A long, curving driveway led up to Birk's place,
and to surprisingly welcoming, but ostentatious, gold double
doors.

Edwin and I didn't have to knock; Birk opened with a flourish. "Thanks for coming so quickly. Come in, come in. I didn't
know if I should call the police today. I didn't want tae earlier,
until I talked tae Delaney, but you didn't call."

"I'm so sorry," I said.

"Anyway, after I heard on the telly about the jawbone,
well . . . I wondered."

Edwin and I shared a look.

The last time I'd been to his house, Birk had been in a robe.
Today, he was dressed as if he was heading out for a golf game:
green golf shirt, with pink and green plaid pants.

"I didn't know what I was buying exactly," he said as he
turned and started walking toward his golden sitting room.

"Here. Look in here." He pointed to a large box that was
propped on a coffee table.

Edwin and I hesitated, but only for a moment. We each
moved to one side of the box and peered in.

A skull peered up at us.

"Oh boy," I said.

"Dastardly-looking thing," Edwin said.

"But there's so much more," Birk said.

We looked at him.

He bit his lip a good long moment, but then continued, "To begin with, I acquired it from someone who said it was a lost victim of Burke and Hare."

"No!" I said. "That's too much of a coincidence."

"Too much of a coincidence? I don't understand," Birk said.

"Burke and Hare have come up a lot lately. Something's going on."

"Well," Birk waved away anything that might not have anything to do with his current problem.

"Birk and Burke," I muttered.

"I do think the name thing is a true coincidence," Birk said. "But, yes, something is definitely going on. I thought it was a joke—a box of bones from 'Burke and Hare days,'" Birk said, laughing once nervously as he made quote marks in the air with his fingers. "I was contacted, and I was curious enough tae make the purchase. Then I received this box. The skull made it much less a joke and much more real. I wanted Delaney tae see it tae tell me if it was from someone recently deceased. I should have called the police."

"I don't know how to assess the age of bones," I said. I left out the part about yes, he should have called the police, but he should have.

The angle at which it sat made it so we couldn't see the entire skull. I tipped up one side of the box so the skull plunked over and we could get a full side view.

"Missing a part of a jawbone," I said to Edwin. Though he hadn't seen the item at the bookshop the day before, he'd heard all about it.

"A match to yours, you think? I saw the report on the telly," Birk said.

"I do," I said.

"What's going on?" Birk asked.

"We need to call the police," I said.

"Oh, how terribly disappointing," Birk said. "So, do you know what this is? Is it really from a Burke and Hare victim?"

"Not sure of that, but . . ." I began. "Who contacted you?"

Birk looked momentarily ashamed. "An email."

I knew by now that emails and Internet communication for the types of items Edwin and Birk acquired was risky at best, criminal at worst. If you didn't know who you were dealing with, in-person meetings were necessary.

"Birk," Edwin admonished.

"I know." Birk waved it away. He sighed dramatically and then sat on a couch. He rubbed his hand over his chin, where there was no sign of a beard. "And they haven't responded tae my most recent emails. They told me they mailed the box last week, and I've been asking for a tracking number ever since. No answer. This arrived a few days ago. I called Delaney, and then I heard about the bone at the bookshop."

"I don't understand." Edwin moved around the table and sat on the other end of the couch. "That doesn't sound like something you would do."

"I bought this after we were talking in the bookshop. Remember our conversation about Burke and Hare?"

Edwin blinked. "Oh. Aye."

"When was this?" I asked.

"Two weeks ago now," Birk said. "You weren't there."

"Birk and I were at the back table and a customer asked if we had any books on the killers," Edwin said.

"Man, woman, old, young?" I said.

"Woman," Edwin said.

"Hair, height, description?"

"Hair pulled back. Trim, attractive." Edwin blinked. "Am I allowed tae say 'attractive' still or does that break a rule?"

I nodded that it was all right.

"Not Sophie or Rena," I said to Edwin. "You remember them?"

"Aye. Not them."

"Curly or straight hair?" I asked.

"Straight, pulled back like Edwin said," Birk said. "Why?"

"Any chance you mentioned the scalpels?"

"I didn't know about them," Edwin said.

"What scalpels?" Birk asked.

"How long after the conversation in the bookshop did you get the email?" I asked Birk.

"The next day."

I thought for a long, almost desperate moment. Was I onto something? If I was, it was a foggy something.

"We need to take this skull to the police," I said. "But we're going to make one stop along the way."

It took us a few minutes too long to get out of the house because no one could figure out who should carry the box. Ultimately, we chose Birk. Edwin steered the Citroën back toward downtown. I sat in the backseat and tried to figure out if the person who'd come into the bookshop could have been Lola, and how that might lead us to a killer.

———

"Oh my goodness," Joshua said. "You really think this had something to do with Burke and Hare?"

"I don't have any idea, but I was thinking about the skull room at the university. Have you received any notices, heard anything new, regarding skulls missing from there?"

"None," Joshua said. He turned to his computer and typed. "No, nothing new at all. Do you think I should inquire? Maybe someone just hasn't noticed? I can say I heard about the jaw-bone that was mentioned in the news. I'll leave this skull out of it for now."

"Good idea," I said.

"All right. I'll send an inquiry right away. If there are skulls missing from the skull room, I'll be a hero," he said.

I couldn't help but hope that skulls were missing from the skull room.

"What about the people who have access to the skull room?" I said. "There's a limited amount, right? Artair has a key. Is there a record of who has the keys somewhere?"

"I don't know how it works. I'll see if I can find out from the director of my museum. She knows how the university does things," Joshua said. He pulled out his phone and sent a text but didn't receive an immediate response. "She'll respond when she can, or wants to, I suppose. She's on holiday, so I don't know."

"I'm sure the skull room isn't the only place for skulls," Edwin said. "It's a medical school. There might be more skulls there than we could conceive of."

I remembered the memorial service. I had no idea how many corpses and skulls and skeletons were nearby, but I was sure there were more than I wanted to dwell on.

"Joshua, do you know anything about a missing Burke and Hare body?" I asked.

"You mean a victim whose body was stolen or not found?

No, nothing. But who's to say? Things were so different back then. Not everyone was accounted for like now. There's a good chance that not all of the victims were found, but the research to confirm that would be daunting, maybe impossible." He thought a moment. "You do know that Burke's skeleton is kept under lock and key at the university, don't you?"

Birk and Edwin nodded, and I said, "You did tell me that, but you don't know where?"

"It's a well-kept secret, but . . . no, it can't be that," he said as he looked at the box.

"Joshua, what?"

"No one knows what happened to Hare after he was released, or his body, at least historically. See what I mean? Less accountability."

We all looked at the box and then at each other.

"No," Birk said. "That would be impossible."

"That would be something," Edwin said.

"I can't think . . ." Joshua said.

"But it's possible, right? I mean, we don't know for sure," I said. "Would there be a way to determine if this is William Hare's skull?"

"DNA, I don't know. Perhaps," Joshua said. "Depends on any artifacts and any DNA left on them."

The notion that there was even a slight chance that we had most of the skull of the killer William Hare was almost too much to grasp. But as exciting and historically significant as this idea was, my hopes for finding Mallory's killer deflated because of it. How could the two of these mysteries be part of the same thing? But how could they not be? How could all of this be happening at once and not be tied together?

"We probably need to get this to Inspector Pierce," I said.

"They can do the proper procedures to find an IP address and track down whoever sent this to Birk, as well as put an age to the skull. Not to mention match it to the jawbone, maybe try to test for DNA."

Of course these mysteries were all connected. Someone just had to figure out how.

Joshua escorted us out of the museum. "I'll let you know if any notices come in, Delaney."

"Thank you. I really hope we don't have William Hare's skull." I looked at the box in Edwin's hands.

Joshua smiled. "Oh, I think it would be pretty cool."

TWENTY-EIGHT

Inspector Pierce was intrigued by the rest of the skull (we assumed now that the jaw piece and the rest of the skull did belong together), but he was mostly intrigued by Birk. He asked Edwin and me to leave the small blue-windowed police station, today much more crowded with three other officers, so he could gather information from Birk alone. My boss and I roamed up toward the castle and back down again just as Birk was being dismissed.

He said that he had agreed to allow the police inside his house and to give them full access to his email account, but that was about it.

Edwin dropped me off at The Cracked Spine and asked me to let Rosie know that he was taking Birk home and would be in later. I found her and Hector sitting at the back table as Hamlet was making stacks of books for her to peruse. I told them about the morning's adventures as I scratched behind Hector's ears. They continued to sort and stack.

"Have you remembered anything else about Dr. Glenn?" I asked Rosie.

"Not much, lass."

"I can't believe Rosie bought the scalpels at a murderer's jumble sale," Hamlet said. He set a book on top of a stack, and a cloud of dust puffed all the way to his nose. I expected him to sneeze, but he didn't.

"I'm going to go grab my laptop. I'll be right back," I said.

As I climbed the stairs, I realized I hadn't seen Hamlet since the morning he'd discovered Mallory's body. School must be taking lots of his time. I missed spending time with him. His intelligent college-age perspective was always refreshing.

The dark side was cold, as usual. I hurried to the warehouse, unlocked the door like an old pro, and then flipped the lights on inside.

Surprisingly, my laptop sat open on a side table. I usually shut it down and closed it at the end of every day. I'd told Edwin the password in case he needed something from it, but he'd protested, saying that my laptop was not to be seen by any other eyes, his included.

It had been a long time since I'd actually done any real work in the warehouse, but a swipe over the mouse pad and the computer came to life. I hadn't even turned it off—since when? Again, I didn't know. I saw that I had twenty-seven new emails. Not a big deal, but this was a computer I used strictly for work, and even with some intermittent junk I usually received only about five new emails a day. Had it been that long since I'd checked?

I clicked on the in-box. A few of the emails were nothing unusual, but six were from Dr. Eban.

The first one from him asked what I'd been doing in his anatomy theater, and had I come to talk to him about the books. The other five seemed to grow increasingly agitated about me having been there. He went from curious at first, to angry, to accusatory, saying that "my friend" and I must be friends with the Clacher clan, and what was going on, did I know anything about Mallory's murder? I read through the emails again. I realized that the threats I sensed were more a part of the tone in my head than the words he used.

I had tried to be open-minded, maybe even like him a little bit. I'd tried to think that maybe his students thought he was odd mostly because of his position of power. But now, in a way, I got what they'd been saying. He was unquestionably odd, though in a way that was still hard to define. Hopefully, he wasn't murderous, too.

These emails would mean nothing to the police, wouldn't lead to a killer, I was sure. I didn't delete them, but I didn't respond, either. I might at some point, but not right now.

I unplugged the laptop and carried it back over to the other side. Rosie and I moved to the front desk, where there was more room.

"I'm just going to ask some questions. Maybe I can prompt some memories," I said.

"Aye."

"Do you know if Dr. Glenn ever had a man over to his place by the name of Dr. Eban? He's from the university."

"No, Delaney, I wouldnae know his visitors. I might know some faces, but I didnae tak tent. There were always people in and oot of the flat, though. They were social."

"I don't know what 'tak tent' means," Hamlet said from the back corner.

" 'Pay attention,' " Rosie said.

I searched on my computer for a picture of Dr. Eban. The first one I found was his university staff picture.

"Aye, I've seen him before," Rosie said, "probably at Dr. Glenn's hoose. A younger version. He was with others, though. I cannae be sure of the specifics, but, aye, he's familiar, and striking, with such sharp features."

I searched again and found Dr. Carson's picture. "Does she look familiar?"

Rosie's eyebrows came together. "Aye. She was there many times, but by herself. I was under the impression that she and Dr. Glenn were . . . weel, I just wasnae sure. She had the exact same hair back then, but only beginning to gray and almost the identical cut."

"You thought Dr. Glenn and Dr. Carson were having an affair?" I asked.

Rosie's mouth pinched tight. It wasn't that she didn't enjoy gossip, or "blether," as she called it; she just liked to make sure it contained more truth than speculation before she indulged too deeply.

"It was a thought I had," she said. "It would have been impossible tae be certain."

"You saw her there, though? Maybe by herself and when Dr. Glenn's wife wasn't home?"

"I did. I think."

"Did you tell the police?"

"When? Why?"

Dr. Glenn and his wife had been gone from Edinburgh for about three months when he'd killed her. Rosie had moved away from their neighboring flat shortly after Paulie died, which was around the same time. She'd been in mourning. Why wouldn't the police have tracked her down and talked to her about her onetime neighbors? And she would never have thought to go talk to them, because she'd been so grief-stricken. It was impossible to know at this point.

"Right," I said. "Why would you? Affairs aren't illegal."

Still, it was important information now. Maybe. Dr. Glenn's relationship with both Dr. Eban and Dr. Carson, and maybe even with Mallory's father—away from the university—must be somehow important.

I searched online for any sort of written information regarding a connection between Dr. Glenn, Boris Clacher, Dr. Eban, and Dr. Carson. There *were* connections, though not as many involving Dr. Glenn as the others. Most were because of the medical school and the sorts of things and events that medical school people attended. I couldn't find much of anything, and I wished I got along better with Bridget. Not everything was online, and old newspapers were a good source. I'd have to check with Artair.

"I'm going to call Inspector Winters," I said absently.

"Tae tell him aboot what I might have seen?"

"Yes. In fact, I'm going to see if he can stop by and talk to us. That okay?"

"Certainly."

———

It was rare that Inspector Winters didn't spend at least a moment wondering where I was going with something I wanted to tell him. Or questioning its importance. As a police officer, he was supposed to doubt and question. I didn't take it personally.

However, this time he was all ears, and focused eyes.

"You saw them together?" he said to Rosie.

"No, I saw her go inside when I knew he was there too and his wife wasnae. I saw it more than one time, which makes me sound nosy. Meebe I am a wee bit, but I remember thinking it was odd and then not wanting tae know more. None of my business."

"More than a few times, though?" Inspector Winters said.

"Aye. Many, many times."

I confessed my visit to the Anatomical Theatre with Elias. He hadn't heard anything about Conn's behavior or about the two of us being there, but he did mention that I should be telling all of this to Inspector Pierce, and that I should also show him the emails from Dr. Eban.

I didn't disagree, but I didn't make any sort of quick move to give the other inspector a call.

I did show Inspector Winters the emails from Dr. Eban. His interpretation was different from mine. He thought that if I was going to intrude on a class, I might need to expect some questions regarding that intrusion. However, he did think everything had the potential to be pertinent to the murder until it proved not to be.

After I felt like we'd told him everything we could and he said he'd find Pierce, I walked him to the door.

"What's so interesting about all of this?" I asked.

"I'm not sure, lass," he said with a rare friendly smile. "But it might prove tae be helpful. I'll talk tae Inspector Pierce, but no guarantee that he won't want tae talk tae you too."

"I understand. I would have called him if . . ."

"If you thought you were onto something important."

"Yeah. Sorry."

"No. I'm happy tae have been a sounding board, but, yes, don't hesitate tae tell Pierce everything."

"Will do. Thank you."

"You know, this is a great bookshop," Inspector Winters said as he hesitated leaving.

"I do know."

"Maybe stick around here and do some work for a wee bit?" He was still smiling, so I smiled back. "I'll give it a try."

He hurried away up Grassmarket Square. I didn't see his vehicle, and I wondered if he'd parked around a corner or if he'd walked the whole way from the bottom of the Royal Mile.

As I was looking out the window, and just after I lost sight of Inspector Winters, I caught sight of someone else, and he was headed this direction.

"What is it?" Rosie said as she moved next to me. "Ye made a curious noise."

"That's Mallory's father, and I think he's coming here." I knew what he looked like mostly because we'd just been looking at pictures of him and his colleagues.

"Aye? Weel, I'll get some coffee. He'll likely be here tae see either you or Edwin. I'll ring Edwin and let him know."

Rosie handed Hector to me and took off for the dark side.

I watched as Boris Clacher, his eyes still wide with grief, looked up and saw me at the window.

There was no mistaking the nod and the small lifting of fingers in a wave. He was coming here.

Hector and I met him at the door.

TWENTY-NINE

"Thank you," he said to Rosie as he took the steaming mug and then sipped from it. "That's very good."

"Ye're welcome. Are ye hungry?"

"No, not at all, thank you."

From the second he'd walked inside, Boris Clacher had been sweet and polite. Did he have to work to not live up to the harsh consonants in his name and his intimidating height and wide shoulders?

"Delaney Nichols?" he'd said as he came in. He'd petted Hector and smiled sadly.

"That's me."

"Pleasure tae meet you, lass. I wonder if you have a minute of time I could steal from you?"

I'd directed him to the chairs we'd left at the front desk just as Rosie had crossed over from the dark side, carrying mugs of coffee. I introduced everyone.

"Lad, I've seen you around the university," Boris said to Hamlet.

"Aye, I'm a student."

Boris surveyed him a long moment. "I remember. I saw one of your presentations, for a biology course, I believe. Your professor had high regard for your mind and wanted me tae encourage you tae consider medical school, but ye're studying literature?"

"Aye."

"I see. Think about it. Ye can still go tae medical school with a literature degree. Ye've studied much of the science, I know. It's all hard work, mind, but there are some who are suited. I believe, based upon what I've heard, that you're suited."

"Thank you. I'll keep it in mind."

"We're very sorry for your loss," I said after I picked up a mug and he turned his attention back to me.

"Thank you." He sniffed and seemed to hold his head higher as he fended off emotions. "I've come tae talk tae you a wee bit about my daughter. Is that all right?"

"Of course, but I didn't know her well. I'd just met her . . . recently," I said.

This was going to be tough.

"I know, but . . . Conn told me you talked tae some of her friends, Sophie and Rena."

"I did. I was hoping that Mallory had confided in them . . . perhaps about Dr. Eban." I swallowed.

"Aye. Conn's a good brother, though a wee bit of an ox in a china chest. He shouldn't have done what he did in Bryon's class, but we were suspicious. Bryon Eban and I used tae be close friends many years ago, and I truly can't imagine him hurting my daughter."

"I hope not." I paused. "What happened to your friendship? Did you have a falling-out?"

"Aye. A man named Glenn fooled us all and we've never

recovered any trust for each other, but that's another story. I came here tae ask you about Sophie and Rena. I've tried tae talk tae them, but they won't respond."

"I'm afraid they didn't tell me anything about Mallory and Dr. Eban." I wasn't going to tell him what they'd told me about Mallory and Dr. Glenn. I couldn't do that to him. If he later learned about it, I hoped Mallory's murder would be solved by then. I would apologize later if he ever learned I'd kept the information from him. It was just too bizarre, too big a pill to swallow.

"Are they . . . are they nice women? Sophie and Rena?" he began.

"I've only known them for a few months, but they've been very nice to me."

"I see." He sipped his coffee and then set it on the desk. "At the risk of sounding terribly snobbish, what can you tell me about their time before medical school? Mallory mentioned them a few times, talked about how they'd come from tough circumstances in Glasgow. I didn't ask her much about them."

"I'm afraid that's all I really know myself, but I believe Rena had it the tougher of the two."

"I see." He paused, as if considering whether or not to go on. He did. "I can't find anything about them."

"What do you mean?"

"I don't have access tae their records at the school. There are privacy laws, and I'm not one of those given access tae student records of any sort. I have friends, of course, but I'm loath tae ask them right now. They would wonder why I was curious. I don't want tae appear . . . paranoid, or as if I'm trying tae influence the women's paths in medical school. Does that make sense?"

"Yes." Though I sensed he was more concerned about later questioning his own judgment during this time of grief than others judging him. "Why do you want to know more about them?"

"Curiosity, I suppose. When they wouldn't talk tae me, I wanted tae . . . Just curiosity."

"I do know that Rena's father had some old medical school books . . . Would you excuse me a moment?"

"Certainly," he said to my back.

I felt everyone's eyes on me as I hurried up the stairs. I practically sprinted to the warehouse, dropping the key once as I fumbled it toward the lock.

I took a breath and told myself to slow down. I unlocked the door and broke a cardinal rule by not locking it again as I went inside. I found the box of books and gathered the piece of paper at the bottom of the box that Rena had originally filled out.

The form was simple. Name, address, phone number, perceived value, desired amount. However, we also asked for a provenance when older books were involved. How far back could ownership be tracked?

Rena had filled out the form, and in the box for the provenance she scribbled, "They were my dad's. He doesn't know who owned them before him, but he's been the owner for at least ten years. Here's his mobile." She included a number.

I hadn't called to confirm the provenance. I was sure Hamlet hadn't either, since I'd been the one who had worked with the women from the beginning, and I was waiting to hear what Edwin wanted to do with the books.

The rule was that we always did our best to research the provenance of all books, and in my case, the provenance of *everything* I researched for Edwin.

I had not done my job.

I grabbed my phone from my pocket and dialed the number listed. I was taken directly to a recording that told me the number wasn't in service.

The unanswered phone number could be a glitch, or a misunderstanding. Maybe I was misreading a number.

I put the paper back into the box, grabbed one of the books, and left the warehouse, making sure I locked the door behind me.

I wasn't in the same hurry as I went back over. Rosie and Hamlet sent me worried glances, and Boris Clacher knew something was wrong when he saw my face.

"Lass?" he said.

I showed him the book. "Do you think this might have come from the university?"

"Maybe," he said. "I know that Dr. Eban has a few collections."

"Have any books gone missing?" I asked.

"Aye, actually. Maybe. Dr. Meg Carson, Dr. Eban's wife, came tae my office not long ago and asked if I knew what happened tae one of our collections. I believe this was a book from that collection. I didn't know of anything gone missing, but she mentioned she might call the police."

"How long ago?"

"About a month or so, I think."

"I think you should go to the police with this information."

"And tell them what? About the books?" he asked.

"Yes. Just trust me—it might help. Let me give you the inspector's number." I pulled up Inspector Pierce's number on my phone and gave it to Boris. "I'll call him too."

Boris looked at me as a new horror pulled at his features.

"Do you think those women, people my daughter thought were friends, killed Mallory? In some way because of the books?"

"No, I really don't," I said, though I had no sense of it at all. "They were friends, Mr. Clacher, no doubt in my mind. But since they were friends, Sophie and Rena might have more information that they're not sharing, or they might have seen something they're afraid to talk about. With what you've told me, that's all I'm thinking right about now."

The horror spread back into sadness and confusion. My heart ached for him.

He blinked it all away, but it would return momentarily. Like all uninvited guests, grief always stayed too long.

"Thank you for your time, Delaney." Boris stood and smoothed the front of his unwrinkled dress shirt and tie. "Please ring me if you think of anything else that might be . . . important tae all of this."

"I will." I took the business card that he'd pulled from his breast pocket. It was simple, with his name, "University of Edinburgh," and a phone number. "Dr. Clacher, is there any chance . . . I mean, you mentioned Dr. Glenn earlier. Do you think he might have come back and is killing . . . killed . . ."

"Oh, goodness, no!" Boris said. "No, he might have been a killer, but he would never have killed my daughter. Never."

I felt a million protests dancing in my head and my mouth, and even in my chest.

I nodded. "Okay."

He bid Rosie, Hector, and Hamlet a polite goodbye and left the shop just as a young couple entered. They were happy to the point of distraction, thankfully, and Rosie and I spent the next twenty minutes helping them.

But after they left I was no longer distracted.

"Rosie, I've got to go talk to someone," I said. "That okay?"

"Lass, no one involved in this mess, I hope."

"No. Just Artair," I said.

"Aye? Weel, then, always a guid visit. Hector and I have things under control here."

THIRTY

I ran into Artair as we were both walking into the university library. He'd smiled when he saw me, sobered as he held the door, and whispered, "Are ye here because of the murder?"

"I am," I'd said.

"Let's get tae work."

I'd been in the subbasements before, so the path to the set of microfiche machines was familiar. The machines down here weren't as often used as some throughout the library and offered us some privacy as we searched.

"When Dr. Glenn's true colors came out . . . weel, it was a sad and tragic time," Artair said when I told him what I was there to look for.

"Do you remember anything about him specifically, before things turned tragic?"

Artair brought his eyebrows together. "He was always curious about the newest medical discoveries, as were many in the medical school, of course, but he even more so. He found me one day and asked me tae be on top of any sort of news. This was at least a decade and a half ago, lass. The Internet was

going strong, but not like it is now. There were items of interest that didn't become readily available immediately like they
do now. I have contacts throughout the world in all sorts of areas of interest. Dr. Glenn was enthusiastic tae know what he
could learn before everyone else."

"Did you find things for him?"

"Aye, but nothing extraordinary. I believe there was some
stem cell research and some promising leukemia treatments that
he was grateful tae know, but if he learned of anything before
anyone else, there was only a brief difference in time."

"Enough that he might have been able to speak intelligently
about topics that were brought up, I bet."

"That's what I thought about when things turned so terrible."

"That had to be rough."

"It was." Artair shook his head. "I even thought long and
hard if I'd somehow contributed tae his wicked ways, but I
couldn't see how, other than he might have been found oot
sooner if I hadn't given him a few bits of information."

"No, Artair, he was evil. His wicked ways were going to happen no matter what."

He thought a moment. "I do remember something else. Have
a seat and I'll be right back."

"Thanks," I said as he disappeared through a doorway into
a microfiche storage room.

I sat and turned to face the machine. It was powered up and
ready when a few moments later Artair returned with a box
full of film.

"There was an event that received a lot of coverage many
years ago. It was a celebration, though I can't remember what

they were celebrating. The medical school held a dance, a formal ball so they could invite dignitaries, I think. Mostly, what I remember is the fallout that occurred. A fight," he said.

"Fisticuffs or yelling?" I asked, watching him find a strip and thread the machine.

"Both, again, if I'm remembering correctly. I've found the university newspaper's coverage, I think. Both doctors, Glenn and Eban, were involved. Maybe Clacher too. Let's see if I can pinpoint it."

I rolled my chair out of his way as he moved another one over and sat. We both loved research, but searching through microfilm wasn't a favorite method for either of us. I waited patiently as Artair scrolled.

"Here we are. Ah, aye, it was something from their drug discovery program. Ultimately, the program was about clinical evaluation that would eventually bring drugs tae consumers. It's a process, of course, but the process, almost accidentally, led to a drug that was being used for one thing tae be helpful in something else." He stopped on an article, and I read over his shoulder.

It wasn't about the celebration, but about the initial discovery. A drug, its name shortened to "Bedhead" for the article's purposes and because, in addition to its intended effect of clearing up eczema, the program at the university found that it also helped patients sleep more soundly, without the side effects that most sleeping pills had.

"This would be on the market by now," I said. "I don't need sleeping pills, but I know people who do. This sounds like a good option for them to look into."

"Aye, it did then," Artair said.

"I heard a 'but' in your tone."

"Correct. It didn't turn out tae be all that it was advertised tae be. Give me another moment and I'll find the other article."

The next article he found spread out over three different pages of the university paper. There were pictures to go along with the words.

In a nutshell, the story began with the initial claim of discovery of Bedhead's additional attributes regarding healthier sleep. In fact, it seems that researchers claimed that Bedhead might actually make people healthier because it worked in conjunction with good hormones, as well as serotonin. Those involved with these initial University of Edinburgh studies were listed, with four doctors as the leading researchers: Dr. Glenn, Dr. Eban, Dr. Clacher, and Dr. Carson.

"The four of them were so connected," I said.

"Aye. Take a look at this picture."

The four doctors stood together. They looked at the camera, smiled just enough not to scowl, and kept enough distance between each other for me to wonder if they'd posed that way on purpose, or if the camera just happened to catch a moment that might be interpreted as aloof. Even Dr. Carson was smiling with less enthusiasm than I'd seen from other pictures from that time.

"They look uncomfortable," I said.

"Not as uncomfortable as this picture." Artair scrolled to the last page of the article. "I remember the day this was published. The picture is tragic, yet one couldn't help but laugh. I'm sairy tae say that I laughed along, guiltily."

It was even more difficult to think that this picture hadn't been somehow staged. It illustrated the aftermath of what must have been a fight, food included.

Dr. Carson was in the middle of the picture, the focal point. She stood with her arms akimbo and her face forever frozen on the page, distraught. She must have been crying or yelling or both as something that looked like pudding rolled down her head, covering half her face just as the camera's shutter clicked.

"Someone poured food on her head?" I said.

"It appears that way, but the food flew because Dr. Eban and Dr. Clacher became angry at Dr. Glenn." Artair pointed at the two men on the side of the picture, Dr. Eban on his back, holding his jaw, and Dr. Glenn sitting up next to him with his hand over his eye. Dr. Clacher wasn't part of that picture. All around the men were spilled food items and serving dishes, as well as onlookers caught right at a moment of supreme shock. I didn't know how the person manning the camera got so lucky, but I'd never seen so many people in such exaggerated poses at the same time. It was indeed tragic. It was unquestionably comical.

We finished reading through the article. It seemed that in the midst of the celebration, the news was delivered that the research had been found to be either compromised or altered, or at the very worst faked. Investigations would ensue as to exactly what had gone wrong, but Doctors Glenn and Eban accused each other of a litany of wrongdoings, with the article writer doing her best to say that the resulting fight was a clash of two very big egos, neither of which wanted to back down in the least. Fists, platters, dinner rolls, and angry words had been the weapons of choice.

Dr. Carson and Dr. Clacher had tried to get the other men under control, but there came a point when it was all too late and the damage that was going to be done was going to happen no matter how they intervened.

"What happened? Was the research faked?"

Artair shook his head. "Later, the university released a statement that the study had been 'compromised,' but that's all they would share. It might have ended up being further investigated, but no doubt something else came along to take up the spotlight. Dr. Glenn's murders didn't occur until about three years later, so that wasn't it."

"Clearly, Doctors Eban, Glenn, Clacher, and Carson knew each other well."

"Aye, but that's not unusual. They were colleagues, and seemingly all involved in medicine. When Dr. Glenn did what he did I remember thinking that the others probably felt horribly betrayed."

I thought about Boris Clacher's words about Dr. Glenn. Had he been talking about more than murder? The past research too? What else might there have been?

"This is a stretch, but Rosie saw Dr. Carson going into Dr. Glenn's flat by herself when she knew Glenn's wife wasn't home. Maybe they were more involved on a personal basis," I said.

"At his flat?" Artair shrugged. "It's possible they were that arrogant." He looked at the article again. "Well, of course they were that arrogant, but I would think they would try tae hide an affair better. Perhaps they were just working together. It's hard tae know."

I nodded. "Right, but if there was an affair, maybe the fight was about so much more. You know Dr. Eban's reputation."

"His oddness?"

I nodded again.

"He *is* particularly taken with the Burke and Hare legend, I do know that. That would make him odd by itself, but I've heard he tries tae play a part in his class—spooky. Wears a cape sometimes," Artair said.

"Yeah, I've heard that too, but I've yet to see anything like that."

Artair shrugged. "Medical school is difficult beyond imagination. I've often wondered if he does that just tae give his students a mental break. Add some drama, and maybe he interprets it as fun."

"He's tough, I hear."

"The toughest, but if any professors need tae be tough, I think medical school professors need to. Though he's thought highly of internationally as well, he's respected, and he's part of the medical school's excellent reputation."

I hadn't even thought of international reputations. I'd been so caught up in our little Scottish world.

"Do you suppose he manipulates the students to do things for grades? The female students?" I asked.

"My dear lass, ye are delicate when speaking tae me and I appreciate that, but there's no need tae be. I've been around the block a time or two."

"Sorry." I smiled.

"Not tae worry. But, no, I don't think he does that. I don't know, mind, but I've never seen anything that would make me think such a thing."

"Do you like him?"

"Ah, there's a question." Artair thought a moment. "I don't dislike him, but he's not someone I would want tae socialize with. I don't want tae discuss Burke and Hare at length, and from what I've heard, that's exactly what he does. In fact, we had a replica death mask of Burke break two weeks ago, and his disappointment was deep; he was on the verge of inconsolable."

"A death mask broke?"

"Aye. Not a valuable one but—"

"Where was it? What happened? How was Dr. Eban involved?" I triggered off the questions.

"Um, weel, just upstairs."

"Take me there while you tell me what happened. Please." I stood and looked at our microfiche mess. "After we clean up."

"I'll clean up later," he said. "Come along and I'll show you where it happened."

Though he didn't understand my urgency, he respected it enough to hurry us up the two flights to a display case under an arched window that looked out toward the medical school buildings.

"There's not much tae tell," he said as we climbed stairs. "We rotate items in the display case, but none of them are valuable. Mostly duplicates, copies, replicas. The case is locked, but not watched all that closely, so museum-quality pieces don't get put there. We like to keep it interesting, though. We asked Dr. Eban for help with a wee Burke and Hare display. He was happy tae help, but he dropped the mask as he was placing it—he insisted on placing it himself. He was upset."

"But it wasn't real?"

"No, not that one. Just a replica, a contemporary plaster casting."

Based upon what Joshua had told me, I knew there were techniques that allowed one to get a pretty good idea of when certain things—materials, apparel, chemical makeup—had been cast in plaster.

"You're sure?"

"That's what Dr. Eban told us, that he had it created just for his own interest."

That was probably true, because if it had been valuable he wouldn't have let them place it in an unwatched display case in the library, but I was just suspicious enough of him to wonder.

"This is the case," Artair said quietly as we came to the window.

There were only books inside it currently, all of them titled something about Culloden.

"We took out the Burke and Hare items last week, and whoever was supposed tae come up with something else hasn't done their job yet apparently. There are usually more than just books."

"Can you remember the other items in the display?" I asked as I crouched and looked around the bottom edges of the case and the surrounding floor area.

"Books, certainly, but also pictures of the murderers. Nothing valuable, Delaney. The death mask might have been the most interesting item if Dr. Eban hadn't broken it."

I stopped my search and looked up at Artair. "Any chance there were scalpels like the ones we saw in the skull room?"

"No, lass, sharp edges like that wouldn't have been allowed. I see you're disappointed. Sorry."

I smiled. "It's okay. I don't know what it would mean anyway, but it might mean something."

I resumed my search, and was well rewarded.

"Artair, look!" I exclaimed as I pointed to the bottom edge of a nearby bookshelf. "What does that look like?"

He crouched as I knee-walked over.

"Looks like the cleaners missed something," he said.

"I bet they didn't see it. It's pretty flush with the shelf. It looks like plaster from a death mask, doesn't it?"

"Aye."

"May I take it?"

"I don't know why not. Wait, what are you going tae do with it?"

"Take it to a newspaper reporter and see if she'll go to the police with me."

"Sounds fairly safe. Take it."

It wasn't about the fingerprints, but I was careful nonetheless, because you never knew when fingerprints might be needed.

It was mostly about seeing if this piece matched Bridget's piece, and if so, maybe that would be evidence that Dr. Eban had been in the close, and if not to kill Mallory Clacher, then why else would he have been there? I'd be happy to give the information to the police and let them figure it out. I just had to convince Bridget to come with me.

Carefully, I wrapped the three-inch piece of plaster in Artair's handkerchief and put it in my bag.

He escorted me to the doors with the promise that he'd call me if he found anything else.

I got on the bus that would take me to the newspaper office, and hoped that Bridget and I might end up seeing eye to eye on more than just the fact that Tom was a really good catch.

THIRTY-ONE

Delaney?" Bridget said as she looked up from her computer screen. I hadn't waited to be greeted or escorted but had walked directly to her.

The rest of the staff watched me cautiously but when Bridget didn't seem in any way scared, they all went back to work.

"I have something," I said. "Can we go somewhere private?"

Like any good journalist that could smell a scoop, she nodded eagerly, stood and led me to a small office in the back. Other than a desk, there was nothing else in the room, not even chairs. But we could close the door.

"What do you have?" she asked.

"This." I pulled out the handkerchief and showed her the plaster I'd found. "I don't know if there's any way to determine that yours and mine are from the same original piece of plaster, but if they are, I just might have a scoop for you."

"I'm listening."

It's never a good idea to accuse anyone of murder unless you

are more than one hundred percent sure he or she did the deed.
I skated around an out-and-out accusation and told Bridget
that it would certainly behoove the police to see if the pieces
went together and if they did, I'd know without a doubt that a
replica of a death mask was at one time in Dr. Eban's posses-
sion, that he was the one who broke it, and that at least my
plaster piece was probably from it.

Before long, we were both boarding a bus for Inspector
Pierce's office.

The blue windows were no less intimidating than they
were the first time. For me. For Bridget, they were just an
obstacle she was challenged to take down, even if she had to
break them. She pounded and yelled, "Help, police!" as if we
were in danger. I was stunned, but I knew I shouldn't have
been.

When Inspector Pierce (and I was glad it was him) opened
the door and saw who was on the other side, I winced a smile
and let Bridget speak.

"We've got something that might be important in the murder of Mallory Clacher," she said.

"By all means then, come in." He held the door wide. "Hello
again, Delaney."

Like the first time I'd been there, he was the only officer in
the place. The addition of Bridget made it feel much more
crowded as we all took a seat around a desk. I wanted to ask
him if they'd found Dr. Glenn or if there was anything new in
the case, but I wouldn't with Bridget in the room.

"What do you need to tell me?" he asked, forcing an even
tone to his voice.

"These." Bridget held out her hand and I gathered the plaster piece from my bag. "These might lead to a killer. I showed

you mine before, but now we've brought two." We placed them on the desk in front of him.

Though Bridget's style was off-putting, Inspector Pierce was interested to hear what we had to say. He definitely wasn't happy we hadn't been more careful about fingerprints (lesson learned) but he was glad we'd come to see him. While we were there, via his radio, he dispatched officers to the close and the library. He told the one going to the library that finding and talking to Artair Fletcher was a priority. I wished for a way to warn Artair, but there wasn't one.

"You can't write about this now. You're part of the story," Inspector Pierce said to Bridget. I thought he was just hoping to trip her up.

She didn't miss a beat. "That's correct, but once it's solved, I'm going to have the best story in town."

She seemed content and Inspector Pierce didn't have a comeback for her, which was probably the main reason she was content.

It was a quick meeting, and as he showed us the door he said, "Be careful, please. Don't do anything stupid."

"Don't plan to," I said.

"You either, Lois Lane," he said to Bridget.

"Did you just make a joke?" I said before I could stop myself.

He didn't answer, but shut the blue door and turned the dead bolt.

"I think he did try a joke," Bridget said. "Come on, I'll buy you a drink."

"It's only one in the afternoon," I said.

"Right. I'll buy you lunch, but you can't look at it as a bribe. You do eat, don't you?"

"All the time," I said.

"Haggis is on me," she said as she signaled me to follow her.

"Uh," I said. If she made me eat haggis, she and I would never get past our issues.

I'd just order something else. Hopefully.

THIRTY-TWO

"Wait here," Bridget said.

The small take-out shop was crowded and it wasn't too cold outside, so I didn't mind waiting. I hoped she didn't think I'd truly eat haggis, but she didn't ask what I wanted.

A few minutes later she exited, balancing two large coffees and two paper-wrapped pastries.

"I was kidding about the haggis," she said as she gave me a coffee and pastry.

It felt like a peace offering.

All the world is made of faith, and trust, and pixie dust, said Peter Pan in my mind.

The bookish voice came out of the blue. Quickly and covertly I scanned the area, but didn't see a bookshop nearby.

Peter must have thought it pretty important for me to get the message. Or maybe that was Tinker Bell.

"Thank you," I said. As I sipped the coffee, my eyes got big at the sight of the cherry pastry.

"You like pastries? Doesn't everyone?"

"I like them very much," I said. It seemed like it would be

rude to pay her back for food and drink, so I just thanked her again.

"This way, I want to show you something," she said as she led the way while we ate the pastries that didn't need much chewing because mine melted the second it came in contact with my tongue. I looked behind as we traveled. I needed to memorize the location of the takeaway shop.

We were on the back side of the Edinburgh Castle, at the bottom of the volcanic cliff that the castle had sat comfortably upon for centuries. The buildings became less adorable as we continued, transforming into more modernish architecture.

"See that place?" she said after she'd licked her fingers. "That's the Argyle House."

"It's an apartment building. Flats, I mean," I said.

The building was huge; even if it hadn't been in Edinburgh, where buildings weren't as big as American buildings, it would have been considered huge. From our angle, it seemed to have two wings, but they weren't at typical angles from each other.

"No, it's business offices," Bridget said. "It's contemporary inside and out. As you can see, it's in between much of the new and the old in Edinburgh."

I looked around as I swallowed my last bite of pastry. "And the castle above."

"Aye."

"Why are you showing it to me?"

"This is the West Port area. This large building sits in the spot where the boardinghouse that Burke and Hare met at was located. I'm sure you've been hearing about them a lot lately if you've heard about Dr. Eban." She looked at me expectantly.

I didn't answer in the way she'd hoped. "Oh, that is interesting." I let my imagination try to superimpose the old over the new. "It was a crowded place back then."

"Without a doubt."

We were both silent a moment as we pondered. I liked it when even the locals enjoyed the history of their city.

"Your bookshop has prints too, doesn't it?" she asked.

"Yes."

"I bet you have a print somewhere of Log's Lodgings. That was the name of the place. They were both Irish immigrants, Burke and Hare," she continued. "They came to Edinburgh to work on the Union Canal. Burke moved here with his partner, Helen McDougal. The boardinghouse was owned by Margaret Laird and William Hare, who lived together; it was named after Margaret's dead first husband. In 1827, a lodger, Donald, died of natural causes and he owed money on his boarding-house bill. It seemed only right to Burke and Hare that they sell Donald's body to Robert Knox for the past amount due. Apparently, murder seemed like the logical next step, or at least the most profitable one."

I'd heard some of this from Joshua, but I didn't mind hearing it again. She spoke about history the way I did, as if we could see the pictures and smell the odors as we said the words.

I wasn't going to interrupt, but something occurred to me. "Wait, you said this is West Port?"

"Aye, that's this district."

"Hang on a second." I pulled out my phone and hit the call button. "Rosie, where did you live in West Port? Where did Dr. Glenn live?"

Using the pen Bridget handed me as she took my coffee cup, I wrote the addresses on the inside of my wrist before I thanked Rosie and hung up.

"Can we find these places?" I said as I showed her my wrist.

"Easily. They're just this way."

Less than a minute later, we'd turned another corner that took us back to the older Edinburgh. Above the businesses that included other takeaway spots, souvenir shops, and the like, we pinpointed Rosie's and Dr. Glenn's old flats.

We looked up, neither of us needing to knock on doors.

"Rosie's was smaller, but right next door. Dr. Glenn's was larger and nicer, if the outsides of the buildings are any indication."

"I don't understand why we're looking at these," Bridget said.

"Rosie, my coworker, lived next door to Dr. Glenn, and I was curious where they lived." I didn't know exactly what Peter or Tink had been trying to tell me earlier, but coffee and the best pastry in the universe weren't quite enough to make me trust Bridget all the way. Almost, but not quite.

"Oh. Interesting. Did she know his family?"

"Not well."

"No good information then?"

"No."

"Shame." We gave Dr. Glenn's old flat a long look. "You know, I felt most sorry for his daughter. Poor girl. I wonder what happened to her. I can't believe I haven't researched that. I'll have to."

"How?"

"Connections." She looked at me. "Can't divulge my sources, but I do have lots of connections. Some in the government. I might be able tae get into the foster care records. Make some calls."

"Can you do that research from The Cracked Spine?" I asked.

"I'd rather do it at my office."

"What if I could try to get that interview with Edwin?"

"Yeah?"

"No promises, but I'd try. For real this time."

"All right."

The trip back to the shop was a matter of getting around the volcanic crag that was holding up the castle. We hurried; we ran and dodged, looking like tourists late for a plane. I was the one who set the pace. A sense of urgency had come over me, but Bridget kept up without complaint.

We burst into the shop, finding Rosie with Hector tucked under her arm at the front desk. Edwin and Hamlet stood at the top of the stairs on the small balcony with a customer. We'd interrupted their conversation.

I cleared my throat. "I'm sorry."

Hector barked once.

"Everything okay?" Edwin asked from above.

"Yes. We'll go to the back," I said.

Edwin eyed the reporter before he and Hamlet turned back to the customer and guided him toward the books on the shelves against the wall.

Bridget, Rosie, and I made our way to the back table.

"This place is amazing," Bridget said in a loud whisper. "I think I would just sit here and smell the books and look around all day."

I smiled briefly at her, but I had more important things to do.

"Rosie," I said, "Bridget is going to see if she can find any information about Dr. Glenn's daughter. Is it okay for her to sit back here?"

"Aye," she said doubtfully.

"I'd rather someplace more private," Bridget said.

"We really don't have anyplace more private," I said. "This corner is quiet. The sound doesn't travel."

Rosie blinked at me, but she went along. "Aye."

I wasn't going to ever let Bridget cross over to the dark side. That was asking for trouble, even if I didn't take her all the way to the warehouse door.

"Well, all right. Pen and paper I could borrow?" Bridget asked.

I'd never known a reporter who didn't have them at the ready all the time, but I gathered the supplies from a shelf and then Bridget started making phone calls.

I stepped back to the front desk with Rosie and Hector.

"What's going on, lass?" she whispered.

"I need to know what happened to Lily," I said. "A picture, if we're that lucky."

"Why?"

"I think either Sophie or Rena is Lily. Most likely Rena, considering the way she talks about her childhood. I think that one or both of them have lied about their age, maybe to keep Rena—Lily—protected. I think Rena moved to Glasgow at the same age Lily's world fell apart. The phone number for her father that she listed on the provenance of the books isn't connected. It's just . . . well, mostly it's a gut instinct."

"Awright," Rosie said. She glanced back to the corner and then back at me. "Should I be friendly tae her? Grab some biscuits?"

I smiled. "It's okay to be friendly, but don't worry about the refreshments." I looked up at the balcony. "I did tell her I would try to get her an interview with Edwin, and this time I meant it. If you get a chance to let him know, that would help."

"I can do that," she said. Hector panted supportively.

"Delaney," Bridget said.

I moved back to the table.

"I put a call into someone in Glasgow, but she hasn't called me back. My colleague at the paper sent me an old picture, though. We never printed it, but it's in the files. He's looking for others." She held her phone toward me. "This is Lily."

The picture was a profile view of a young girl, barely beginning to look like a teenager. A scarf covered her hair.

"That doesn't tell me much," I said.

"I know. I think that's why we kept the picture. If we ever wanted tae print a picture, this would still keep her identity pretty well hidden."

Rosie and Hector joined us. I held the phone toward Rosie.

"You know what Sophie and Rena look like. Is there any chance at all that one of them is Dr. Glenn's Lily?"

"Lass, that picture doesnae tell me much at all," Rosie said.

"Anything else?" I said to Bridget.

"I'm waiting right now," she said. "Why is this so important? Sophie and Rena are two women in Mallory's building, right?"

I nodded but didn't expound. I saw her eyes light up though. This could definitely be a big story.

I said, "I think if Lily was in town, it would be more likely that Dr. Glenn truly had resurfaced, and Lily could help the police find him. No matter what, he's a killer on the loose."

"And you think you might know someone who used tae be Lily?" Bridget asked.

"I'm not sure, but it feels like a good guess."

"Sophie or Rena?"

Bridget's phone rang as I avoided the direct question. I glanced at the number before I handed the phone back to her. I didn't recognize the caller.

"Hey," she answered.

Rosie, Hector, and I observed her on the call, even after she sent us a look that said she'd rather we wouldn't. It was a quick call.

"I just got sent another picture." She scrolled on her phone and then held it out to me.

This one was of Lily and Dr. Glenn. She was younger than in the first one, but there was more of her to see, even in black-and-white. She was adorable, with a long brown ponytail, a button nose, and big eyes I was sure were blue. The hat on her father's head convinced me even more. His head was turned slightly to the left, as if he had a crook in his neck like Rosie had mentioned. But it was the hat combined with the partial profile that made it all become clear.

It had been on Saturday that I'd seen Lola on campus, allegedly meeting people to work on a group project. She'd met a man outside a building and they'd hurried inside. He'd worn a knit cap and had a profile almost identical to that of the man in the picture. I hadn't registered that he'd seemed older because I hadn't looked that closely, but now I wondered if he wore the hat to cover gray hair. As I thought some more, I wondered if I'd noticed a strange angle to the man's neck. Had it been a little crooked?

It made so much sense. Lily couldn't handle medical school, just as her father hadn't been able to. He'd faked it, and she was just doing whatever she could to be around it.

"Oh dear," I said.

"What?" Rosie and Bridget said.

"Let's call the police," I said. "I know who Lily is, and I'm sure Dr. Glenn has returned."

THIRTY-THREE

"Inspector Pierce, I know I've been . . . This is Delaney. Call me as soon as you are available. I think Dr. Glenn has definitely resurfaced, and I think a woman named Lola who lives in the same building Mallory did is actually Lily, Dr. Glenn's daughter."

I hesitated before I ended the call. Bridget, Rosie, and Hector watched me with wide approving eyes, but it certainly felt strange to say such things, particularly in a message form. I looked at the picture on Bridget's phone again. Yes, I was sure. I hung up.

I'd been about to call Inspector Winters when Tom and Gaylord walked into the shop.

"Delaney, you've been talking tae the police," Gaylord said.

I didn't point out that technically he probably couldn't represent me anyway.

"Actually, I just left a message for Inspector Pierce," I said.

"Delaney."

I shook my head. "None of that matters now. Come on, let us show you what we've got."

Tom and Gaylord joined Bridget and me at the back table. Rosie and Hector watched the front of the store, and I happened to catch Edwin and Hamlet leaving through the front door with the customer. Edwin was doing everything he could to get away from Bridget. I'd get them together later. Besides, she knew her story was already big without him.

I told everybody everything. I didn't leave out one thing I knew. Bridget took notes on paper, not on her hands or her arms. I was sure she was having visions of Pulitzer.

Gaylord, his mouth slightly agape, shook his head. "My goodness."

"I know, it's crazy, isn't it?" I said.

Tom jumped in, "Aye, but I'm still curious about the books and why the phone number Rena gave you is disconnected, as well as the email you read."

"Me too, but at least I know she's not Lily. Well, I'm almost certain. I think there's so much more to what's been going on with Sophie, Rena, Mallory, Lola, and all the doctors. The important thing is to find Mallory's killer. Dr. Glenn has resurfaced, I'm almost one hundred percent certain. He must have killed Mallory."

"Because she didn't want tae live with his daughter?" Bridget said, seemingly thinking out loud. "No, that wasn't it. He's just a killer. He had access."

"But why outside the bookshop?" Gaylord asked.

"I don't know. Maybe Mallory just came exploring based upon Dr. Eban's question about the scalpel, and he followed her. The dark close would be an appealing place to commit murder if you had murder on your mind," I said.

"But . . . the affair that your friends seemed tae know about, between Dr. Glenn and Mallory?" Bridget said.

"I don't know, maybe they were wrong, or scared. Or, if there was an affair, it was Dr. Glenn's way of trapping his victim," I said. "I don't think there was anything between Mallory and Dr. Eban. I think Conn Clacher overreacted to something he thought he'd put together in his mind. But I just don't know."

"The police need this information as soon as possible," Gaylord said.

I held up my phone. "I left a message."

"No, we'll need to do more," Gaylord said.

"I can call Inspector Winters," I said.

"I'll take you tae him," Tom said as he stood.

Bridget and Gaylord wanted to go with us, but Tom told them to meet us there. We told Rosie and Hector our plans and left, still in a hurry.

Bridget didn't even notice that Edwin was already gone.

THIRTY-FOUR

Inspector Winters would talk to me only with my attorney present. We all pretended Gaylord was my attorney, though even Inspector Winters figured out there was a conflict of representation. Neither Inspector Winters nor Gaylord cared. They just wanted things done as correctly as possible by then, and they were both glad an attorney was in the room, perhaps as just another witness.

After I told the entire story again, Inspector Winters dismissed us, with assurances that he'd take care of everything.

Bridget was disappointed that Gaylord wouldn't let me tell her anything new that had come up in the conversation in the interview room. Nothing new had, anyway. Tom gave Gaylord his car keys and told him to make sure Bridget got to where she needed to go, that he'd get the car back later, and that he and I were walking to Grassmarket.

But we didn't go straight back.

"We're taking some time," Tom said. "We don't have tae talk, just walk is fine. Time tae clear your head, take a breath."

Before long, we'd taken a path toward the library, and decided to stop by and see if Artair was there.

I didn't realize how long it had been since we'd walked the city streets and just chatted about normal things, but it had been long enough that the moments passed by quickly and infused me with a sense of calm and peacefulness that had been missing for a few days at least. Edinburgh had become home. Leaving someday was something I chose not to think about very often, but my time with Tom, while perfect for the most part, sometimes left me sad about a potential future when we had to live in different cities. In different countries.

But today, I was walking, hand in hand, cobalt eyes smiling at me frequently, with my very own pub owner. For a few moments, I'd just focus on that. And maybe think about how good he looked in a kilt.

We found Artair right inside the library doors. He greeted us with happy surprise, and I knew immediately our calm moments were over again.

"I've found a wee bit, Delaney, but not much. Come to my office," he said.

"I didn't know you had an office," I said. "You're usually working on something in specific areas of the building."

Inspector Winters had commanded me not to tell even one more person what I'd told him. I didn't think Artair counted, but Tom sent me a small head shake. I wouldn't tell Artair anything. For now.

"Ye'll have tae forgive the mess, but, aye, I have an office."

I expected something hidden, like the subbasements or Joshua's small office in the museum, but Artair's office was down a hallway and set in between other matching rooms. It seemed too businesslike for the larger-than-life library.

I might have bet that the inside of it held more books than the library itself.

"Oh my!" I said. Stacks of books teetered everywhere: floor, desk, shelves, couch. A book labyrinth.

"I know. I've a million projects," Artair said. "Make your way tae a couple chairs and I'll gather the things."

Tom and I sat on one side of the desk just as Artair slid a short stack of papers in between us all.

"I found a picture of Lily," Artair said as he pulled it from a small pile. "I didn't find much, but, aye, here's a picture."

I took it and didn't say I'd seen it just a short time earlier; it was the picture with the man in the cap, the infamous Dr. Glenn. The picture must have been circulated at one time.

"That's a clear picture. I wonder what happened to her. Such a sad story," I said.

"Aye," Tom said.

"I thought this picture was interesting too," Artair said.

He slid a copied piece of paper my direction, and I looked at Tom. It wasn't fair that Artair was doing all this work, yet couldn't be told of the recent developments. But Tom shook his head again.

In the picture, Doctors Eban, Glenn, and Clacher were younger, standing together, laughing, probably making a toast if the shot glasses were any indication. Dr. Carson was there too. She had her arm crooked in Dr. Glenn's, her admiring full smile aimed his direction.

Rosie had said they'd spent time together at Dr. Glenn's flat.

I read the caption: "Medical school personnel and their

families enjoying a warmer than normal summer day." It was from a picnic or some outside gathering, something casual.

"That's all I found," Artair said. "I wish there were more."

"No, this is great. Thank you, Artair." I fell into thought. Was there something important about the past relationship between Meg Carson and Jack Glenn?

"Lad, come help me carry up some boxes from the other side of the library. I couldn't find a cart and you're here now."

I barely noticed them leaving, but when I realized I was alone, I stood and walked around some book stacks to get to the arched, paned window. Even the windows in Scotland were architecturally interesting. And the views. The current one looked out to George Square, the patch of short trees and green grass that students passed through, the space Lola had seemed to look at suspiciously when I first ran into her on campus.

There was no sun out today. No rain at the moment, but some clouds threatened at least a drizzle. The green area was populated only by moving pedestrians. I didn't spot anyone relaxing or chatting.

But I did see something strange. Or I thought I did. It was a moment when I hadn't been paying close enough attention, just letting my eyes scan. Thankfully a bookish voice spoke up.

Listen to the trees as they sway in the wind. Their leaves are telling secrets.

It was from Hamlet's desk calendar. Quotes from the Perpetual Calendar of Inspiration, transcribed onto a tear-away-a-page-a-day calendar. Maybe the strangest place I'd ever received a bookish voice communication from.

Okay, I needed to listen to the trees. I moved my eyes back to the tree line I'd already scanned.

I still didn't see it at first, but at third glance I saw what the voice, and my instincts, were telling me to look at.

A man held too tightly to a young woman's arm and guided her way too forcefully toward a building on the far side. I was turned around and wasn't positive, but I thought the building was the one in which Dr. Eban's anatomy theater was located.

I only slightly recognized the tall gray-haired man as the one I'd seen in the pub the night Mallory was killed, but I couldn't mistake the tilt to his head. "Dr. Glenn?" I said aloud.

I recognized the women right off. Lola. Lily.

I hurried out of the office, hoping I'd run into Tom and Artair on the way. I didn't spot them, but I made my way toward the doors I thought they'd gone toward. I pulled out my phone and hit Tom's number as I set off in a fast walk. As much as I wanted to run, it was a library.

My phone eventually took me to voice mail, and I left a message that was sure to scare him to an unreasonable state, but a killer was forcing Lily into that building. Even if he was her father, he was a killer. I couldn't wait for Tom and Artair to return before I hurried to help her.

I put the phone into my pocket and took off in a run. Librarians everywhere would be unhappy, but I'd make it up to them.

The distance across the green seemed so far; I started pumping my legs and arms even faster, but it still took forever to get across. Snippets of thoughts ran through my mind: yell for someone to call the police, yell to someone to go find Tom, yell to someone to come help you.

I ruled out the last one quickly; if harm was being done, I wouldn't want to put anyone else in its way. As far as yelling to call the police or Tom: a request to call the police could cause panic, and it would have taken too much time to try to explain who Tom was and where they could find him. No time. Hurry!

I kept running. Breathing heavily, I pulled open the door to the building and propelled myself inside. I quickly determined that this was indeed the building with the anatomy theater, though I'd come inside it from a different door than before.

I didn't even consider that they'd gone anywhere other than the theater. I hoped I'd picked the right way. I didn't see anyone else in the building, and another flash of a thought went through my mind: Dr. Glenn had known the building would be quiet.

As I turned a corner, though, the population in the hallway went from just me to two. With all the grace of someone in too much of a hurry, I ran into Dr. Meg Carson.

Noises of surprise bounced off all the plaster, lath, and linoleum as we both stumbled backward. I was grateful that neither of us went down.

"Goodness, lass, why do I so often come upon you in hallways?" Dr. Carson said after we'd both recovered our balance. "You're not even a student here."

I was happy to run into someone fierce. "I'm so sorry, Dr. Carson, but please, let me explain later. For now, come with me if you want, but I need to get up to your husband's anatomy theater."

"He's not there," she said, a deeply suspicious tone to her voice. Again, I'd heard that tone a few times before from other women who didn't trust their husbands.

"I know. Please, come if you want." I started to walk away, but she grabbed my arm and yanked me backward.

"Ouch," I said.

I wrestled my arm free and sent her my best scowl. "Don't

touch me, Dr. Carson. Come with me or not, but I'm going to the theater."

I turned and started moving away, the spark of anger giving me renewed purpose.

Dr. Carson double-timed and started walking with me.

"Why?" she asked. "What's going on with you and my husband?"

"I don't even like your husband," I said, but I knew that sounded childish, and wasn't true. I actually liked what I knew of him. "Nothing is going on. I met him less than a week ago. I don't know him."

"Why are you going to his theater then?"

"Because I saw something and I'm worried about someone, and something tells me they went to the theater."

"In that case then," she said. I heard the eye-roll.

"You don't have to come with me."

"Oh yes I do."

I should have been paying better attention. Looking back at that specific moment and her clipped words, I should have been paying much better attention to the word everyone had been using to describe her. She wasn't being sarcastic at all. It's too bad I didn't see that at the time.

With a matching double-step climb, we took the stairway in record time.

"Where is everybody?" I asked.

"Classes are over for the day. No Wednesday afternoon classes or labs."

"That must be why he brought her here," I said.

"Who are we talking about?"

"I don't know for sure. I'm not even certain I'm going to the right spot. I hope my instincts are on track, though."

"Should I call the police?"

"Probably."

We'd made it to the next floor, but she didn't pull out her cell phone. She kept walking right along with me.

We reached the theater, and I put my hand on the door as I looked at her.

"Hang on. Let me look," I said.

"All right." She pulled her phone from her pocket and held it at the ready.

I opened the door and peered carefully inside. I was shocked but not surprised to see Lola and the man who'd been manhandling her. They were seated in the back row, one empty seat between them. It looked like I'd interrupted a conversation, not a murder.

"Delaney?" Lola said as she stood.

The man turned his face away as if he didn't want me to see it. I'd been just about to ask if everything was okay when everything suddenly became not okay.

Dr. Carson shoved me, causing me to be flung backward down the concrete stairs that led to the stage.

I didn't hit my head only because I managed to stop myself from more than one roll by catching my hand on the last chair of the third row down. I twisted muscles in my back and shoulder, but adrenaline kept the pain from going beyond that initial twinge that promised much more agony later.

I heard Lola scream and Dr. Carson yelling for her to shut up.

"What's wrong with you?" Lola continued loudly.

I looked up toward the door. Lola had joined Dr. Carson, who seemed to be latching the door with some sort of pin. I had a memory of seeing such a mechanism at one time, but it had been a while. Were there other doors? Yes! Dr. Eban had entered through one at the back of the stage when I'd been there before.

"Shut up," Dr. Carson told Lola again.

I was trying to figure out how to get out of there, but it would have been impossible not to wonder about the other people in the room.

"What the hell, Dr. Carson?" I croaked. "What's going on?"

She didn't look at me. She turned her attention to Lola. "I'm doing this to protect you and your father."

"I don't want you to protect me by knocking someone down the stairs!" She started to descend toward me.

I put my hand up to stop her. I wasn't going to trust any of them. I figured chances were about 93 percent that one of these people had killed Mallory.

"Stay away," I said.

"Oh, Delaney, I'm not going to hurt you," she said.

I looked at her and remembered our conversation as we walked across campus. She'd seemed so young, but she'd said she was a senior.

"You're Lily, aren't you?" I said as a few more tiny pieces came together.

She sighed. "I am. I'm not going to hurt you."

"The man. He's your father. He's Dr. Glenn."

"He is, but Delaney, he's not a killer. He never . . . Oh, Delaney, your arm looks funny. Let me help you."

"Stay away."

"All right." She turned back to Dr. Carson. "I don't want to be protected; neither does my dad. Come on, let us get some help for Delaney."

She made a move toward the door, but Dr. Carson pointed something at her. A scalpel. A modern one.

"What the hell?" I said. "What's going on?"

I hefted myself upright and stood. My shoulder was either broken or out of joint. Either way, even the adrenaline wasn't going to keep the pain at bay much longer.

"Stop it, Meg," Dr. Glenn stood too, and came around the seats toward the two women.

"Stay back," she said as she grabbed Lola and twisted her around, holding the scalpel at her throat.

"Don't!" I yelled. "Let her go."

"Meg!" Dr. Glenn said.

"Why can't everybody just do what I say?" Dr. Carson said.

Dr. Glenn looked at me and then at Meg. "We will, Meg. We'll do whatever you want us to do."

I nodded, but the motion hurt all the way to Kansas and back. My eyes filled with tears.

"She's the one who killed Mallory," Lily said between clenched teeth.

"Shut up, Lily," I said.

"Of course I killed Mallory. You destroy me, I destroy you. I've killed before."

Dr. Glenn was seething. I could almost see the smoke coming out of his ears.

"Did you kill anyone?" I couldn't help but ask him.

"No!" Lily croaked. "She did it all. She set my dad up. It was all her."

I couldn't believe that Dr. Carson wasn't slitting Lily's throat, but the doctor seemed to be enjoying the sudden notoriety instead. She smiled, some evil mixed with some satisfaction. Dr. Glenn had gotten all the credit for murdering people, but now at least one other person knew differently. If I wasn't being fed lies.

"I didn't kill anyone," Dr. Glenn said. "But she set me up, and good. All evidence points undeniably to me. There's no doubt I would have been found guilty."

He was a handsome man, his thick gray hair bushy but neat. The lines around his mouth and eyes were deeper than they should have been, but the younger man I'd seen in the pictures was still there.

"You're really a doctor?" I said.

Shame pinched at the lines around his eyes. "No."

"I see. You did fake that part?" He nodded. I looked at Dr. Carson. "And you worked it. You found out and killed all those people and blamed it on him."

"He wouldn't leave her!"

"Wait, who wouldn't he leave? His wife?" Pain muddled my mind, but I could still think a little bit. "This was about that? About him not leaving his wife for you?"

"Yes!"

"You killed Mallory too?" I asked.

She laughed cruelly. It was almost a cartoonish noise. "She had to go."

"Mallory and my dad met when she and I were roommates," Lola interjected. "She didn't know who he was. They . . . they fell in love."

A May-December romance to be sure, but that was the least weird thing about it.

More pieces came together tighter in my mind, even if I still didn't understand it all.

"Your husband? He has an eye for the girls, right? He wasn't having affairs, forcing women to do things for grades?"

Dr. Carson laughed again. "Not a chance. There's not a woman interested in him. He was easy to frame, though, much easier than Dr. Jack Glenn," she sent him a venomous glare, "was all those years ago. A skull here, a jawbone there. That bookshop of yours. When those men were talking about Burke and Hare, I knew I could use you all."

"The bookshop? You were just there one day and heard Edwin and a friend talking about Burke and Hare? You cooked all this up from that?"

"No! I was at the bookshop because I figured out my husband gave those two stupid women some of our books to keep them quiet about Mallory and Jack. I found out they'd sold them to Edwin MacAlister! I visited the shop, and he and his friend were talking about Burke and Hare. It was a sign, something telling me I could frame my idiot husband easily. That's when I started cooking all of this up."

Oh! I thought. Sophie and Rena were given the books to bribe them to keep quiet about Mallory having an affair with an older man. Who, I wondered, did they think he was? If it wasn't until after Mallory's murder that they realized he was Dr. Glenn, no wonder they behaved the way they did.

"Well . . ." I said. She was brilliant and fierce, but I didn't want to give her credit for either.

Though I wasn't sure exactly what to believe, it had become clear that the only thing that could save the people who remained alive, the only hope really, was me. No one would believe anyone but me if they were to hear what had transpired in this anatomy theater. In fact, they might not believe me the whole way, but I stood a better chance than anyone else. I had to survive and talk to the police, tell them what Meg Carson had confessed.

But Lily had to survive too. She shouldn't have to suffer anymore. I didn't know how much longer Dr. Carson would revel in her glories. She was going to kill more people if she wasn't stopped. Immediately. I shared a quick look with Jack Glenn, only long enough so we'd get on the same page, have the same plan.

If he charged at the same time I did, hopefully we could stop Dr. Carson before the scalpel hit home.

A blink and a half later we were charging.

THIRTY-FIVE

I let loose a string of the worst words you could think of, used in the most terrible ways possible.

"I know, that hurt. You'll feel better in a second," Jack Glenn said after he put my shoulder back into place.

He wasn't really a doctor, but he sure knew how to put a shoulder back into place. My arm had been hanging funny, but the paramedics hadn't arrived yet. He'd offered to put me back together. Caught in the moment and in more pain than anyone should be, I told him it was okay.

We'd charged. And somehow, we saved his daughter from too much damage. The scalpel grazed her forearm before it pierced Meg Carson's shoe and foot, causing her to forget she was planning another killing spree.

Tom answered when I called, after I called the police while Jack held Meg Carson down. She couldn't have gone far anyway.

"Where'd you go?" he asked.

I told him, and he and Artair arrived right after my shoulder was fixed.

Inspector Pierce put Dr. Carson, her foot wrapped by a paramedic, in a police car and then turned to face Jack, Lily, Tom, Artair, me, and Dr. Eban, who'd shown up with big freaked-out eyes. He handcuffed Jack even after I gave him a rundown of Dr. Carson's confession.

"I need a room where we can all go and talk about what's going on here. You're probably all going to be under arrest for something, but I'd prefer to get some facts here first." He looked at me. "Call your attorneys if you want to."

Artair guided us to a conference room in the library. I'm sure there was a moment of humor in our march across George Square, Artair in the lead, Inspector Pierce and another officer, Reynolds, following behind, but none of us were laughing. In turn, Inspector Pierce, Tom, Artair, and Gaylord asked if I needed to be taken to the hospital. I told them that I was sore, but could move everything just fine. I was eventually going to be really sore and bruised, but I wanted to get this over with.

Tom called Gaylord, who ended up being the only attorney in the room, but stated that he wasn't officially representing anyone. No protests were voiced.

"What happened to lead you over to the anatomy theater?" Inspector Piece began with me after we all sat down.

Instead of just answering the question, I gave him the entire rundown of what had happened at the bookshop with Bridget beforehand. Those in the room, even those who'd already heard the story, gave me their undivided attention.

"Wait, though," Inspector Pierce said. "This man," he nodded at Jack, "was forcing you to go into the theater?" He looked at Lily.

"No, not forcing," she said. "We were just going inside in a hurry. He's not really recognizable, but we try to be careful, and we often meet in George Square and Dr. Eban's theater."

"Yes," Dr. Eban said. "They were welcome to go to my theater anytime."

"How long has this been going on?" Inspector Pierce asked.

Lily looked like she didn't want to answer.

"I've seen my daughter every week since Meg Carson killed her mother, and almost every day since she began school here," Jack said.

A hum of disbelief filled the room, but Inspector Pierce held up his hand to end it. He looked at Jack. "All the evidence pointed to you. I'm still not convinced you aren't a killer."

"She framed me," Dr. Glenn repeated.

"She confessed in the theater," I repeated. "She confessed to everything, Inspector Pierce."

"Did you record it?" he asked me.

"No," I said. "But I'll testify."

Gaylord nodded approvingly.

"You still impersonated a doctor a decade ago," Inspector Pierce said. "You're in some trouble."

"I'm aware."

"He's a good man," Dr. Eban said. "He wasn't properly educated, but he's brilliant. I fell for his act at first too, back then, but when it became clear that he really wasn't a doctor, I had a hard time not forgiving him. He really was brilliant, self-educated in ways he never would have been in medical school. I'm not justifying his actions, but I will testify on his behalf in whatever way he requires."

Dr. Eban had been shaken. His wife's evil had been exposed, and he was confessing to having known about Jack's activities and whereabouts. However, at some point since we'd come into the library, a calm had overtaken him. I wondered if the truth was setting him free.

"I don't understand why in the world no one came forward to vouch for Jack, tell the police the killer was Dr. Carson. That makes no earthly sense to me," Inspector Pierce said.

"She was that good, Inspector," Dr. Eban said. "She had us all where she wanted us. The evidence of murder would only have pointed to Dr. Glenn. She would have won. You were looking at me for Mallory. She would have accomplished framing me too, given just a little more time."

Who had won now? I wondered, but didn't say it out loud.

Inspector Pierce looked at Jack again. "You had an affair with Mallory?"

"I did. I loved her. She loved me," he said. "If not for everything else, we would just have been an old guy with a young woman, maybe laughed at, mocked, gossiped about. When Mallory understood who I was, she loved me enough to keep the secret. I can't give you a better answer than that, but I'm devastated that she's gone."

"Were you at the pub where Mallory was the night she was killed?" I asked. No one seemed bothered by the question.

"I was. I often went places she or Lily were, just to be near them."

I wished I'd somehow put all of that together sooner, but I didn't know how I could have.

"How did Dr. Carson get Mallory to the close?" I asked. Inspector Pierce sent me a look of impatience this time, but he didn't retract the question.

"I don't know. None of us knows," Dr. Glenn said.

I wished I'd asked her, but time had been running out in the anatomy theater.

"She confessed to killing Mallory, though?" Inspector Pierce asked me again.

"She did." I looked at Dr. Eban. "You gave the books to Sophie and Rena to keep them quiet about Mallory and Dr. Glenn?"

Dr. Eban nodded. "About Mallory and an older man. They didn't know who he was. They were upset when they realized it."

"Which was when?" I asked.

"The morning of the service for the corpses. That's why we were there together after the service in the kirk; I was trying to ease their new concerns. I managed tae calm them down, but mostly because you were there tae distract them." He paused, but we knew he had more to say. "If Meg hadn't discovered that the books were missing from my collection, none of this would have happened. That's what sent her looking into things."

"Why did you stay with her? Even before she began trying to frame you for Mallory's murder, she had to be a . . . challenge," Inspector Pierce said.

Dr. Eban smiled sadly. "If I'd left her, she would have done something horrible and made me look guilty of it; it would have been just a matter of time. We were married, but we weren't together."

He was odd, yes, and desperately lonely. I could see that now. I felt sorry for him, and I liked him; however, there might have been a way to make a better life for himself. But who knew what went on in other people's lives? And it was impossible to understand others' motivations without walking in their shoes.

I sighed.

"You asked me about the scalpels?" I said. "How did you know they were at the shop?"

"That's how we picked a bookshop for Sophie and Rena tae try tae sell the books. Dr. Glenn, Jack, had not too long ago told me about selling them years ago tae a woman who worked in a bookshop. He said that over the years, the legend of there being a room with treasures in it had grown. He wondered if that's where they'd ended up. It was a casual conversation at the time."

"They were Dr. Knox's?" I asked.

"They aren't real," Jack said. "Just things I got at a conference I attended. A gimmick."

I nodded, but wasn't sure I believed him.

Inspector Pierce rubbed his hand over his chin and looked at each of us, one at a time. I didn't know if he was looking for something or trying to convey a message.

Finally, he spoke. "All right. Jack Glenn, Dr. Eban, and Lily, you're coming with us. The rest of you may go," Inspector Pierce said.

As we left, I looked back at the three who were going with the police. They were scared, yes, but I saw something else too. A dim light of relief in their eyes, and maybe some hope. The lies were done, over. Tragedy had occurred, and it would be impossible to ever fully accept the murders, but at least these people's lies could end.

It was good to be outside, good to be free. Tom insisted on taking me to the hospital, but I said, "I'm fine," as I sent one more look back at the building with the anatomy theater.

I was really glad I'd survived.

THIRTY-SIX

"I am going to ace that test," Sophie said with a fist pump.

Rena and I laughed.

"We have no doubt," I said.

"Drinks on me, ladies. Tom, pour us all something," Sophie said to my pub owner.

"Happy tae!" Tom said. He winked at me and grabbed some shot glasses. My friends would enjoy the whisky. He'd pour me something tamer.

Rena lifted her shot glass. Sophie and I joined her.

"To Mallory," Rena said with a sad smile.

"To Mallory," Sophie and I said.

Sophie and Rena had wanted to meet me at Tom's pub tonight. We were part of an enthusiast crowd watching a football game on the television Tom had mounted on the wall.

Sophie and Rena had stayed in school, realizing that it *would* have been what Mallory wanted. They were still mourning their friend, probably would in one way or another forever, but hopefully honoring her too. They told me it had been a tough month, and they wanted to thank me and see Tom, since they hadn't seen him in some time either.

"Oh, that's so good," Sophie said as she set the glass down for Tom to pour another. He did.

"You know," Rena said to me, "we're sorry we were so mysterious tae you. That night, I knew about Mallory seeing an older man, but I tried to divert you with a lie about Sophie because I thought she'd told you something she shouldn't have when you two were in the loo—that she'd seen Mallory and the man together, that we thought we'd figured out who he was, and why we had the books, and . . . well, it was such a mess. After I got home that night, I went back out tae meet Dr. Eban. It was a planned meeting—we had to meet late at night, in places his wife wouldn't find us. She was everywhere and into everything. Anyway, I wanted tae tell him that I wanted tae get the books back from the shop and return the money, but he convinced me not tae. By then, though, it was too late to change anything."

It had been too late. In fact, Dr. Meg Carson had lured Mallory to the bookshop with her own lie. She'd confessed to telling Mallory that if she didn't break into the bookshop and retrieve the books that Dr. Eban gave to Sophie and Rena to keep them quiet, she would tell Boris Clacher that his daughter was having an affair with the one and only murderer, Dr. Glenn. The scalpels had had nothing to do with the murder. Dr. Carson had even jimmied the lock of the bookshop's front door and left it slightly open, just to confuse whoever found it that way.

Both Dr. Carson and Dr. Eban knew what books I was referring to when I went to the university to allegedly find out more information about them. Apparently, Dr. Carson pretended not to know to see if there was any way she could frame me or Edwin for any of her evil deeds. Dr. Eban had just played along with the act, thinking that his curiosity might somehow help. Yes, it was a huge mess.

With Joshua's help, I'd researched the scalpels. They weren't trinkets—they were the real thing. I wasn't sure what I would do with that information at this point, but for now, it was just another secret, another one for the secret room in the greatest bookshop of all time.

"I'm so sorry about it all," Rena continued.

"Me too," Sophie said. "Me too."

I nodded.

Sophie and Rena's medical school paperwork was found. They were who they said they were. Rena *had* written down an incorrect phone number for her father regarding the provenance of the books, but that was only because she was trying to hide the fact they were from Dr. Eban. Dr. Eban refused to further admit that the books were used for blackmail. After that day in the library, he stuck by the story that he'd just given them the books out of the kindness of his heart. Sophie and Rena were in no trouble at all, except for the pain from Mallory's murder that would always be a part of their lives.

"We're either going tae give the money back tae your boss or the medical school for research," Sophie said.

"And he'll give the school the books. They can doubly benefit." That was one transaction I knew I didn't need to get approved.

"Aye? That's too much tae ask," Rena said.

"Edwin would be thrilled," I said.

"This is the best whisky I've ever tasted," Sophie said.

I made note to watch my back for spills tonight.

Two of the soccer fans, in a moment of celebration over a

goal being scored, walked over and introduced themselves to Sophie and Rena. I already knew them as regulars. They greeted me, then asked Sophie and Rena to join them the few steps away at their table for some celebratory drinks.

I told them to go and have fun.

I sidled up to a stool and watched my pub owner as he waited on another customer. He was fun to watch.

Dr. Glenn, now known only as Jack Glenn, had been arrested, but charges were pending and muddled. A trial date had yet to be set, and I wondered if the police just wanted to put him somewhere until they could make sure he really hadn't killed anyone. His daughter, Lily, was now in a flat all her own, and no longer a student at the university. She visited her father in prison every day.

Lily knew what had happened to Mallory, or at least she'd guessed. She also knew she had to keep her father hidden. She knew the rumors were that Mallory was having an affair with an older man, so she had mentioned Dr. Eban to me, in a shock and fear-induced reaction to Mallory's murder. She'd seen her lie as a way to continue to keep her father's whereabouts hidden, or not even considered. She and I hadn't spoken after we saved each other in the theater, but I hoped to talk to her someday. Her life had been bizarre and punctuated by so much violence, and I still thought she would ultimately be okay. The resiliency of the human spirit. I couldn't believe that she and her father had been in Edinburgh, him not far away undercover in a distant land. He'd been hiding in plain sight, maybe. There was no grandfather in Virginia; that was another lie. I didn't know where Lily would end up, but truthfully, I was fascinated by her and her father.

Dr. Eban was also in some trouble, but he hadn't been arrested. Though I hadn't seen him again, I'd thought about taking him the scalpels. I liked the guy, and felt maybe he should be the one to have them. I hadn't decided yet.

Meg Carson was a criminal mastermind. Fierce, intelligent, and now in prison for the rest of her life. Driven by a need to control everyone and everything, and to be worshipped and obeyed, she had killed, and she had left ruination in her wake. I hoped all truths would come out, but much of the damage done couldn't be undone. I was more sickened than fascinated by her, and I had no desire to ever see her again.

"Where're your thoughts?" Tom asked as he came back over to my side of the bar.

"On you," I said in my best flirtatious voice.

Tom laughed. I wasn't very good with flirtatious voices.

"Here, I'd like you tae try something." He reached under the bar and pulled out a shot glass and set it in front of me.

"Oh. What is it?" I asked, still not into the Scottish spirit of drinking.

"Just try it," he said with a smile.

"You have amazing eyes," I said as I lifted the glass.

He reached out and stopped my hands from making it all the way to my mouth. "You need tae stop looking at my eyes, as much as I enjoy looking right back at yours, and look at the glass."

I did.

"What?!" I proclaimed.

"Marry me?" he said so casually that I almost asked him to repeat it.

Rodger appeared over his shoulder. "I told him this was not the right way."

"Rodger," Tom said. "This is perfect."

A ring took up the space that a good shot of Scottish whisky normally would have. I had to blink away a million tears to see it clearly, and stop myself from hyperventilating to say anything else.

"We're in my pub, soon tae be hopefully ours, where we had our first date. Delaney had no idea this was coming," Tom said, but he looked at me, not Rodger. "She'll never forget it."

He took my hands in his. I was still holding the glass. "I love you, Delaney Nichols, from Kansas in America. Marry me. Please." He fished out the ring and placed it on my shaking finger.

"Well?" Rodger asked.

I sniffed and wiped my nose with the hand that didn't have the ring.

"Tom was right," I said. "This is perfect."

Someone must have scored another goal, because more cheering ensued.

THE VICTIMS OF
WILLIAM BURKE AND WILLIAM HARE

Joseph the Miller

Abigail Simpson

An Englishman

An old woman

Mary Paterson

Effie

A drunk woman

An old woman and her
deaf grandson

Mrs. Ostler

Ann McDougal

Mary Haldane

Peggy Haldane

James Wilson

Mary Docherty